Rebirth
Julia Starr

First Edition: 2025
ISBN 979-8-9913342-0-4 (paperback)
ISBN 979-8-99133 42-1-1 (hardcover)
ISBN 979-8-9913342-2-8 (e-book)
Book format by Nathan C. Collins
Book cover designed by Sydney J. Rooney
This is a work of fiction. All of the characters, organizations, and events portrayed in this novel are products of the author's imagination.

This book is dedicated to my father. Thank you Dad for putting books in my hands and for always having unwavering faith and support in my dreams. You are the reason I can now call myself a published author.

Chapter One
Sunday, February 26th

My skin is gelid. The majority of my body is wrapped in tight bandages. I am forced to confront the haunting image of myself in the mirror on the ceiling, and feel the chill that follows like a thousand pinpricks into my soul.

A padded cage holds me in. I am unaware of my surroundings due to the windowless room, but my body senses a gentle sway. It rocks me, like a natural lullaby cooing a newborn to sleep. But I'm not a newborn, I can see that from the length of my body and the nutmeg colored hair that grows rather unnaturally from the crown of my head.

But then why does my brain feel empty? I am nameless and I have no history. Why am I here? Where is here? Why is my face covered?

The pattern of my breathing intensifies as a large wall panel slides open across the room. I try to pinch myself awake from whatever nightmare I slipped into, but my body is overtaken by paralysis and tingles, so all that moves is my eyes. At first, nothing exudes from the other side of the door except a black quiet, but then out steps a woman in white scrubs, her hair slicked back into a tight bun.

I call to her but all that escapes my mouth is a whimper. Where are my words? I try again. Nothing but a squeak slips out. I prod my tongue around my mouth and bite the inside of my cheek in an attempt to wake up the nerves and muscles that allow me to talk, to ask questions. But it's not working. I keep biting, over and over again, and I don't stop until my taste buds register a metallic flavor that wets my dry mouth.

"Please don't make me sedate you, Miss. Weiss."

Weiss. Is that my name? Why can't I remember my name?

"Would you like some water to wash the blood out of your mouth?"
I instinctively try to nod but my head stills, and the pain that follows after is unbearable.

"Apologies, I didn't realize that your motion is still so limited. As for your throat, it's likely still hoarse, making it difficult to produce sound," she notes clearly unbothered by my current state. "Could you blink once for yes and twice for no?"

I squeeze my eyes tightly shut and open them with dramatic force. I wait a beat longer so that she really understands. In response, the woman walks over and places her hand on the only hard section of the otherwise padded wall, next to the closed door. An outline of her hand lights up in green. As soon as she pulls away, the panel pops open with a gentle click. Water and a round container sit in the pocket of the wall like an offering.

"You should try to eat something solid, considering you have been fed only liquid nutrients for the past few days."

Is that how long I've been asleep?!

The nurse brings the items over to me and places them on a metal rolling cart next to my bed before using a remote to prop me up. The motion startles me. My body tenses even more so when she moves me forward to fluff the life back into the pillows I am laying on.

"Open your mouth for me."

This is the only command I can obey, and as I do, she begins to unscrew the cap off of the unlabeled water bottle and pours the liquid into my mouth. I grasp for the droplets

with my tongue, trying to lick up any bit of liquid falling
through the air while mourning the tiniest spillage on my
paper-thin gown. It soaks through the material and dresses my
thigh with a refreshing coolness. I wonder when the last time I
bathed was.

"The doctor will check on you in a bit. Until then, it is
imperative that you eat."

She twists off the cap of the container, and I recognize
the food on top as bread. She leaves whatever fills up the
rest of the oval dish on the table, as she breaks the bread up
between her gloved fingers into tiny, uneven, chunks. My
mouth begins to salivate uncontrollably as I observe her out
of the corner of my eyes. I yearn to swipe the drool away
from my mouth in embarrassment before she notices, but
the excruciating pain that follows leaves me powerless. My
struggle brings her attention back to me, and she drops the
broken bread into the lid of the oval before taking a cloth
from her pocket. Her mouth is set in a thin, concentrated line
as she dabs away the bodily fluid that has leaked from me.
With her being this close, I can now see that her forehead
is covered in a light layer of sweat despite the chilled
environment of the room. She pulls back before I can dwell on
that thought any further.

When she's done she lifts the second lid to reveal a
beige liquid mixed with vegetables and chicken. Soup. I think
I like soup.

"Open your mouth please," the woman instructs as she
drops a few crumbs of baguette into the broth.

I do as she asks, closing my eyes along with it. The
spoonful of warmth that follows does nothing to quell my
hunger, but instead intensifies it. I need more. The way
the chicken falls apart between my teeth and the ease of
swallowing when just moments earlier the taste of my saliva
was stiff and bitter. I lock eyes with the nurse, hoping she
understands my pleas. I can tell she does when she brings
another spoonful my way.

The door doesn't open again until I finish sipping the

last bit of broth from the bowl. There is still bread left on the other side of the split container but the nurse steps away without a word with the rest of the food as another woman in a lab coat steps in. She pulls a swivel chair along with her and rolls it to the edge of my bed. She doesn't sit though, instead, she stands stiffly beside it.

"My name is Jackie, I am the head doctor in charge of your procedures. I understand that you are likely very confused but all will be explained in due time by your assigned Rebirth counselor. My job is simply to follow up on your physical health after the surgeries."

Surgeries, plural? What happened to me? Wait. Rebirth? The word sounds foreign yet familiar. Where have I heard that before?

"Could you try to move your toes for me?"

I brace myself for the pain that should follow, but with minimal effort, my toes seem to awake from their slumber. They wiggle, which makes me want to laugh. The sensation of truly feeling is thrilling.

"Great. Now try moving your fingers."

I once again prepare my mind for the disappointment and my body for the punishment. Then I will my fingers to move, even an inch. They don't, but at least the pain doesn't follow.

"Try again please."

Exhale, inhale, move. Still nothing. And just like that, my hope is stolen from me despite my cautious manner. The doctor makes a note of this in her chart and then finally takes a seat in the swivel chair.

"For some reason, Miss Weiss the reconstructive pills are moving through you much slower than they should be. You reported that you took the vitamins that we instructed you to take before you got here, which is why this is odd. However, it is nothing to be too worried about. Your body is likely just reacting slower and will catch itself up soon, but I am requiring you to stay with us for at least an additional day because of this. I will update your Rebirth counselor and he will plan accordingly. Until then, I will ask Nurse Renne to take you on a walk. Some fresh air might be what you need." She finishes scribbling on her pad of paper then clicks her pen shut and dismisses herself, the nurse following after her.

I wait for her to come back. It takes a while, but eventually the door opens again just as the silence begins to sit a little too long. Except the girl that walks in this time is younger and has her hair in two short braids. She comes in with a man and a wooden chair on wheels.

"Let's get you out of that bed," she lulls sweetly.

The man gently wedges his hands behind my back and under my legs, picking me up with ease and placing me in the wheelchair. The new nurse, whom I now know as Renne based on her name tag and the doctor's introduction, thanks the man as he leaves.

"It's going to be quite bright out since the sun has just risen," she explains as she places bulky, black glasses over my eyes. She then positions my hands comfortably in my lap before pushing me out the open door.

The wheels catch on the poorly installed flooring as soon as we get into the hallway. The slight jerking motion every foot or so starts to aggrevate me as we approach the door that leads us outside. Renne warns me once again about the light as she steps around me to push open the heavy metal door.

As she does, rays of warmth cover me like a blanket. I instinctively close my eyes and simply feel comfort in the sun. I am content leaving my eyes closed forever, but the squawk of an animal pulls me from my peace. I observe the bird that makes the noise as it flies overhead, swooping and swerving in abstract directions until it glides across the endless ocean. I watch it until it leaves my eyeline.

Renne turns me at that moment and pushes me along what I now realize is the deck of a boat. To my left is the ocean and straight before me is even more ocean. I wonder if I've ever been on a boat before.

"Which direction would you like to go?" Renne asks

before catching herself. "Sorry, I keep forgetting. I'm so used to the patients being able to talk by now. We'll go this way," she decides for me. She pushes the wheelchair to the left and we begin walking towards the back of the boat.

Is my situation an unusual occurrence? Are people typically able to talk by now? The idea worries me and I beg to ask about it.

We do a lap or two around the deck in silence before Renne decides to change course and go in the opposite direction. We have yet to encounter another living being, aside from the animals that soar past us. I can't help but feel jealous that they have control over where they go.

It isn't until the fourth time of passing the stern of the ship that Renne speaks again to ask if I would like to try to move my body once more. She establishes the same blinking system that the first nurse used. Blink once for yes and twice for no. I blink once rather aggressively to clearly signal my decision and Renne locks the wheels of the chair and moves in front to guide me.

Slowly I follow her words and move my toes. Then she asks if I can try squeezing her fingers. I concentrate and beg my body to push away the feeling of static in my blood. It doesn't work. I try again. It still doesn't work. Why won't it work?! Anger boils in me, threatening to spill over in the form of indignant tears.

I don't know who I am. No one will tell me. I can't even ask. I can't even move. Why am I here? Why can't I fucking move?!

"I'm sorry, I shouldn't have-," Renne pulls away remorsefully, "especially not without Dr. Jackie present."

But just as her fingers are about to lose touch with mine, I grasp them with a force so hard she jumps. This triggers tears that slip out and are now proof of victory instead of failure.

Chapter Two
Monday, February 27th

The mirror hanging above mocks me again, taunting my very existence and amplifying the repulsive sound of my urine trickling through a tube. The presence of it is especially apparent when the night nurse, the first one I met yesterday, comes to change the bag connected to my catheter. With an unyielding gaze, the glass compels me to confront my helplessness, as if I needed any further reminder.

All I can do to pass the time is to both mourn and appreciate free will so I begin to play mind games with myself, trying to exercise my memory. I dream of what my life was like when I knew it and I dream of what my life can be when I figure it out. I also play a solo game of trivia, quizzing myself on simple certitudes.

What year do I last remember it being? 1998. What month? February. Where did I live? I don't remember. What are the four nations of the world? Accrington, Alnerwick, Altone, and Aelville. What was my job? I'm not sure. Who are the current four leaders of the world? Garrison Hays, Camille Morin, Lian Gui, and Felipe Perez. Why can I remember the lives of others but not my own?

I play this game until five in the morning. I can tell that this is the time because that's when the night nurse said she would check on me next.

"I see that you're still awake. You should try to sleep before the doctor comes in a few hours."

I don't want to sleep, I try to say to her. All that comes out is rasp. I had been asleep for about four days and that's plenty of sleep for me.

"The plan today is to take off your bandages once your Rebirth counselor gets here and try to get more of your muscles going," she explains while simultaneously glancing at the monitor next to my bed and making notes in a chart. "They don't want to release you though until you can walk, talk, and go to the bathroom on your own so we'll see how today goes and evaluate from there."

Fortunately, I have also been practicing moving my neck and other limbs throughout the night, despite Dr. Jackie asking me not to. But the look on her face when she sees how much progress I've made overnight will all be worth the pain I have endured.

Renne was a huge help as well and upped my dosage of painkillers before she left for the night as soon as she understood what I was trying to do. She held up a finger to her mouth to mime that she wasn't supposed to be doing so though. What was I going to do? Tell someone?

An eternity seems to pass before Dr. Jackie comes to see me again. I greet her first by turning my head to the side, taking her all in. She attempts to hide her surprise but I can tell that this has caught her at least slightly off guard based on her body language.

"Can you move your head the other way for me, Miss Weiss?" I do so and she makes note of it. "What about your fingers?"

I move them up and down, side to side, and for extra measure, I even grasp at the scratchy sheets below me to show that I can not only move but hold as well. But Renne and I knew this already.

Speaking of, where is she? I wanted her to see the rest

of my progress and was hoping that she would have come in first.

"Lovely. Anything else?"

For the grand finale, I exhale shakily and then begin to raise my right arm. Slowly at first, and with extreme effort, my fingertips reach toward the ceiling. The higher the ligament rises the easier it becomes, and in no time the task is accomplished. I do the same with my left hand and a cry of triumph escapes when I finish. Now the surprise is more difficult for her to hide.

"Extraordinary." She allows herself to indulge in my advancements for only a moment before switching tracks. "Unfortunately, I do have some slightly off-putting news, Miss Weiss. I was hoping to take off your bandages now but your Rebirth counselor is running a little behind and has asked me to wait for him so that he can help you through the process of accepting your new image as well as work through any conflicts with you and your current state. However, he should be here within the next few hours which will provide the perfect opportunity for rest since I hear that you were up all night. And I do insist that you do so." Outwardly I nod but on the inside I string together a few curse words, at least I can remember those. "Maybe we could get you up and walking by the end of the day."

Her goals excite me but so far all that I've been able to move on the lower half of my body are my toes, so the prospect of this does not seem all too likely.

"Anyways, I will have Renne come bring you breakfast in a moment and then I seriously do need you to give yourself a break before you strain your muscles."

I nod once more to signal to her that I understand but I am unsure if I mean it. My body is running on adrenaline and faith right now and I can't afford to stop.

Shortly after Dr. Jackie leaves Renne stops in with some sort of soft pastry and yogurt to fill me until lunch. I show her the skills I practiced overnight and she tells me about visiting her new nephew in the NICU after leaving work. She even holds up a tiny Polaroid photo for me to see. I can relate quite a bit to the crying, innocent baby that she described. We both truly know nothing and no one in the world.

After she leaves I become consumed with loneliness. I let my eyes close and finally allow myself to sleep just to give my body something to do.

I don't wake until Renne sets down a tray of meat and cheese with crackers around noon. "Would you like some lunch and then another walk? We're still waiting on your Rebirth counselor so it is unfortunately going to be a bit longer." She's sympathetic as she delivers this news.

This must be some sort of sick joke. My Rebirth counselor's absence is my only roadblock in discovering who the fuck I am and what I look like, so where are they? And what exactly is Rebirth? The memory of knowing is right on the edge of my brain but getting to it is like trying to find my way out of a room full of fog.

"Miss Weiss, are you hungry?" I am not, so I move my head slowly and horizontally. "Okay, how about that walk then?" She abandons the tray of untouched food on the metal bedside table and walks over to an intercom button on the wall to call for help.

I can't weigh more than a hundred and thirty pounds but for little Renne, who weighs much less than that, I can see why she needs the backup. So once again the man from yesterday comes to help me into a wooden wheelchair and once again Renne pushes me across the bumpy floor of the hallway till we reach the exit.

Today the clouds hang low in the sky and there's a more comfortable breeze than the one I felt yesterday. It isn't until I turn the corner of the ship that I understand why though. We are docked. My head moves up towards Renne as if to question where we are.

She understands what I am asking and answers with, "Accrington."

Why are we here? And if this is our final destination

then where did we depart from?

"Did you want to try speaking again today?" Do I? Yes. Will I most likely be able to? No. And do I want to be disappointed? No. "What if you try choosing a simple word? How about hello?" She continues to coax, clearly sensing my unease.

I prepare my tongue to sit behind my bottom teeth. Slowly, my mouth huffs out the sound of an h. The noise has a layer of rasp, but the sound is undeniably veracious. Then my tongue maneuvers to the back of my top teeth as I try to force out the double l's. Renne, as hopeful as ever, watches my face, which is scrunched in concentration. Just as I make it to the final letter, the o gets caught in my throat and nothing will come out.

"It's okay, that was so close. Maybe if you drink some more water your voice won't give out so much. Shall I go ask someone to get you a glass?" Renne coaxes as she lowers herself to my level and places her hands on mine. She gives a gentle squeeze of encouragement but I pull away as a singular drip of salt marks a pathway down my cheek.

According to the clock, hanging from the wall of my recovery room/cell, it is five minutes past the time Renne said dinner would be brought to me. She knows that I skipped lunch too which if anything would make her inclined to be early.

Just then the door slides open and I use my hands as leverage to attempt to sit myself up higher. I don't end up accomplishing much with my limited function though.

"Miss Weiss, I would like you to meet your Rebirth counselor," Dr. Jackie introduces. "This is Mr. Hartman." The doctor steps aside and gestures to the man who has followed her in.

"Please call me Miles," he counters warmly with a smile and a subtle squint of his eyes.

The color reminds me of kiwis. And the way he talks

seems different compared to everybody else, but in a way I find it hard to explain. I also pictured him to be a bit older, not in his mid twenties.

As I'm overtaken by the distraction of him my mind subconsciously forces my lips to hum. "Mmm," I take a steady breath, preparing myself to try again, with more awareness this time. "Mmmm-iles," I hiss out forcefully.

I did it. The smile that overtakes me hurts and pulls at the bandages still covering my face but it doesn't matter. I don't think I've smiled at all yet since waking up yesterday.

Miles makes notes on a pad of paper and nods his head in a way that not only communicates approval but what I detect to be pride as well.

"That's the first word that-"

"I know," Miles confirms. "Now why don't we get these bandages off of her?"

"Yes, of course."

Dr. Jackie pulls the swivel chair that was pushed to the corner of the room beside the bed to sit on. It squeaks under her as she continuously moves and unravels the compression wrap. The more her arms circle my head the more my skin becomes exposed to the air. She takes a moment to admire her work once finished and then hovers a handheld mirror out in front of me.

I close my eyes to keep the object of glass and iron out of my field of vision. I want to see, so what is holding me back? Maybe it is the lingering stares of the people in front of me, waiting to see my reaction.

"It's alright, you don't have to look right now. It's okay to take your time," Miles notes.

"N-no. I w-want to."

"Okay, would you like us to look away?" He offers.

I nod.

The mirror gets placed in my hands before I hear their bodies reposition themselves, turning towards the walls nearest them. I wait a few more moments before opening my eyes and hover them just over the mirror's frame, to make sure that no one is looking. They aren't, so slowly I bring the reflective glass more into my view.

I catch the gentle curve of my chin as it becomes exposed, then the arch of my cheekbones. My skin is still swollen and bruised, which leaves me curious as to what and just how much of my facial structure was changed. Keep going, I urge myself. I continue looking now, noticing the thin nose and doe-like eyes that I've been given. The color of which are as gray as a cloud compacted with rain. Conclusively, I bring the mirror closer to take up the full space of the frame. I look beautiful, but feel a strange sensation within me, as if I am an imposter. But how can I feel like an imposter if I don't know what my face looked like before this? Why did I want to change these things about myself in the first place? I seem devoid of color now with my gray eyes and pale skin, not that I have a before image of myself to compare to.

"How are you feeling?" Miles asks while still facing the wall.

I can tell that Dr. Jackie itches to turn back around when her body cheats out to catch a glimpse. Miles places a hand on her back, stopping her from doing so.

"I don't k-know." The words come very slowly as my brain seems to be relearning phonetics.

"May we turn back around now?"

"Y-yes," I confirm.

The doctor happily obliges and immediately gapes at me as if I am some masterpiece in a museum and her scalpel cuts are equivalent to calculated strokes of paint. Miles once again corrects her with his own firm look and she snaps out of her trance with a harsh cough.

"Would you like to go someplace else for our debriefing Miss Weiss? I'm sure you're tired of these four walls."

It's almost as if he can read my mind.

Miles pushes a button on the elevator and the doors glide close. The space is cramped and the machinery old and unreliable yet he seems unbothered anytime we lurch one way or another. He spends the short duration of the ride glancing over his notes and only stops when the elevator emits a melodic ding.

He smiles, tucks the manilla folder he's been going over under his arm, and pushes me onto the open, top deck of the ship. It's smaller than the main deck but it provides for a new view with more to see so I can't complain. Dusk has just fallen and the air is decently chilly but I'm grateful to be out of my cage and away from the circus ringmaster.

"Doctor Jackie has informed me that you are currently able to move your toes, fingers, arms, and neck. Is that correct?" He asks as he pushes me over to the railing and locks the wheels.

"Y-yes," I state with time but confidently, thankful to finally be able to communicate at least something.

"Good, and we have recently come to the realization that your speech is developing again as well. Anything else I should know before I fill you in on everything?" I shake my head no and restlessly await the knowledge that I have been craving. "Very well." Miles pulls one of the deck chairs over and positions it across from me. "First off I would like to apologize for my tardiness, there was a family matter that I had to attend to." He reopens the manilla folder in his lap and clicks open the pen that he had tucked behind his ear. "Next. I would like to ask you what you know or remember already about Rebirth."

"N-nothing much."

"Interesting," he whispers while making another note on his yellow paper. "Usually clients remember at least the general gist of the program but in this case, I will explain." He clears his throat before going on, "Rebirth is a company created in 1949 amidst the aftermath of the Second World War, the one that ended up uniting our nations. At first, the law restricted us to only serving veterans or those with debilitating post-traumatic stress disorder symptoms, but after the protests of '78, we were allowed to open our limits to accommodate a wider demand and help those in witness protection, abusive situations et cetera The first step of going through the Rebirth process is to sit down with a designer and figure out your new life. These details include everything- name, looks, living situation. During this stage you also fill out an extensive survey, pick your package based on affordability, and meet with your surgeon. The second step however was primarily out of your hands as you waited for the board to approve you. While you awaited approval you were preparing to leave behind the life you knew and confirming final details. Then there's the third step, surgery and recovery, which you are currently going through. This is when they erase any memories of a former life and along with it the trauma you've experienced, whatever that may be. They also perform all alterations that have been asked for which is when I come in; although I am most heavily involved in the fourth and final stage, reintegration and adjustment. Is everything making sense so far?"

"I c-choose this?"

"Yes."

"W-why?"

"That information was asked to not be released to you, Miss Weiss."

"By w-who?!" I demand seethingly. The stutter steals some of the power from my statement.

"By you. Well, by the former you."

"But w-why?"

"I think that this is enough information for today, Miss Weiss. I don't want to push you too quickly. I will return early tomorrow morning to explain the rest."

"B-"

I try to protest but the last bit of words seems to catch in my sore and scratched throat as the locks on my chair are released. I am consumed with rage at the number of questions still left unanswered but I can do nothing but comply as I am wheeled out from under the canopy of stars and into the dingy elevator that will send me straight back to my padded cage.

Chapter Three
Tuesday, February 28th

I fake sleep when the night nurse comes in, like a child caught playing past bedtime. My rouse is spotted rather quickly though.

"Would you like to take a walk?" She offers with a bothered sigh. I wish it was Renee here with me instead.

I open just one eye and wait a moment to judge whether I should go or not before beginning to push myself upright. Then she helps me maneuver my legs over the edge of the bed.

"I mean a real walk by the way. We have to try to get those legs of yours moving."

"N-no!"

"You haven't even tried."

There's a moment of fearful silence when all that moves is the sheets under my now tight grip. On one hand, she's right, I haven't really tried yet. But on the other hand, walking feels like the most dangerous thing to do on my own. But I guess I wouldn't exactly be alone.

"We'll start you in the chair but once we're outside you should try to stand yourself. Okay?"

There is no way that I am walking. And what is she going to do about it? Leave me? But still, I say, "Okay."

She left me. She really, truly left me on the main deck in the middle of the night with only the blanket on my lap and two crutch contraptions leaning against my chair. She just had to "tie her shoes," she said, and the next thing I know I'm alone.

I dejectedly push the crutches onto the wood deck and wheel myself back towards the door. I'm going to get her license revoked. You can't just leave a disabled patient alone.

The door's locked. I need a key card to get in. Fuck. I bang my hands against the door with the full force of my anger and don't stop until my skin is red and the muscles underneath start to sore. Then I shrink into my chair.

What now? Is she really not going to let me in until I walk? How would she even know if I did so? She must be watching. How chilling.

I take in my surroundings, surveying for another entrance into the warmth of the ship. There's another door about twenty feet from this one and in between them lays something small on the deck. I pull the wheels back, away from the door, before pushing them towards the object. The closer I get, the more my hope of it being what I think it is rises in me. A slim, medical, key card with the night nurse's somewhat frowning face on it now lays in front of me and I can't help but smile at the correct identification of it. The nurse's name is Carla and she's from Alnerwick.

I hold onto the back of my chair with one hand for balance and lean towards the ID with the other. I outstretch my arm till I'm teetering on falling but it works because the tips of my fingers squeeze the card and pull it back towards me. I give a victorious laugh and swiftly wheel back over towards the nearest door.

I reach the ID up to tap it against the chip reading square on the wall but it's once again very much out of my reach and no amount of stretching will save me this time. Carla's forcing me to stand.

I could try. Or I could flop onto the deck of the ship

like a fish losing oxygen and use the last of my effort to roll underneath the railing into the sea. No, I want to at least find out my full name before I seriously contemplate the option of death. But it depends on how good this name I choose for myself is, that could make or break my decision.

I use my arms to lift my bare legs onto the cold deck. A shiver runs its way up my spine along with a blinding pain. "Bitch," the word is spoken into the wind but directed at Carla.

I aggressively slap my legs to help wake the muscles before leaning one way and then the other to test my weight. I then use what little arm strength I possess to push my upper body into a standing position. The second I do my legs become liquid and my body slams against the metal door.

I look down at my hands to find the left one cut open from a sharp corner of the door handle. "What the fuck!" I scream into the dark abyss. This is the longest sentence and the most vocal energy I've been able to produce so far.

I'm starting to re-contemplate letting myself be taken by the frigid ocean waves and having the moonlight as my only witness when Carla instructs me to get up from the shadows. I turn to catch her with my eyes but she moves farther away as I do, making it hard to track her. I can't tell if I'm shaking more from anger or the early onset of frostbite that must be infecting my body.

"Let. Me. In."

"No." I can finally see the silhouette of her body as she walks along the railing of the ship before leaning against it, observing me as if I am once again the circus freak in a ring doing a trick for her amusement.

"You're going to b-be in s-so much trouble," I groan between clenched teeth.

"Really? Because the way I see it you manipulated me into taking a walk late at night. I knew it was wrong but my empathetic heart just felt so bad for you," she cries out with mock regret. "Then when we got outside you tried to steal my keycard and roll away with it but failed. I have no idea why you did that but I am pregnant and therefore simply could not keep up." She places a hand on her barely showing stomach which I thought was just bloating that had been poorly concealed by her nurse's scrubs. She should consider sizing up soon. "Your move." She grins, clearly satisfied with herself.

"Oh Carla," a lower voice croons in disappointment.

She jumps. "Mr. Hartman, I was just giving the girl some fresh air and she fell from her ch-chair. I was just about to pick her up but thought that she would want to see if she could walk first."

"Please, save your breath."

Miles steps out of the shadows and grabs the wheelchair to roll closer to me. He's wearing plain clothes and his face holds signs of tiredness that did not show previously. He locks the wheels as Carla attempts once more to escape her lies.

"Could you grab the blanket from over there?" He interrupts, pointing to where the thin fabric fell away from me at some point.

Carla hastily dashes for it and upon returning attempts to defend herself a final time. Miles gently takes the blanket clutched in her hands and shakes his head in disapproval. This silences her for good and her deep peach checks become a rosy maroon as soon as Miles hands her the key card back.

"You should go," he commands bitterly.

"Yes, of course." Then she hurries away, towards another entrance near the bow of the ship.

"I am so sorry about her. May I?" He asks, gesturing toward the chair. I nod.

He gives me an awkward half-smile before gently putting one arm under the crease of my knees and the other behind my back. He lifts me with ease and places me down lightly in the chair. He then takes the blanket he draped over the back and lays it across my shoulders. I adjust it to shield more of my skin away from the night chill as I urge the chattering of my teeth to stop.

"Would you like to go inside now?"

"Yes, please."

He presses his own keycard to the sensor and maneuvers around me to push the door open after it unlocks. The warmth of the hallway heaters greet me as I am rolled back inside. Behind us, the door mechanics slot back into place. I expect him to drop me back off in my room without another word but instead, he brings me past the door labeled 337.

"Where would you like to go?"

"Excuse m-me?"

"If you want to go to bed I can bring you back to your room. I just figured that the reason you two were out was because you were tired of the same scenery." I shrug as we turn the corner. The only places that I have seen are my cell and the outdoor decks. "Can I bring you to my favorite place on the ship?" Miles asks with a profuse amount of excitement.

"O-only if you tell me more about who I am."

"Deal."

He stops at an elevator in the middle of the hall and pushes the button to call it to us. The doors open quickly, and upon stepping inside, Miles presses the bottommost number on the wall panel. I stare at the elevator numbers as we travel down. Floor eight, floor six.

"Close your eyes. I'll tell you when to open them."

I'm unsure if I should or not considering the last and pretty recent time I was blindsided I was left alone to crawl and freeze on the deck of the ship.

"Please."

I read that we are now on level four as I sigh and close my eyes.

"Thank you."

I hear the electronic dings signaling that we have gone down three more floors. Then the doors slide open with another ding and Miles is wheeling me out. We don't go very far though before he instructs me to open my eyes. I do so, slowly.

The sight around me makes my breath catch and my tongue feel loose and unable to convey words. We're in a hallway, except not a normal one. The floor and convexed walls are made of glass, showcasing schools of vibrant fish and other wildlife on the other side. The only source of brightness illuminating the space is from the blue-tinted ceiling lights.

I wheel myself closer to one of the curved walls and place my hand against the cool glass. Miles comes to stand next to me as I do.

"Pretty cool, huh?"

"Yeah," I breathe out, still stuck in a state of astonishment.

Just then a leopard-printed animal swims close to the glass causing me to pull back with a jump. Miles laughs.

"That's a small spotted catshark. Very common in The North Sea." I look up at him with questioning eyes. He shrugs, "I've always had a fascination with animals. And I did a report on sharks in grade school," he confesses.

I can't help but chuckle. Oh my god, I haven't laughed since waking up to this nightmare. It feels nice but I have to stay focused. We made a deal.

"What's my name?"

"I notice that you've been stuttering less."

"You didn't answer my question."

"You're right, my apologies. The name that you have given yourself is Emily. Emily Jane Weiss."

"Emily," I test the sound out. I like the way he says it better, it sounds less plain. "Why did I sign up for Rebirth?"

"You did not want that information available to you. All that you wanted to know in this life was the name Wren and that he is dangerous," he explains in a cautious manner as he leans against one of the glass walls.

"Dangerous how?"

"I'm not sure."

"What do you mean? Isn't that something you would have thought to ask?"

"We did, you choose not to share the specifics."

We both take a moment of silence. I mourn and Miles pays his respects. Then I pick back up into our cadence of questions. "Where are we?"

"Didn't I just say? We're in The North Sea," he teases.

"I mean where are we docked genius."

"Accrington."

"Yes, I know that. What part?"

"Croyden. But you choose to live in a cute little town about an hour from here, New Cresthill."

"Interesting. What day is it today?"

"As of a few hours ago it is February 28th."

"What was my job? You know, before my memory was stripped from me."

"You were a freelance screenplay writer."

"So you can tell me that but nothing else about my life?"

"You mean past life," he corrects.

"Right."

"I can tell you this piece of information because you stated that you would prefer to continue with this career. But of course, if you don't want to then you don't have to. There were many other careers recommended to you based on your interests- the top three being a librarian, actress, and literary critic."

I take a moment to digest everything that's being thrown at me. My given name is Emily, I was a screenplay writer, I am now going to live in New Cresthill- wherever that may be- and I have no idea where I lived before. Also, there's a dangerous person named Wren that could be the very reason for me doing this to myself.

"So when do I get to see this new home of mine?"

"Tomorrow. Hopefully, we can get your feet working by then because the house isn't very handicap friendly and-"

"And?"

"I didn't say and."

"Yes, you did."

He pauses for a long while, "Dr. Jackie wanted to tell you herself but if you don't regain function by tomorrow then there is a higher chance of permanent paralysis."

"P-permanent?" Fuck, I was just getting a hold of that stupid stutter.

"Yes, unfortunately."

I turn my chair away from him to face the opposite wall. "Could I have a moment alone?"

"I'm sorry, but you're not supposed to be unattended."

"Please." My voice cracks at the end of the word in desperation. I can see that he is still debating on whether he should move or not. "I w-woke up a few days ago not being able to speak, move, or remember anything about my life. And then just now I was abandoned, outside, on the floor by a nurse who was supposed to be helping me, a-and to put the icing on the f-fucking cake I just found out that I might be paralyzed for the rest of my life so please, please can you just go for a moment?!" I scream at him. My tongue trips over the s's and p's but I force them out for the sake of making my point.

He looks around the linear hallway before swiping his key card and dismissing himself behind one of the unmarked doors. "I'll check on you in five," he informs before I'm left alone to my own devices.

For the next five minutes my eyes multitask as I try to keep track of the small spotted catshark while also mourning the potential loss of my legs. The occasional blur of my vision makes it out to be a hard task, but I like pretending that I am the animal, able to swim with ease and at will.

In reality I am not the animal, and knowing so makes the tears falling from my eyes come with more force now. The only way the two of us can truly relate is because we are both currently trying to make it through a stream of salt. But even this fact is clouded by the realization that the animal can swim, whereas I can't help but drown.

Chapter Four
Wednesday, March 1st

The rest of yesterday was spent sleeping and in physical therapy for my legs. I was able to move my hips more with the activities I was given, but after about four hours of work, that's all that was able to be accomplished.

I also told Renne about what the night nurse did early yesterday morning and how Miles found me while out on his walk. Together the two of them reported Carla and they reassured me that she has been immediately pulled from my case and her license suspended until an investigation can be done.

It's not like I would have to deal with her again though, because today I am going home. Not to a home that I recognize but instead a place with four walls and a roof. Sheler feels like a more correct term I guess. This home that I have been assigned to is an empty shell of a house that holds nothing more than the most basic of furniture.

Miles, Dr. Jackie, and the rest of my medical team are stopping by within the next hour to discharge me but until then Renne helps me to get ready. She assists me with bathing for the first time since my surgeries and brushes the knots out of my matted hair afterward. She even offers to style it. When I agree, she eagerly sits on the edge of the bed and begins to braid starting from my scalp. Her legs dangle off the side but don't quite reach the floor, so now and again they bang against the bed.

She finishes off the second braid with a small tie before applying both a hydration and steroid cream to my face and figure. The medicinal components cause a tingling sensation that makes me feel more clean and refreshed than I've been in days. The swelling and bruising have also drastically decreased since the bandages came off two days ago but hints of my facial reconstruction still show if you stare long enough.

I pull the towel around me tighter as it begins to slip, retucking the corner. It's all that has been covering me since my bath. I am about to ask for real clothes when Renne holds a small tablet to my face. Options worn by faceless models fill the screen. All of my options are bleak and colorless. I guess the Rebirth package I chose must have been the most basic. I end up going with a pair of jeans, a brown oversized sweater and boots.

To retrieve them Renne presses her hand against the panel in the wall, the one used to deliver any goods, and they appear instantly along with socks and undergarments. She grabs them and assists me with putting them on. I have no problems fastening the bra and I can pull the sweater on myself, but when it's time to put the bottoms on I am unable to do so alone. Renne helps by putting the beige underwear and blue jeans on my lower legs and allowing me to pull them up myself. Somehow it's more vulnerable than when she was helping me to bathe, perhaps from the lack of bubbles I previously used to cover myself.

When we are done, she stands back to observe me as if I am her doll that she has prepared for a beauty pageant. "I'm not supposed to do this, but here," she takes a pink tube from her pocket and unscrews the lid. "Pucker your lips like this," she makes an odd shape with her lips which I try to mimic. Renne giggles at the way I copy her face as she begins to apply a thin layer of gloss to my lips. "I wish I had my mascara with me too. You have the most wonderful eyelashes."

"Thank you, Renne. Your kindness has meant everything to me these past few days."

"Of course. I'm just saddened to see you go without the full function of your legs."

"How uncommon is this?" I dare to ask as I look down to my legs.

"Well, this has only happened once before in my two years of being with this program, and we help about ten thousand a year. I wasn't personally working on the case, just heard about it through the grapevine, so that's all I know. It occurred in our Altone location."

"R-really?"

She seems to have realized the bluntness of her tone rather quickly and attempts to backtrack, "Oh yeah but I don't mean to frighten you. The doctor you've been transferred to is quite good and has a very successful rate of rec-"

"Good morning." The main door bursts open and Dr. Jackie along with a team of other random doctors flood the space, intruding on mine and Renne's moment. "We'll keep this short since you have quite a day of travel and adjusting ahead of you. I just need to do a last-minute checkup and have you sign some documents and then you're solely Mr. Hartman's responsibility. First off, would you like to try walking again?"

I do want to but the numerous, unknown spectators with notepads make my throat dry and my muscles tense. I don't need this many people to witness me fall. Why are they even here if not to document my failures? I believe Dr. Jackie can sense the source of my hesitation since she then introduces the people as student interns and informs them to observe through the glass window in the viewing room instead. I wasn't even aware that there was a viewing area for my room. The interns leave and then it is just me, Renne, Dr. Jackie, and Miles- who had come in with the rest of the group but stood removed from them.

"Would you like to try now?" Dr. Jackie asks again.

I want to tell her no because not having them in my eyeline or peripheral vision doesn't mean I'm not aware that I am still in theirs. But Renne and Miles wear encouraging expressions so I feel obligated to try, if not for me then for them.

"S-sure."

"Wonderful. Why don't you try putting your feet on the ground first."

I use my hands to help pilot my legs to the side of the bed. They fall limply to the floor, hanging lifelessly. I glance around for something to grab onto when I inevitably fall, but there's nothing but people and the bed. Someone whispers words of encouragement to me, though I am too focused to pay any attention as to who said them.

I take a tentative breath before leaning to my left and then my right, I can't feel much of a difference in comparison to when I did this last. Before I change my mind though I push myself off of the bed. My weak arms shake and shortly after begin to buckle under the weight of holding up my body. I am forced to slowly lower myself till I rely fully and completely on my feet. I can feel my toes and my hips, I remind myself. Maybe today I will be able to feel my knees too.

Once I make unmitigated contact with the floor my legs give out and down I fall. Luckily no smack of my lifeless legs hitting the tile occurs because I am caught by both Renne and Miles. Dr. Jackie callously makes a note in her chart.

"Try again."

"What?" Didn't she see what just happened?

"Try again."

I look up at Renne and Miles. Their faces echo my concerns. "Can I at least receive help this time?"

"Fine, yes. One person may assist you."

"One?"

"Yes, Miles can."

"Fine." I'll take what I can get.

Renne slowly lets go of me and cautiously backs away.

Miles then moves to stand behind me and supports my upper body by placing his arms under mine.

"The doctor's just annoyed that this has to happen in front of her students. But you have nothing to prove." Miles whispers in my ear, which tickles the hairs on my skin. "Ready?"

"I think so."

"Okay, I'm going to hold you up but try to move your legs as if you're riding a bicycle. Can you do that for me?"

I put my hands on his for support as I prepare to move. I want to remind him that I might not even know how to ride a bike but this isn't the best time. At first, all that seems to come to life are my hips, and then after a moment, the muscles in my ankles begin to loosen up as well. They flop somewhat loosely as if the tether from the muscles to my brain is still fractured but regardless they are going in the direction that I want them to.

"Good," he encourages. I can tell through his words that he is smiling. "Keep going." I can't help but wear a matching grin myself as I continue moving.

A few more seconds pass before Miles has to adjust, switching his grip to my lower waist. I'm glad he does so as the pressure of lifting me was starting to hurt my underarms. Somehow, his grip has been staying stiff throughout the whole process, refusing to shake or waver. However, unsurprisingly, no change has occurred since my ankles were revived.

"How much longer do you want me to do this?" I ask the doctor, beginning to tire.

"Just another minute."

As she says this my knees unlock and start to move in motion with my hips and feet though it's still as if my body parts are moving separately from each other and my brain isn't entirely sure where the nerves should be connected. This must be a funny sight as I likely look like a fish out of water, but it doesn't matter because I am pushing myself to move faster and in more aggressive circles, progressively growing more at ease with my movements.

For a bit everything is great. I am not becoming just another statistic. But then my foot collides with Miles's kneecap, causing it to buckle, and the two of us collapse to the ground.

Renne runs to our side while Dr. Jackie's grin slips from her face. "Thank you, that is enough for today. Renne will finish up the rest of the checkup and I'll send in one of the students to help you out with the paperwork. It was a pleasure treating you Miss Weiss, have a nice day." She waits till Miles sits me back on the bed to shake my hand formally. Then she leaves.

"Are you okay?" Miles asks, straightening out his collared shirt.

I press my lips together to keep from laughing but the air still escapes my nose, making a funny noise. I clamp my hand over my mouth but that does nothing to conceal the fit of uncontrollable laughter that inevitably comes out.

"Is she okay?" He directs the question to Renne. She shrugs.

"I just I- I did it. Kinda. I- I did something."

Renne pushes my chair until we get to the gangway that leads off of the ship. From there Miles takes over, picking me up and helping me into the car waiting for us on land. As he places me down on the seat I find myself having trouble wanting to let go of his shirt. I watch in entirety as he breaks down the wheelchair and places it in the back. I don't let my eyes wander until he's seated across from me. He has the answers I need. He is safe. I need him.

The driver starts the car and I roll down the window nearest me to wave a final goodbye to Renne as Miles clicks his seatbelt in place. Then we start towards my new home.

We're halfway there with another thirty minutes to go. I've spent the entire time so far admiring the colorful buildings and tiny hills, but we lost the mass groupings of apartments and public spaces a while back, so now there's only the occasional house or town every few miles.

"I have a question."

"What is it?"

"Why was Carla so distasteful towards me? Is she like that with everyone?"

He takes his time coming up with an answer, pausing his charting to do so. "I don't know her very well. She only works night shifts and doesn't usually have much contact with patients since most of them are sleeping during her rounds. But sometimes nurses have off days or sometimes-"

"Sometimes what?"

"Nothing."

"I don't like when you do that."

"Do what?"

"Not finish your sentences, it's annoying."

"Sorry. It's just-" he pauses to redirect. "Sometimes there are rumors that go around about why clients choose to go through the Rebirth process. It's a daunting task to wipe your memory and start entirely anew, staff members simply get curious as to why since no one in the company is legally allowed to ask or know unless the client allows us to have acess to that information, in order to protect your privacy."

"So what do they think my reasoning is?" I re-evaluate and counter with another question. "Do you know the reason?"

"It is not my job to know that. And again I don't know if they heard anything about you, I was simply saying that it's a possibility."

"Okay."

I let this sink in for a moment as I stare back out the window. We pass over a small stone bridge with a sign off to the side, announcing that we've crossed over into the town of New Cresthill.

"Are there any other questions that you have?"

I ponder for a moment on whether I should broach the

subject or not. "I have been thinking about something else actually. You told me yesterday that my old self only wanted me to know the name Wren and that he is dangerous. Who do you think that could be?"

"I'm not at liberty to say nor influence."

"So you do know who Wren is?" A million emotions flash through my brain: anger, hope, excitement. But I keep my cool.

"No. But I am saying that even if I did know. I would not be able to tell you."

"Fine."

I accept defeat and crack the window to let the cold breeze in. As the air hits my face I let my thoughts take me away to a time when I had a family and probably friends, maybe even a dog or cat that depended on me for food, and water, and walks in the park.

Miles calls my name, coaxing me out of my daydreams. "We're here."
I glance out the car's glass as we pull in front of a cottage with a thatched roof. There are two tiny windows in the front, both decorated with a flower box underneath. The flowers, freshly planted with beautiful tulips of every color, are the only thing new about this place. The unmistakable signs of aging are evident in the intricate cracks that adorn the surface of the beige brick while the windows appear to be layered in a film of dust that creates an odd distortion over the glass that can be seen even from here. The shutters, that are currently pushed away from the windows, are colored in a deep green and feature heart-shaped cutouts for handles.

There's only one other house in sight and it exists about a quarter mile from this one on the opposite side of the road.

"Reclusivity does seem to be perfect for someone who can't completely walk yet," I spit out sarcastically.

"Your temporary paralysis is an unforeseen defect that

was not expected and it's what you requested. Luckily though that house over there," he points to the matching lonesome structure that I had just noticed, "has been assigned to me."

"You'll live here too?"

"All Rebirth mentors move as close to their patients as possible to provide the best quality care and 24/7 availability." That does make me feel a bit better about everything.

"So how long does it take to get into town from here?" I ask as he lifts me into a wheelchair.

"It's about a fifteen-minute walk or a five-minute bike ride."

"Bike ride? They don't do cars here?"

"A bike is the only vehicle that is included in your Rebirth plan."

"Oh."

"But there is also a twenty-four-hour cab service at your disposal." He informs me as I am pushed towards the wooden door, which is stained a deep brown.

He pulls out a ring of keys as I notice that one of the hinges is screwed on incorrectly, leading to an unfortunate finger width of wiggle room between the bottom of the door and the frame.

"Your key should be on the table inside," he informs as he places the correct piece of metal into the lock and twists.

He pushes the door open lightly, leans the chair back to bring the wheels over the small stone slab outside the front door, and rolls me into the house, making sure to kick the door closed with his foot. Outside I hear the car pull out of the gravel driveway.

"Here we are. If you would like to rest I can help you into bed and come back later."

"No!" I object. "The last thing that I want to do is spend another minute in bed."

"Okay. Then why don't I give you a tour?"

Though there's not much of a tour to give, still I say, "sure."

Most of the floor plan is small and open with the

kitchen, living and dining room being in the same space. Each room has basic furniture that is unfortunately damaged in one way or another. There is the couch with a large rip in the back, counters that have deeply embedded stains from past cooking endeavors, and a table with chipping paint. There are no pictures or artwork, which I guess makes sense considering I have none.

The bedroom and bathroom on the other hand are off to the side of the house. The bed is covered in an ugly quilted pattern comforter and the washer and dryer are shoved into the already cramped closet, but overall it could be worse.

"There's one more thing I have to show you. May I?" Miles gestures toward the handles of my chair as I had begun pushing myself around since coming inside. I nod, giving him the go ahead.

He pushes me out the front door and around to the side of the house. The wheels are difficult on the wet dirt and sink into the land countless times, but Miles is determined and continues onward. The exterior is infested with ivy which hangs over the one window that lets splotchy light into the kitchen.

When we reach the back we come into contact with a grand section of land cordoned off by a stone wall and a small green fence gate. Miles pushes up the latch and pulls me inside, which is when I notice that if I was just a bit taller, or really if I could stand, then I would have seen this sight from my bedroom window.

"You mentioned in your forms that you also wanted to try out gardening and I know it's not growing season for another month or so but I was thinking maybe we could do some arugula over here and maybe broccoli and cauliflower over there?"

"Broccoli and cauliflower?" I question with a raise of my eyebrows.

"Well, it's your garden, whatever you want to plant we can."

"We?"

"You. Whatever you want to plant you can," he corrects. "I'll only assist if that's what you wish."

I didn't mind his inclusion, it's just the lack of discussion that confused me. "I think I would like a lemon tree or two and maybe a couple of different types of berries."

The garden mirrors the rest of the house, overgrown and falling apart. It's nothing special but I appreciate the potential to see beyond the damage. Maybe one day, when I do have all of my leg strength restored, I can make this place what it should be, but for now, I can only plan.

"Are you hungry? It's just about dinner time."

"Starving actually." I have been repressing the sounds of my stomach grumbling since about half-way through the drive. I'm sure if I asked for something to eat they would have provided but I didn't want to be a bother.

"Your cupboards have already been filled with a month's supply of food so we can make something for you here or we could go to the diner in town if you would like to get out and explore a bit. If that's what you wish then I can call the car to come back."

I stare out into the empty abyss of land that shows nothing nearby except for Miles's house, as I mull over my options. "I think I'll just stay here for tonight, but maybe you can show me around town tomorrow."

"Of course."

After having Miles call out the ingredients in my pantry we settle on a simple chicken soup. He pulls the metal lid off of the can of broth and dumps it into a pot sitting on the stovetop. While it heats the two of us sit in silence at the dining room table. He cuts up the celery while I do the carrots.

"Are you alright?" He asks as he notices me place my knife down despite the partly cut vegetable in front of me.

"My hand is cramping.I guess my muscles just aren't that strong yet."

"Don't worry, they'll get there. If you want I can schedule your first appointment with Dr. Pierce for tomorrow to try to get a move on the recovery of those joints."

"Sure, that would be nice."

He acknowledges my response and then scrapes the cut-up celery pieces off his cutting board and into the pot. He then runs the board under cold water before preparing the chicken.

"Miles."

"Yes?"

"Do I have a bank account?"

"Yes, with around two thousand dollars currently deposited into it." He stirs the broth as he talks. "While we're on the topic of money, I should inform you that your monthly rent is six hundred and fifty dollars so we should look into potential job opportunities in the area sometime soon but for today you should worry only about adjusting."

I nod my head as I pick the knife back up and continue to cut the carrots. There's only a tiny nub left but I'm set on seeing it through to the end. Meanwhile, Miles takes his spot back across from me with the chicken.

Chapter Five
Thursday, March 2nd

The home phone awakens me around nine. I pull the pillow over my eyes as it rings through its cycle the first time. But just as it ends it picks back up again. I groan and drag my legs to the edge of the bed. Luckily Miles left the wheelchair close to me last night after helping me get under the covers. I pull it near me and sit atop the cushionless, caned seat. I wheel myself out of the bedroom with the ugly bedspread and towards the front door where the phone has fallen off its base. It hangs loosely by its cord and for a moment I debate grabbing the kitchen scissors and snipping the wire. Instead, I pick it up.

"Hello," I answer groggily.

"Morning," Miles's voice chirps back. "I'll be over in a few minutes so start getting ready. You have your first appointment with Dr. Pierce at ten. See you in a minute!"

He hangs up and I leave the phone to dangle, since I realize that I can't reach to put it back on the wall where it should be. Then I push myself towards the bedroom.

Upon opening my daytime clothes dresser drawer I discover that these options are just as plain as what I wore yesterday. I guess I'll have to add shopping to my to-do list. And not just for clothes, furniture too. Everything in here is so outdated and impersonal.

I settle on brown corduroy pants and an even darker brown turtleneck, laying everything out on the bed before going to the bathroom to brush my teeth. I opened the beige toothbrush from its packaging last night along with shampoo, conditioner, face wash, and other sanitary items I was given in a nicely wrapped box placed under the sink.

I wonder if I had a routine before, one that I followed through with consistently every morning. I wonder if these are the products that I used prior to my memory being usurped. And were these the clothes that I would wear? If so then I needed better taste.

The second I finish freshening up there's a knock on the main door. I bump into the doorframe, a result of trying to get out of the bathroom quickly, before maneuvering myself into earshot range.

"It's open," I call out before shuffling around to continue getting ready.

The squeak of the doors hinges let me know that Miles has come inside. "Hey, how are you this morning? Have you been adjusting nicely?" He asks professionally as he closes the door behind him.

I hear him hang up the telephone and place something heavy on the ground. Curiosity gets the best of me so I pull the wheels of my chair backwards till I can see into the living room. He's brought with him a red, rusted toolbox that he searches through for screws, pulling up different ones to match them to the one in the door.

Suddenly I remember to answer him, "well, I can't exactly see into the bathroom mirror so that's fun."

"This place wasn't exactly designed with accessibility in mind, unfortunately," he reminds me. "I can try to fix that issue for you if you would like though."

"It's alright, I don't plan to be in this chair much longer."

Miles stops turning the screwdriver placed against the door hinge for a moment to smile at me. He must have taken my comment as optimism despite the clear ring of annoyance behind the words.

"Anyway I was wondering if you wanted to get breakfast after the appointment."

"Uh, sure."

"Great. If you want to finish getting ready we should be on our way soon."

I push the bedroom door shut so that I can get dressed as he continues fiddling with the hinge. I once again have no issue getting a bra and the top on but the second I am tasked with my underwear it proves difficult. I try to hook the garment around my left foot as I hold it up with my opposite hand but it's like trying to throw a line in the same spot every time you fish.

"Are you okay in there?" Miles asks with a gentle knock on the door after some time has passed. "I don't mean to rush you, just checking in."

"Oh, uh, yeah. I'm doing great."

"I'm done with the door. Will you be ready to go soon?"

"Uh, yeah, yeah. Just give me five more minutes"

"Okay."

Maybe I could go without the underwear for today? But on second thought, if the doctor at this appointment asks me to get into a gown like the one I was wearing yesterday I would probably feel most comfortable with something underneath.

I hold the underwear more steady and controlled this time with both hands and place it at my feet. It hangs, balanced in the middle, before I lift my leg with one hand and pull with the other. When the clothing reaches my hips I lift them up and then adjust to make them comfortable. I did it. I put them on by myself!

Rejuvenated by a newfound confidence I try the pants but they are larger and bulkier. After a few attempts that do not prevail I admit defeat and mumble a string of curse words together.

"Miles? There is something that I could… could you

just... could you come in please?"

"Sure."

"But just so you know I'm not wearing any-"

"Oh."

"Pants," I finish the sentence pathetically despite him already infiltrating the space. He squeezes his eyes shut and places a hand over his face for extra measure. "No, you see, that's actually what I need your help with…"

"Oh!" He exlaims as the realization comes to him. He sheepishly lowers his hand but the green of his eyes still hide mostly behind his eyelashes.

"Yeah."

He comes to sit by my side. "I wasn't made aware by your medical team that you still couldn't dress yourself. How did you change clothes last night?"

"It took a while."

"I see."

"I managed my underwear just now but the pants are going to take longer as it's a more strenuous process," I explain as I offer over the piece of clothing. He takes them from me.

"May I?"

He gestures towards my exposed legs and we both become painfully aware of just how uncomfortable this truly is. Either way, I nod, because what other choice do I have? Leaving the house without pants would be far more embarrassing.

He kneels at my feet and bunches up one pant leg and then the other so that it's easier to slip on. I use my arms to lift my feet into both legs and then Miles pulls them up halfway for me. His cold fingers graze my skin up until my knees, which is where I take over. Our fingers overlap during the transfer of clothing and he gently pulls away after a moment of contact, even turning his back in respect as I lift my hips to pull the pants around my butt.

"Ready?" He asks once I pull up the zipper and push the button through the hole.

"Yeah."

The wheels are unsteady on the dirt road. The motion makes me feel queasy and I want nothing more than to get out of this chair. Miles checks in on me now and then but if he saw the unusual paleness of my face he would realize how contradictory my statements of reassurance have been to him.

We're so close to town now. I estimate that we've been walking for about seven minutes already, and mostly in silence. It's a comfortable silence though, a safe silence.

"How are you doing? Still good?"

"Yeah, how about you?"

"Oh I'm fine, don't worry about me."

I look up at him in curiosity. He's barely struggling and yet he's been pushing me through unruly ground for minutes on end. He notices me staring and smiles down at me. Any normal person would look away but I don't. And he doesn't either, which causes me to fall to the dirt when he steers me right into a large rock that hits the wheel at an odd angle.

"Are you okay? I'm so sorry I didn't see the-"

"I'm fine, it's all good." I brush myself off and check my limbs for any scrapes or tender spots that might feature future bruising. Nothing. "See," I turn my arms over for him to examine.

"Okay, but I think it might just be easier if I carry you the rest of the way. Would that be alright?"

"Carry me? And do what with the chair?"

"We'll leave it here, on the side of the road, till we can come back for it anyways."

"That's crazy," I spat out with a laugh. "You're not worried that somebody's going to steal it?"

"Not at all, the crime rate here is practically non-existent. Now if you were assigned to live in Croyden then that's a different story."

"So you're going to carry me?"

"If that's okay with you."

"I guess."

Miles bends down and wipes the dirt from my pants before instructing me to place my arms behind his neck. I do so and he counts down from three before lifting me with ease. Then we start back towards town and once again fall into silence, except this time it's not comfortable, at least not for me. I overthink every breath and readjustment. We only have a few more yards to go and with each step I slightly bump against him. I pretend to be back in the chair instead of crumpled and crippled in his arms to save myself from feeling the full force of my embarrassment.

"Here we are," he announces as he carries me up the steps that lead to one of the houses on the outskirts of the town. To the side of the steps is an elongated, paved, stone ramp.

Miles knocks on the door. The sound of dropping metal and banging copper comes from inside as well as a gruff, indistinguishable voice. Then the old door is aggressively pulled open and in its place is an even older man.

"Mr. Hartman? Miss Weiss?"

It takes me a minute to realize that the lanky man with a head full of silver hair is referring to me. I guess I'm still getting used to my name.

"Yes," Miles responds once he realizes that it will not be me who does the talking.

"Come on in."

He waits for us to just cross the border between out and in before slamming the door shut with just as much force as he used to pull it open. He pushes a wheelchair over for me and Miles gently bends to place me on the seat. Once I am comfortably situated I notice something caught underneath one of the wheels. I lean over to pick it up and see that it is a sketch of a person's left leg with the bones, muscles, and joints labeled. The man snatches the paper from me and places it on a table in front of the window with a rock overtop of it to act as a weight. This brings my attention to a nearby wall of poorly tacked-up papers which must have gone through a frenzy when the breeze swept through them.

"Right this way."

Miles pushes me into an adjacent room, which is surprisingly more modern in comparison to the tiny waiting area we were just in that held no more than a desk and three poorly constructed chairs.

"The goal is to get you walking Miss Weiss," the doctor says as he sits down and opens up a paper file. There's one dingy computer in the room but it doesn't appear to be in working condition based on the cracked screen and glitching pixels. "My first suggestion is to build strength in the muscles that you already have complete function of, as you started to do under Dr. Jackie's care. Then I would like to get you standing by the end of the hour that we have together today. Does that all sound okay?"

"Yes, that sounds manageable Doctor…" I drag out the r a bit in hopes of him filling in the blank for me. I don't remember his name though I know that Miles has said it in the past.

"Lovely, then in that case I would like you to simply straighten and bend your knees for me about ten times on each side. Mr. Hartman will observe while I go check on something."

"His name is Dr. Pierce," Miles informs me after the man excuses himself from the room.

The first half hour of the appointment is filled with what should be particularly easy instructions. "Tighten the upper thigh muscle." "Lift your legs one at a time." But it's not easy. For some reason, it is very difficult and excruciatingly frustrating. I understand the point, logistically it makes sense, but my body begs me to slow down with leg cramps and the feeling of exhaustion.

"How are we doing?" Dr. Pierce asks as he rubs at least an ounce of sanitizer into his hands. He's been absent half of the time so far, bouncing back and forth between me and whoever is in the next room over.

"It's been fine."

He looks to Miles for the truth, clearly not believing my unconvincing tone. "There's been some struggle but the more she does it the easier it gets," he confides.

Dr. Pierce nods, accepting this answer with more ease. "Would you like to try to stand now Miss Weiss?"

"I-I'm not sure. Maybe I should just stick to the exercises for today?" My muscles are screaming for a break. I am not ready to stand yet no matter how much I want to.

"Your counselor and I will be right next to you the whole time and you will be holding onto something."

He must be able to tell that I'm still unconvinced because he uses a key to unlock the closet in the room and pulls out a walker. At first, I think it's for him but then he places it in front of me and stands back. I look down at it almost offended. Someone my age should not be using this.

"How about you just try to hold yourself up for now," Dr. Pierce suggests.

"The last time we did this it didn't go so well," I mumble.

"Just try it, Emily. We'll be right here if you fall."

No, you'll be right there. The old guy might break his brittle bones if I fall on him. I want to speak my mind but I bite my tongue. Instead, all I say is, "Fine."

I scooch to the edge of the chair and use my arms to lift myself up and above the walker. I dangle for a minute, relying on my hands and the strength of my arms.

"Great, now straighten your feet and place them on the ground."

I roll my eyes, ultimately knowing how this will turn out. But still, the joints in my knees straighten and the bottom of my boots graze the floor.

"Can you try to put some pressure on your lower body?"

"Sure, but it won't work, not for long at least."

"Quite the optimist, aren't you?" The doctor sneers.

"At least I'm not pushy," I reply.

"I'd rather be pushy and get results than scared and go nowhere in life, literally." He looks me up and down, his eyes searing me with judgment.

"Fine. You want me to move? I'll move."

I lock my knees and waste no time putting weight on my feet. I stay up for no more than a moment before my muscles throb, pulse, and give out. I fall on my hands and knees, which will most definitely cause a bruise to appear on my thigh later.

"Was that enough proof for you?" I fume from the floor.

"Depends. Would you rather damage your skin for change or stick with your broken body? Because one is a matter of temporary color and soreness while the other… well, really you must ask yourself what is worth sacrificing?"

The purpose of his final words seems clouded, as if they are aimed at more than the subject of my legs. Or maybe I am just misdirecting my anger. I have no idea why I chose to do what I did, but it is done, and I must live with it. I must live with my unworking bones and my absent memory. But if I don't try to make the best of it then what was it all for? I pull myself up.

I grab the walker and use it as leverage. My legs limply hang below me until I place my feet back on the floor again. This time around I decide to slowly put pressure on my feet. I stand for twice as long, but I am still not upright for more than five seconds before I am once again on the wood floor. I think a splinter might have lodged into my red hands.

"Very good. We'll try this again next time. Between now and then do more of those strength exercises in the chair, but please do not attempt to walk without an aid nearby."

"That's it? You're going to push me just to call five seconds good enough?"

"It's progress. Compared to where you were yesterday, I'll take it."

"Progress, right," I scoff.

"Yes, and if you want to continue making any more, you might want to drop the attitude."

Drop the attitude? I don't know who my father is but I know that he sure as hell isn't this guy.

"Would you like to go to breakfast now?" Miles asks, clearly in an attempt to divert the current tension. He has been silently observing in the corner, wincing when I would fall and twitching when he knew it would be frowned upon by this new man to help me up.

"No. Just take me home, please."

"Are you sure? You-"

"Just get me out of here."

Chapter Six
Friday, March 3rd

I spend the morning in bed, snuggled inside the plaid comforter like a caterpillar in a red cocoon. I do not get up when my stomach grumbles or when the pitcher on my bedside table drains empty. I do not get up when the strong winds move the bent lock and blow the bedroom window open, or even when there's a knock on the door and Miles calls out my name. I tell him to go away. I do, however, get curious when faint scratching comes from the wall behind me.

I lift my head. At first, I wonder if I'm about to have my first encounter with a mouse, but the noise appears to be coming from outside. But mice can still be outside, I remind myself. The wind covers the dainty sound of claws dragging across the wall for a moment but after it dies down it gets harder to ignore and more difficult to restrain my curiosity.

I sit up in bed and pull my chair over from where it's been residing since Miles brought me home yesterday. I wasn't in the mood to see anyone after that appointment so I shooed him away as soon as he helped me into bed and gave me painkillers. He wasn't too happy at the prospect of leaving me alone, but I found out that I can be quite persuasive with my words if there is something I truly want.

The scratching becomes more urgent as I transfer myself from bed to chair and wheel myself out the room's door. The sound disappears behind me.

"I'm coming," I whisper to no one.

I travel through the main living space, out the door and, around the path to the side of the house before I hear the scratching once more. This time a faint cry comes as well, an inhuman one.

I wheel myself as close as I can get in the chair before I ungracefully let myself fall to the soft dirt next to a large patch of overgrown weeds. One last anguished cry, this one as close as ever, comes from the patch. I start gently piloting the grass around with my fingers till I see what has concealed itself in the strands of earth.

A tiny, brown kitten with one green eye has managed to get tangled within the grass, trapped by mere nodes. One must be quite weak to not be able to fight off even the smallest of enemies, or quite strong to continue trying. It depends on how you look at it I guess.

"Shhh" I whisper in an attempt at comfort as it tries to squirm away from me. The more the animal wiggles the harder it is to set free. "Please just stay still," I plead with the kitten. I know logically that it can't understand what I have just said, but for some reason, the cat settles down anyway. "Thank you."

I finish pulling the strands of grass away and gently pick up the animal. It shakes in my hands as I bring it in closer to take a better look at what I am dealing with. Its brown fur is matted against its rib bones and the poor thing is actually missing an eye, it wasn't a trick of the light. This animal has been brought into the world, stripped of part of its basic rights. Or maybe it was a casualty of life, like my legs.

"You have the strength of a bear," I whisper to the cat as I pet the tiny creature with two fingers. It looks at me with wary curiosity.

Once it assesses that there is no danger, the animal gradually stops shaking and begins nuzzling into my hand.

Our peace in the overgrown garden is gone too soon though when I hear someone call out my name and a moment later Miles rounds the corner.

"Emily! Are you alright?"

"I'm fine." I stay focused on the cat.

"Is that a-"

"Could you help me back into my chair so that I can feed him? He's malnourished."

"Him?"

"Well I don't know if it's a boy or not, I'm just assuming so." I lift the cat slightly above my eyeline view and peek underneath its frail body. "It's hard to tell with the fur," I conclude.

He blinks away his shock and sets into motion, helping to lift me back into my chair.

"What are you doing?" I chastise Miles as he pours milk into a cup, splashing a puddle on the floor in the process. "Kittens can't drink cow's milk. Pour some water for her instead."

He puts the cup on the dining room table as fast as if it were poison and follows my instructions. "How do you know that?" He asks as he turns the faucet on.

"I don't know, I just do." The cat purrs satisfyingly in my hand as I show him attention. "Can you run out into town and grab some cat food for me?"

Miles doesn't seem too eager at the idea of me being alone again but he caves quickly. "Fine, but please no more solo adventures to the backyard before your legs start working again. I don't know how you would have gotten back inside if I hadn't shown up."

"I would've managed."

"Even so I'm not leaving until you promise me."

"Yes, yes I promise." I place the kitten on my lap and wheel towards him till he's cornered near the door. "Now go, I'll be fine and we'll see you in twenty?"

"It will probably be closer to thirty bu-"

"Doesn't matter, go." I jokingly shoo him away,

pushing closer until he's backed against the wall. He tries to say something again but I cut him off once more, "Do you want Bear to starve?"

"Bear?" He chuckles.

"Yes, it's what I've decided to name him."

"That's cute."

I open the door for him and tug on the sleeve of his button-up to usher him outside. "Go," is the last thing Miles hears before the door is slammed and we are separated. "Now, let's go give you a bath," I narrate to the kitten kneading his claws into my muddy nightgown.

It is not until an hour later that Miles returns amid a moderate downpour.

"Where have you been?" I take the cat food from his hands and open one of the cans to put into a bowl. "I'm glad that I got to him while I did. There's no way that he would have survived this storm. I bathed him while you were gone by the way, luckily I didn't find any fleas."

"Have you eaten?" Miles asks, completely disregarding everything I have said.

I pet the cat as I watch him graciously lick up the food he has now been given. Maybe a little too graciously. "Hey, could you grab some paper towels? I have a feeling he might throw some of this up in a bit."

"Emily."

"What?" I look at him now. His button-up has been stripped and left in a heap on the floor along with his coat and boots. He's only wearing socks, a see through undershirt and pants.

"I asked if you have eaten anything today."

"Oh, no I haven't. Can you grab me the paper towels?"

"I am going to make you food. What would you like?" He opens some of the cabinets, searching for ingredients.

"I would like for you to get me the paper towels."

"I will once you tell me what you would like for

lunch."

"Hasn't lunch already passed?"

"Fine, dinner then. What would you like for dinner?" I can tell he is starting to get impatient with me, which means I'm winning.

"I'm not hungry." But of course just as I say so my stomach has to disagree with me.

"Does pasta and sweet potatoes sound okay?"

"Depends, what type of pasta?"

"Linguini?" He suggests.

I pretend to think it over. "Nah. What's the status on those paper towels?"

"What's wrong with linguini? You can have the soup leftovers instead?" He suggests. I ignore him, too preoccupied on making sure Bear eats in moderation. "Emily you have to eat."

"Paper towels ple--"

Before I can finish the cat backs away from the now cleared-out bowl and retches up half of its contents back on the dining table. I huff frustratedly at Miles as I come toward the counter to grab them myself.

"I'm sorry," he says as he puts both hands on my chair to stop me from moving. He is so close I can smell the lingering aftershave he must have used this morning and the fabric sheets he tosses in the dryer. His chest is currently in my eyeline so I can see a bit more of his figure than I'm supposed to. "Please let me make you some food and take care of the mess."

"That does seem only fair."

"Meanwhile, you can sit up here."

He lifts me from the chair in one fast swoop that makes me grab onto him so hard I'm sure I'll leave indents on his skin when I let go. He places me on top of the dining room table, along with the cat now licking up its regurgitated food. I cringe at the sight and close my eyes until Miles finishes cleaning it up. Bear then climbs onto my lap and situates himself within the dip where my legs meet.

"Is this allowed?" I ask while stroking Bear's freshly cleansed fur.

"Is what allowed?" Miles turns the stove to low and fills a pot with water.

"Holding your clients hostage and forcing them to ingest toxins."

"Toxins?" Miles laughs. "I'm insulted. You seemed to like my soap last night."

"Technically it was our soup, and I only helped so that I could make sure you didn't poison it."

"Oh, is that so?"

"Yes," I state proudly, even though we both know that this is not true.

"You are something else."

"What does that mean?" I retaliate defensively.

"I'm not sure, give me a moment to think about it."

"When you figure it out, let me know. Until then I choose to interpret it negatively and have decided that I am hurt by your words."

"Oh, is that so?"

"Yes."

"Fine then, take it however you wish. Meanwhile, I know exactly what to make."

The kitchen smells of herbs and butter by the time Miles is through cooking and ready to present his finished masterpiece, lemon-coated chicken with linguine and asparagus.

"Where did you learn to cook like this?" I ask through a mouth full of chicken.

"Food is very important in my family. My parents even own a restaurant in Croyden."

I wipe leftover butter from my mouth with my napkin before I speak next, "Tell me more."

"About what?"

"Your family. I know so little-" I stop myself. "I

know nothing of mine. I think it would be nice to hear about somebody else's."

Bear's whiskers itch my hand as he tries to get around to my plate. I place him on my lap instead. I'm not sure if this food will agree with his stomach.

"I don't know, that might overstep boundaries."

"Oh, okay."

Forks scrape, heavy rain beats on the window glass, and the cat in my lap purrs. There is no more exchange of words. The topic has fallen somber.

"Do you think that I had a good family?" I ask. "I feel as if I probably didn't considering I didn't, care to stick around."

"Emily, it's not that your family wasn't good, it's just-" he struggles to find the right words. "It was complicated."

"So you know why I did this to myself?"

"I don't know the full story, but I do know some things."

"What kinds of things?"

Miles hesitates before going on. "All I know is that you did it for your safety."

"For my safety?" I let this information sink in. "Do you think it has something to do with Wren?"

A blinding flash of light takes me off guard and a nearby crack of thunder rumbles quickly behind it, shaking the house. Then the power goes out, and we are covered in a blanket of darkness.

Chapter Seven
Saturday, March 4th

Candles cast volatile shadows on the walls. The oil lamps on the other hand are much more reliant. Luckily there was some in the closet, hidden behind a typewriter on the top shelf. There weren't many, only two of each. Bear stumbles blindly into the leg of the table, rebounding into my foot as Miles puts kerosene into the last lamp. The canister he found below the sink should last us a few days if need be. But god I hope we don't need it to be.

"You should stay the night," I respectfully suggest while fluffing up a tattered pillow and smoothing out the gingham blanket on the back of the couch.

He takes a moment to think about the offer. "Are you sure?" He scoops Bear up and gently begins to massage his fur. The kitten dodges the attempt at first but quickly warms up once he understands the intentions.

"Yeah, you probably wouldn't be able to see more than two feet in front of you in this weather." I wheel myself towards the window to double-check the accuracy of my statement. It's true.

"Okay, thanks. I promise not to be a bother and I'll finish cleaning up dinner." He lays the kitten in my lap and goes over to the table to gather the leftovers.

"Of course. Have a good night."

"You too Emily. And don't forget that you have your second appointment at nine tomorrow and this time you're not getting out of breakfast."

"Fine."

I can't sleep. According to the clock on the wall, it's been three hours since I laid down. I can shut my eyes, squeeze them with all the force I can muster, but nothing will shut my brain off. I feel like a broken dam of never-ending thoughts, and always the same ones, the same water that keeps coming through. It's as if the water gets confused as to why it's not being repurposed into electricity and instead stored inside. I don't want to keep it inside, I want to find answers. I want to know who I am. I want to know why I still can't walk. I want to know what I am going to do. Why can't I know these things? Why are these questions running through my brain, storing themselves on top of each other while the dam continues cracking? I wonder when I will inevitably break loose and let the water all come out.

I feel infected with imposter syndrome.

Another hour has passed and the only thing I've done since the last time the little hand on the clock went around was breathe. Breathe and think. I'm starting to get tired of both.

The storm is still raging on, fueling my dam and my sheets. I didn't expect the slew of humidity that has followed this weather. It's been making me sweat, especially considering the time of year. My fresh pajamas are no longer fresh and my clean skin is no longer clean.

Before bed I ran myself a bath, the first one I've done on my own. It was a challenge but I never faltered. I was determined to get the stains of grass and dirt off of my knees.

Bear is cuddled up within the crease of my elbow. I have been a statue staring at the plastered ceiling these past few hours because of this.

I think that I should bring him to the vet tomorrow once the storm has gone, maybe after my own appointment. And after that, I can go furniture shopping to bring some life back into this place. Speaking of, I have to ask Miles how to access my bank account. I wonder if he's up now too.

Okay, that's it. Hour five is my breaking point. I had to put up with just my mind on the ship but I have a lot more function of my body now. I refuse to waste it.

I shake the joints I have control over to wake them up before pulling my chair over. But where am I going to go? I'm practically confined to my bedroom now that Miles is occupying my main living space. Maybe this could be a prime opportunity. Dr. Pierce said not to try without somebody nearby but technically, there is now someone nearby.

I start with a few reps of the chair exercises, which isn't much but, by the time I'm done the strain causes my legs to feel like loose jelly. I am determined to move on to the skill of standing, but I don't know if my body will work with me on that one just yet so I give myself a moment and a few sips of water before starting up again.

I must have completed at least fifty of each exercise by now but I lost track a while back. My goal is to take a step, or at least stand for more than fifteen seconds. I must. But in order to do so I have to stop procrastinating.

I grab onto the corner of the taller of my two dressers and slowly pull myself up until I am leaning all of my body weight into the drawers. The handle of the top one pokes my right rib while the lower ones stab me in the waist, but at least it proves that I still have feeling down there. I repeatedly push myself away from the green and gold dresser, trying to catch my weight underneath me. Every time I don't, I go tumbling back into the dresser, narrowly catching myself each time. I'm prepping to push myself off for the fourth or fifth time when Miles comes barging through the door, startling Bear from sleep.

"What's going on?" His voice is filled with panic. The moment he sees me crumpled up pathetically against the dresser I notice a look of sympathy slip into his eyes, which is exactly what causes me to push myself up for the final time.

I brace myself for another fall and stab in the ribs but it doesn't come. I open my eyes to make sure it isn't Miles holding me upright. It's not. He's drawn closer but he isn't touching me. I'm doing it again and this time completely self-sufficient, there's no walker or hand-holding. Miles and I stare at each other in bewildered amusement.

"You're doing it!"

"I know!" I falter and we both brace ourselves for the fall but instead, I hold my arms out for additional balance. "Do you remember when I started?" I ask as I redirect my eyes to the clock.

"Maybe five or ten seconds ago?"

I nod so he knows that I heard him. "Eleven, twelve, thirteen, fourteen…" I begin whispering under my breath, going higher as each tiny tick moves behind the glass.

"Fifteen, sixteen, seventeen, eighteen," Miles joins in.

By the time we get to sixty I am biting my lip to keep from crying because if there is one thing that I have discovered lately it is that I hate crying, especially in front of other people.

"Do you want to try taking a step?" Miles suggests once we hit sixty-eight. "You can hold onto something if it makes you feel better."

I stop counting to think this over. I have made so much progress tonight. I don't particularly care to have this victory spoiled by the reminder of me not being able to walk. Plus I've been keeping my body so tense and still that I'm beginning to shake, not a notable amount from where Miles is standing, but enough to cause concern up close. I have to let up soon, but maybe that can be after I walk.

"Yes, but I don't want to hold onto anything."

"Okay." I can tell that he is wary of the idea since he

subtly steps even closer to me. "Ready?"

"Yes."

I gradually relax my muscles, starting from my upper body and working my way down. Once I get to my hips I leave just enough tension to keep upright. I have to do this quickly. I can already feel my body giving out from exhaustion. I look to Miles for encouragement as I pick up my left foot and let my weight fall into the right. Halfway there. I can tell that he wants to move closer but he stays firmly planted where he is, trusting that I can do this. I need to fully trust in myself that I can do this. I lose the connection between brain and foot for a moment as it dangles limply in the air, causing a second of panic.

"Just breathe Em."

He's never called me that before. I like it. It gets me out of my head.

"Try another one," Miles encourages with a level of excitement that is only comparable to a child on Christmas morning.

Another one? But I haven't even finished the first step. Right? I look down at my left foot now in front of my right, firmly planted on the ground. I just took a step.

I sway a little in shock as the world around me blurs. Miles begins chanting muffled words of encouragement as my feet move not one, but two more steps ahead of the previous ones.

Then the world goes dark.

Miles dabs an ice-cold washcloth over my face. When I come to it takes a minute for my vision to settle. I am in bed now.

"What time is it?"

"Well, you first woke up a few seconds after you fell, but now it's almost noon sleepyhead."

"Noon?! But wasn't my appointment at nine?" I try to sit myself up but my arms give out, forcing me back down.

"I rescheduled it to tomorrow, I figured that you could use a break after all the work you did this morning. And I caught your head before you fell so I doubt there's any chance of concussion, but the doctor can take a look tomorrow."

Oh good, it wasn't a dream. Part of me is glad that the appointment was canceled. I'm not sure if I can do what I did again. But, most of me wants to rub my victory into Dr. Pierce's face, in case I can do it again.

"Did Bear get fed this morning?"

"Yes, and I even let him take a gander outside to use the bathroom."

"Good, thank you," I groan as I push myself up in bed.

He walks into the adjoining bathroom and wrings the rest of the washcloth into the sink. "He doesn't have a litter box yet. We could go and purchase one today if you'd like?"

"Sure, and can we grab some decorations for the house too? I still feel as if I'm intruding on somebody else's property."

"That sounds like a fabulous use of the day."

Miles pulls the chair around for me and helps me in, allowing me to do the majority of the work. I appreciate the freedom but loathe the pain that comes with it. I might have pushed myself a little too far and too fast earlier.

"Are we going to leave my wheelchair on the side of the road again?" I query as the uneven section of the path just outside of town approaches.

"No, the rain wore it down a bit so that shouldn't be necessary."

"Oh."

He's right. The ride is much smoother compared to yesterday but the wheels are still going to need a good wash before going back in the house.

"Why didn't we just take a car into town?"

"Walking allows you to be out in the open air and is proven to improve morality and spirits."

"Oh."

I wonder if he knows what was going on in my head when I was on the ship deck, my contemplation of death and lack of willpower. I saw a copy of his degree while in the car a few days ago. He studied psychology so he must be well versed on cues of depression.

"Did you want to get some food first before shopping? You promised," he reminds me.

I can't remember if I truly did or not but either way I go with it because I am hungry from skipping breakfast this morning. "Sure."

We continue traveling towards the middle of the little city. As we do I begin to notice how inaccessible all of these buildings are with their elevated porches, many steps and lack of ramps. When we make it to the diner Miles even has to flag a stranger down to help get me inside. It is utterly embarrassing and further proves the need for more accessibility in this town.

The stranger asks for permission to lift me, which I appreciate and grant as Miles brings my chair to the top of the steps. The burly man grabs hold of me and follows after him, placing me back down accordingly. Miles thanks him and they exchange a quick yet polite conversation.

"Do you know him?" I ask Miles once the man leaves.

"He's the husband of one of my first ever clients. I check on her now and then. They moved out here from a city in Aelville a few months ago. This place comes highly recommended among Rebirth customers who want a smaller town feel."

"Oh."

I want to ask how many people there are in town that have been in my position, but I doubt that he would be able to tell me for legality purposes. I wonder if he would be allowed to share or connect me with one of them if I asked.

Once inside, an older waitress with glasses directs us to a booth. To make things easier I stay seated in the chair and lock the wheels once I get situated at the end of the table. The waitress introduces herself as Gloria as she places two water cups, a saucer of lemons, and a singular menu on the wood tabletop.

"Can I get you folks any drinks besides water?"

"A coffee for me please and my usual."

"Of course. And for you?"

"I'm go-"

But Miles cuts me off, "She'll have whatever milkshake special you have this week."

"Wonderful, and I'll come back for the lady's food order in just a moment," Gloria announces.

No, not wonderful. "What did you just order for me?"

"The milkshake special," he replies nonchalantly before taking a small bite of lemon and squeezing the rest into his water.

"Yeah, I got that. Why?"

"Because you have to try it. I'm kind of a milkshake connoisseur, and I can confirm that this place has the best."

"A milkshake concierge?" I raise an eyebrow at his self-proclaimed title.

"Yeah, this job takes me everywhere so I've tried a lot. That's why I do most of the sampling for new dishes at my parent's restaurant and why I joined Rebirth in the first place."

"To try different milkshakes from around the world?"

"Well, yes." He chuckles. "But mostly to help people in some way and to travel in general."

"How long have you been doing this job?" I don't know Miles's age but he seems rather young, no older than twenty-six if I had to guess.

"I've only been in the business for four years but I've visited all four countries and most of their states."

"Do you know if I've done any traveling in my lifetime?"

"I am not sure, but if that's something that interests you now I can help arrange that."

I'm about to continue further with this subject when the waitress comes back with a cup of freshly brewed coffee and a container filled with sugar. "Have you decided what you would like to eat dear?"

I hadn't even looked at the menu, but I guess since I'm already taking a chance on the milkshake, why not do so with the whole meal?

"Whatever Miles got is fine."

"Alrighty, I'll be back."

Another wait staff member brings over the milkshake and two straws just as Gloria leaves. Whipped cream and sprinkles are piled on top of the pink drink along with an ice cream bar and cupcake. Miles opens both straws and sticks them in the shake, one on my side and the other on his. He gestures for me to try first. I lean closer to the table to not spill.

The liquid moves through the straw and past my tongue. The texture is equally thick yet smooth. My tastebuds register the flavor but my brain has trouble pairing it with its food counterpart.

"So?" Miles prompts.

"It's good, but what is that?"

Miles takes his turn now, sipping from the straw. His eyes widen at first and then melt peacefully to a close as he savors what's in front of him. "Fruity pebbles," he answers back confidently. He puts his mouth to the straw again. "Now do you believe me that this is the best milkshake?"

"Well, considering I have no recollection of trying any other milkshakes, I'm forced to say yes."

"Hey, a win is a win."

Miles takes the skewer out of the ice cream bar then holds it out for me to take a bite from. I slowly let my teeth sink into the cold dessert with a strawberry coating. After I pull away, Miles takes his own bite from the opposite side. We continue on this way until nothing is left but the stick.

"Here you two are. Can I get you anything else?" She offers while placing two plates on the table.

"Thank you, that should be all Gloria."

"My pleasure, I'll be sitting at the booth taking my

break if you need anything."

"Wow," I express as I stare at the stacked pancakes layered with icing and blueberries. Hash browns sit off to the side as well. "This is your usual?"

"Yep, the only thing I've ordered while stationed here."

"And how long have you been assigned to this jurisdiction?"

"Well, you're the second person I've mentored here now, so probably close to five months, which now that I'm thinking about it, is the longest time I've been in the same area since graduating from university." He takes a moment to think this realization over before rebounding back into the conversation. "Ninety percent of Rebirth mentors stop counseling before the six month mark, although with the updated information the doctor and I have been providing, I believe your statistics estimate our time together to be a bit longer, mostly due to your current medical condition. Hopefully you don't get too sick of me," he teases.

Nothing about that answer was expected. First of all, I would have figured that the company would want their brainless customers more scattered, to brag about numbers and expansion. But more importantly, I was estimated to take more than six months to recover, which is apparently unusual and does not leave me feeling confident.

"I can get you in contact with others who have gone through what you are experiencing, if you would like," he suggests.

"I'll think about it."

We spend the rest of lunch eating in silence, except for near the end when Miles pulls out his fancy work tablet to show me how to access my bank account information and activate my debit card. I even insist on paying the bill at the end, going through the instructions to do so exactly as he tells me to. Once the payment goes through, a sense of purpose and accomplishment arises within me. That feeling ceases though when I watch the money ingrained in a small corner of the card deplete from what little savings I have. A pit in the center of my stomach grows and a new anxiety is formed. I need a job.

Another kind townsperson passing by offers to carry me back down the steps of the diner on our way out as Miles once again carries my chair. Though I am grateful to the stranger, I feel as if I would be much more comfortable wrapping my arms around someone I semi-know.

"Onto the pet store?" Miles asks as he takes up the space behind me, wrapping his fingers around the handles of my chair.

"Yes please."

The pet store isn't too far, just a block down and around the corner. Luckily it only has a small lip of concrete to conquer before heading inside instead of an unnecessary amount of stairs.

The interior of the building is quaint and light music plays as we walk around, or as Miles walks and I get pushed. I make him stop in front of the cat food section and listen to all of the brands that the owner recommends to make sure that Miles grabbed the best one for Bear. He did. I don't find out until the end of the conversation that the man had already gone over this with Miles the day prior when he had also asked.

Just as we finish the conversation with the store owner another customer requests assistance and he has to hurry off, so we move on to the toys. I pick a few that I hold onto in my lap which then turns into a mountain. When my pile starts to overflow Miles cuts me off, recommending a spending limit. I'm quick to agree when I remember the numbers in my account. The last item we grab is a small box of litter.

Eventually, the owner rings us up. Miles places the bag of toys on one of the wheelchair handles and I hold the extra bags of cat food and litter in my lap.

"Did you still want to stop somewhere else to get

things for the house?"

I do, but where would it fit? I can't carry a comforter set and paintings in my lap as well. "Maybe another day, when there's more storage to help get the items home."

"I can always call for a car," he suggests.

"What about all of that stuff you said about the air and morale?" I tease. His facial expression becomes serious as he thinks of what to respond with. "I'm kidding."

"Did you want me to call for one though? That way we can still do the shopping that you intended to get done."

"That's alright, I want to get back to Bear anyway. However, next time please do so that I don't have to suffer through another long walk."

"You really didn't like our walk?"

"Too much air and morale," I kid.

He rolls his eyes but I can see the smile he holds back in the slight upturn of his lips.

Chapter Eight
Sunday, March 5th

On our walk home yesterday afternoon between the silence and the odd tension, that probably only existed from my perspective, Miles brought up my career. He asked me if I had thought about it at all, to which I answered yes. He then asked what my plans were, to which I did not have an answer to. He didn't continue to push, but it did get me thinking.

I was a screenplay writer in my past life, but I do not know what I have created. It could be utter garbage. This thought kept me up for half the night. Therefore, once the clock hit a respectable hour, five in the morning, I brewed myself some coffee and called up Miles, asking him to bring over any work of mine. I'm afraid I must have woken him up because he comes over an hour or so later, still in plaid pajama pants.

"Do you want some coffee?" I offer as he yawns for the third time in under ten minutes. "I feel bad that I made you get up so early."

"That would be lovely actually. And don't, this is my job."

"Right. Hot or cold?" I ask as I wheel my way into the kitchen.

"Hot please."

I hold onto the counter with a tight grip and pull

myself up to reach the cabinets. I grab a bland, white cup and saucer before brewing more coffee, since the machine only makes enough for one at a time. As it pours, I try to think back to the diner yesterday to decide if I should put milk and sugar in the drink or not. I can't remember so I end up asking. Sugar, no milk. Thankfully, I left the sugar out from when I used it this morning. I pull out a little spoon from the drawer in front of me and dump in a moderate amount before stirring it together.

"Thank you," he says through a yawn. He takes the cup from the counter and heads back over to the couch. I follow after him. "I printed every script of yours that I could find. Unfortunately, any non-published works of yours are inaccessible unless you previously transferred them to our database for restoration and there was only one that you chose to do that with. I have printed it for you as well."

"May I see that one first?" It seems like a safe place to start.

"Of course."

Miles attempts to neatly go through the stacks of paper in piles around the dining room table. Eventually, he pulls out a singular sheet of paper and hands it to me. The page only has writing in the top quarter and upon further inspection, I realize that it is the same word written over and over again. Wren. That one name runs from corner to corner. Sometimes it has typos or a random capital letter inserted in as if it was written in a rush, but ultimately, it is all the same.

"Is it good? I didn't look while I was printing because I wanted you to see it first."

"Can you do me a favor?" I counter, ignoring what he has just said. Panic sets into the soul of my chest but I attempt to appear collected still.

"Uh sure, what is it?"

"Can you look up the name Wren?"

He seems wary but even still pulls out a tablet and stylus from his bag, the one he uses for work. He wordlessly taps a couple of buttons on the device before tentatively handing it to me. I scroll for a minute, looking at numerous faces, descriptions, schooling levels and relationship statuses. The level of detail and depth I have access to right now feels unsettling and illegal… actually, it most definitely is illegal. There is no way that I am authorized to be looking at this information.

I try to put the thought of Miles risking his job for me out of my head and continue on. There are many variations of the name, elongated versions and such, that come close but don't quite hit the mark. Only one man comes up with exactly the name Wren. I click on the profile and scroll through it. He's a bit older than I, graduated from somewhere in Altone and now lives with… his wife and three kids. Why would I want to remember him?

"I don't think that's who you are referring to," Miles seconds, matching my thoughts. I nod to show him my agreement. "The person you're referring to might not even be listed. The Rebirth database is meant to hold people registered within our own system, or those who have downloaded certain apps that allow for us to collect their information."

"Oh, okay." I give in and hand the tablet back to Miles.

He powers the device off and recommends just focusing on the other documents in front of us. However, the paper still in my hands won't leave my mind until I get rid of it. So I crumple up the useless scrap and give it to Bear to bat around.

Some of the scripts I read in full and some I just thumb through. I wrote mostly short films for festivals. Some of them have won local awards for best picture or best screenwriting but only one was picked up by a big budget studio on the western side of Alnerwick to turn into a full-length feature film.

According to Miles, casting was already done when the project got postponed a month due to an injury the leading actress sustained. Apparently no one wanted to replace her because she was some big shot with a large following. Somewhere in that month, though, production was permanently canceled for reasons unknown to the general public. It's no mystery to me though why the movie was scrapped considering the article he reads off is dated the day that I woke up.

"We should watch that one. Well, the short film version of it at least," I suggest after my third cup of coffee.

"Watching anything right now might send me snoring. Even the caffeine isn't helping anymore."

"Did you get any sleep last night?"

"Not much, I was catching up on paperwork."

"Would you like to go home and-"

"No, no thats okay. I want to help."

"Okay."

He smiles at me before typing words into his device. "There is one DVD available on this side of Accrington but it's a good sixty-mile drive," he announces with regret.

"Oh, that's okay. Thanks for looking." I try to hide my disappointment as he gives me an apologetic half-smile.

I wait for him to finish reading the last page of the script currently in his hands before holding out the one that I have just finished. He flips back to the front page before handing that one over to me as well. We exchange offerings at the same time.

I begin to read. This story is about a girl from the city who travels to the country to meet her biological father for the first time. I just get to the part where her best friend offers to roadtrip with her when my eyes get heavy and my head begins to lean to the side.

I had a dream, but I don't remember it. How on brand. I wonder if I'm still dreaming. I'm warm, and not just from being wrapped up in a blanket. There's something else contributing to my body temperature. It almost feels as if someone else's body heat is blending with mine. Is this what a lucid dream feels like? And who am I laying with? Whoever it is has their arm around my waist. I'm tempted to open my eyes and find out, but they feel so heavy.

A noise from the kitchen startles me, forcing me to sit up anyways. Bear looks at me from the kitchen counter, innocently pawing another loud, clangy, utensil to the floor. I scold him in a whisper, and he only listens after knocking down yet another item. I wince as it hits the tile, hoping my companion, who has turned out to be Miles, does not wake up before I get a chance to compose myself.

How did we end up so close to each other? I swear that we were on opposite ends of the couch, though it's not all that big.

I smooth down my hair and pick up the papers that fell to the floor. I need to get up before he wakes. I pull my chair over, but of course, it hits the leg of the coffee table, immediately pulling Miles from his sleep.

"Sorry, I didn't mean to wake you."

"I fell asleep?"

"Yeah, we both did," I confirm after deciding that transparency is the best choice.

"I'm so sorry. This is entirely unprofessional." He shuffles around as he starts to collect his belongings.

"It's-"

"What time is it?!" He interrupts frantically as he smooths his sweatshirt and collects the coffee cups to put in the sink, despite mine still having perfectly good caffeine inside. Although, it's most likely cold by now. "Em, what time is it?"

There's that nickname again. "Oh, uh, fifteen minutes until noon."

"Crap, we have to get you to your appointment. Can you get ready in ten? I'm going to run back to my house and send a car over to pick us both up, okay?" He stumbles to put his shoes on as he speaks and rushes out the door, only stopping momentarily to pet Bear.

"Okay," I whisper back to no one.

A black car with tinted windows, similar to the one we rode to New Cresthill in, pulls into the house's short adjoining driveway exactly fifteen minutes later. The driver doesn't say a word as he helps me and Bear in before folding up my wheelchair to put in the back.

I missed being in a functioning vehicle and not having to make the bumpy ride into town, plus it's faster. However, something saddens me about missing out on a potential walk with Miles, even if only one of us is good at the walking part.

"I called Dr. Pierce and told him that we would be a few minutes late by the way," he says the moment he gets in the car. "What is the cat doing here?"

"Cat?" I draw back, clearly offended.

"Okay sorry, what is Bear doing here?"

"Much better. And I thought that we could take him to the vet after my appointment. That was the original plan the other day, remember?"

"Right. And that will actually be easier than you think."

"What do you mean?"

Miles attempts to answer but is cut off by the ringing of his cell. He checks the screen for the caller ID and puts his fingers to the bridge of his nose, rubbing in a circular motion as he picks up. He shoots me an apologetic look and holds up a finger while beginning to whisper talk to the person on the other end.

The conversation is short, most likely since I am near, but the strain is clear. It shows in his now hunched shoulders that have been nothing but upright and confident within the past few days. And he's wearing glasses for the first time since we've met. Maybe he was too tired to bother with contacts, which I am just now realizing he must wear. The frames of the glasses are bulky and ill-fitting. They give him a dorky, down-to-earth appearance than is different from his usually put together, fancy clothes wearing self. Somehow both looks fit him.

"Everything alright?" I ask.

"Not really." For a moment it seems as if he might elaborate. Instead, he says, "We're here." Wow, I grossly misjudged the difference between walking and driving distances.

Miles takes Bear from me so that the driver can easily help me out of the car and into my chair. Once Bear curls back up into my lap, climbing up my sweater to play with the ends of my hair, we start up the ramp. The driver takes off as we head inside.

"Ah, there they are."

The clinic is harshly quiet right now. There is no one in the waiting room and both exam room doors are wide open, awaiting their victims. There is only us and the receptionist. And by us, I mean me, Bear, Miles and, Dr. Pierce.

"Am I checking this little guy out today too?" The doctor asks, scratching a soft spot under Bear's chin.

"You're a veterinarian and a people doctor?"

He gestures to four picture frames on the wall behind him, his degrees. "I had two majors in my undergrad. Then I went to medical school and a few years after finishing that education level I enrolled in veterinary school," he explains.

I wonder if I went to school for something, english or film maybe. But if I'm twenty now then I either dropped out early, graduated ahead of time, or never went.

"Who do you want in which room?" Miles asks for me.

"Miss Weiss can take the one on the left."

I start to head towards the exam room when Dr. Pierce places his foot in front of one of the wheels, causing me to stop. He looks me in the eye with a guileful smirk before instructing me to walk there instead.

I am appalled. I know I wanted to show him what I can do, but I'm not at that level of confidence yet. I planned on standing on my own for a bit and pretending that was all of my progress. Then, right before he gives me a list of exercises, I would hold my hand out to Miles and we would take a nice boastful stride around the room or at least a few steps. I daydreamed about this moment. I want my moment. I do not want this. I still need the help.

"Can you walk to the room, Emily?" He asks now, reiterating his demand.

I don't like the way he says my name, full of condescension. Does he not think that I am trying hard enough?

"She only just started walking, I'm not sure if she can do it without assistance yet," Miles lightly protests in my defense when he sees me struggling to find the words.

"Thank you for your input Mr. Hartman, but I would like to hear from Emily." Dr. Pierce folds his palms together in front of him. I can tell that the receptionist is trying to mind her own business, but I catch her staring.

"I can do it." I whisper the words to myself in an attempt to trick my confidence into complying. They are not for him. They are a motivation to me and for me.

I give Bear to Miles and put my feet on the floor to go through my routine: slight pressure on the feet, ease my body weight into it, and stand. Okay, good. It's time to pick up my feet now. Left foot first, I decide. Shakily, I raise my left shoe a few inches from the ground and slam it down a bit ahead of me. The balance in my body falters and my limbs sway.

Now it's the right foot's turn, but my muscles are already growing tense as my body prepares itself for the further strain that's about to follow. I have to get past just one step. That can't be all I do. My right foot goes up, and with slightly more grace, falls to the floor in front of me. I do this four more times. Different muscles in my legs contract, as if confused about which one should be put to work but I'm doing it.

After four more steps I reach the door frame. I grip the wood so hard that I leave nail marks, but I must keep my balance. I can not show how unstable I am right now.

"So someone has been doing their homework." Dr. Pierce studies me with clear respect. "Great, now take a breather and relax those joints while I check out this little guy." He takes Bear from Miles and struts into the other exam room, closing the door behind him.

Miles rushes over then to help me the extra few feet to the exam table. He takes one of my hands in his and supports the other behind my back. Once we get there I lean against it for support. He gives me a moment before offering to help me get on. I take him up on it, and let him grab hold of my waist. I close my eyes as he lifts me, waiting for my heart to steady. It doesn't until Miles lets go and takes a seat in one of the visitor's chairs off to the side.

The effort that it took to get over here has conjured up a dizzy spell and a pounding headache at the base of my temples that I can tell will not be going away easily.

"Are you okay?"

"That was nauseating," I confess.

In response Miles turns out the lights and pulls the garbage pail closer. "I can't believe that you just did that. You deserve a treat or something. Oh shit, that sounds bad, sorry," he backpedals. "I didn't mean for it to sound like I was calling you an animal. But celebratory ice cream might be in order after this."

"It's alright, I didn't take it that way. And ice cream sounds great. Do you think that we could stop by the library before heading home too? I was hoping to maybe see if they are hiring."

I had the idea this morning while we were going through the scripts. My writing is honestly quite good, but I need some sort of income now. I can't afford to wait however long it will take me to write a new script, pitch it, and receive royalties or a flat rate.

"I think that that would be a lovely idea."

Eventually, Dr. Pierce comes back to finish my exam and update us on Bear's, the results of which are that he is in top-notch health. At the end of my appointment Dr. Pierce recommends staying in the wheelchair just a bit more for longer outings, but using crutches instead while traveling shorter distances and moving about the house. Miles and I both agree with this plan and schedule to see each other again in a few days to revisit and revise my care plan. We then check out at the front desk and head outside towards the library.

"I don't think that there are any pets allowed, so I'll stay outside with Bear while you head in," Miles offers once we approach the double doors with stained glass. The words "New Cresthill Library" are etched into the stone above the doorway.

"Are you sure?"

"Yeah, of course."

"Okay, I shouldn't be too long."

"Take your time, we'll be out here." He takes Bear from me before I head to the entrance. Thankfully there is a ramp off to the side that I can use. "You got this Em."

"Thanks."

I pass through the doorway and make my way to the front desk, holding my head a degree higher even though there are a million things to fear right now.

"Excuse me?"

"Mhm?" An older lady wearing a red scarf, despite being inside, leans over the desk to look down at me. "May I help you?" Her breath lingers, leaving a smoky smell behind.

"I was wondering if you are hiring."

"Maybe." She shrugs and puts her book down, dog earring the corner to mark her place.

"Maybe?" I question.

She pulls a loose string from her scarf before continuing to speak, "I am currently the only one who works here and there's never been enough business for two. So why should I hire you?"

I sneak a glance around me to confirm the amount of truth behind her statement. Only one person occupies a table near the far back corner, other than that there is no business.

This is when I get my first good look at the place. The space isn't all that large. But the ceilings are raised to a striking level, accommodating tall shelves full of aged and worn books. And there's a separate, clearly unused community room in the back with a glass door which gives me an idea.

"Because I can help you."

"Help me how?"

"Well, if I worked here I would hold more events to bring people in. Maybe some storytelling hours for children and a cheese and wine book club for the adults. You can even run them at the same time to maximize attendance. And you can rent out that space in the back for members to take classes on poetry or contemporary writing and such. As for the aesthetics, I would recommend a more cozy atmosphere, maybe opt for more couches instead of wooden chairs. And another computer or two wouldn't hurt."

She digs in her drawer and pulls out a pack of cigarettes and a lighter. She takes one out from the case and puts the butt in her mouth as she flips the lighter open, lighting the flame that starts the flow of poison traveling to her lungs.

"Do you know how expensive those are, missy?" She lectures casually after taking a deep inhale and exhale of the tobacco. "The computers are a big no, but your other ideas are good. I'm Tabitha, by the way."

"Emily."

"Nice to meet you, Emily."

"So can I have a job or do you just plan on stealing all of my ideas the second I walk out of here?" On the inside I am shaking and praying, but on the outside, I hold a confident facade. Or at least I try to.

The woman seems to think it over for a moment as she takes another inhale of her cigarette. "How about a trial run? Come back tomorrow at eleven for your first day, we'll talk pay and all that then."

"Oh, thank you Tabitha!" In my fit of excitement I grab for her hand, shaking it firmly. She's thrown off guard for a moment but quickly regains her composure. "I'll see you tomorrow!"

Then I wheel myself out before she has a chance to take in the chair any further and second-guess her decision. I wouldn't have judged her if she hadn't hired me due to my condition, as it's not exactly easy to attain books on higher shelves when you're confined to a height just tall enough to reach the bottom of your kitchen cabinets, but I sure am glad that she has put her faith in me.

As I come down the ramp to leave, I decide to make it my goal tomorrow to prove to Tabitha that she made the right choice and the only way to do that is by getting as comfortable on my feet as I can be, as soon as possible.

"How did it go?" Miles asks as he stands from the bench he was sitting on. He gently picks up a sleeping Bear, who was lying on his lap, and places him back down onto mine.

"Well…" I lead him on with a look of faux disappointment.

"Oh, I'm sorry. There are many other places though that might need assistance. What about the diner?"

"I'm just kidding, I got the job!" I exclaim giddily once I get him right where I want him. "Well kinda, we're going to do a trial run. I have to be here at eleven tomorrow for my first day."

"That's great, now there's two reasons for ice cream!" He moves behind me to help maneuver my chair. "Speaking of, shall we?"

"We shall."

The diner closed early today for some small renovations, according to the sign taped on the door and the loud drill sounds coming from the open windows. Instead, we sit on a bench outside of the one convenience store in town. Miles is biting into some red superhero popsicle like a child while I scoop tiny, rolled circles of ice cream into my mouth.

Once he eats a sufficient amount he holds the popsicle to my lap for Bear to finish off, which I scold him for. He doesn't listen though until a vibrant red stain ends up displaying itself on my clothes.

"Sorry," he sheepishly apologies. He tries to bite back a smile and so do I, neither of us succeed. "Is there any place else that you would like to stop before heading home?"

I'm about to decline when I remember another unchecked box at the bottom of the to-do list in my head, something I did not want to do until I got a job.

"There is actually..."

Chapter Nine
Monday, March 6th

Paint samples dry on the paneled wall in the living room. I stare at them for the hundredth time since Miles put them up this morning. Do I like the cream or the pale yellow better? Or maybe the classic eggshell white is what's best, but the sage green also compliments nicely. Or maybe I should just put up wallpaper to match the floral one in the bedroom. No, I would never be able to find an exact match.

"Have you decided?" Miles shouts from the bathroom.

"Not yet."

I move into the kitchen to study the ugly brown cabinets. I have already chosen the white color for them with brass handles. Plus Miles is going to install the white backsplash tile that we got. So, maybe we can rule out white for the walls, that would seem a little much. The countertops, though, will remain their current light beige wood color.

I use my crutches to get into the bedroom to see what progress has been made there since I last checked in. Miles has already changed my bed set and put up the generic pictures in gold frames that we found at the antique shop. I hope to replace them eventually with pictures of me and my life instead of somebody else's, but for now they will do.

He is now working in the bathroom where he has just finished installing a shower rod and curtain. He climbs down from the side of the tub and starts to gather all of the tools he will need to change the rusting lighting fixtures next to the mirror.

"It looks great so far."

"Thanks." When he turns towards me to acknowledge my compliment I notice a black smudge of something on his cheek, as if he's been working on cars all morning and not on faucets and drains.

I point to the exact spot on my face. He quickly gets the memo and wipes his face with the back of his hand. This simply ends up spreading the mark more.

"Better?"

"Not at all actually."

He wipes at the same area again, stepping closer so that I can get a better look. "How about now?"

"Absolutely not."

Without thinking I take the cloth hanging from the belt loop of his jeans and adjust the crutches under my arms to run it under warm water. Then I hold his chin steady between my fingertips and start wiping gently at the black streak until it transfers to the cloth.

"Thanks," he practically whispers.

His soft eyes study my face as he lays his hand over mine to take the cloth from me and pull my arm away slowly. I'm immediately embarrassed by the interaction and drop the cloth, turning away before he can see the physical representation of my feelings displayed on my face.

"Of course. Hey, what time is it by the way?" I ask, frantically trying to change the tone between us. I wish Rebirth could take this memory from me too.

"Shit, it's 10:30. We better call a car for you."

I turn back towards him now that my face has had the opportunity to return to its normal color. "Are you not coming too?"

"Why would I come to your first day of work?" He chuckles as he twists a screw. "I'm going to stay here and finish up some things before you get home if that's alright."

"Of course, right. Thank you."

It makes sense that he wouldn't come with me today now that I think about it but he's gone everywhere with me, so it's a knee-jerk reaction to assume today would be the same. I haven't left the house without him the past few days, six to be exact. Wow. I've already lived here almost a whole week.

"I am going to need you to make a decision on that wall color before you leave by the way."

Tabitha unlocks the building's two main doors as she inquires on my preference of tea. My options are earl gray, lemon, and peach. I chose peach as she holds the door open for me, allowing me to enter the library first.

Once we're both inside she flicks on the lights and heads towards the back hallway, gesturing for me to follow. We make our way into a small kitchen with a table off to the side.

She begins boiling the tea as she speaks. "Here's the deal- you can come in whenever you would like while we're open, do the tasks I assign for you, and then you can leave whenever you please. You'll be paid eight an hour for every hour you work and I suggest you don't try to negotiate on this considering the minimum wage is five fifty right now in three out of the four countries. I will also need you to provide all of your banking information as well as proof of citizenship. You can leave those papers on my desk at the start of your next work day. As for this trial run of ours, I have decided to give you the next seven days to prove yourself. If your work is subpar I will let you go. However, if you turn out to be exceptional you can continue on here like normal without a peep from me. Is all of this clear?"

"Yes, Ma'am."

"Oh, please. My name is Tabitha and that is what I would like for you to call me."

"Of course m- Tabitha." She gives me a testing look as I catch myself.

"Dear, if you don't mind me asking, what is the situation with those legs of yours? Injury?"

I look down at the base of my crutches and my untrustworthy feet that have so far done alright by me today. "I lost function of them after an operation that I had, but I'm slowly gaining mobility again."

"I see. Well, I don't think that it should impede on the tasks I have for you today, but if you are having trouble please let me know and I will arrange something else to occupy your time."

The kettle on the stove releases steam and a high-pitched scream before Tabitha takes it off of the burner. She picks out two cups from the scarcely stocked cabinet and pours an equal amount of water into both before setting one of the cups in front of me along with the unopened tea bag. I rip the packaging and begin steeping it, dragging the string in and out of the water.

"What would you like for me to do first?"

"I wrote up a list last night before leaving, it should be on my desk when you're ready."

Tabitha picks up our beverages to take into the other room, beckoning for me to once again follow after her. Together we travel back to the part of the building that is open to the public.

She places my tea, still piping with steam, down on her desk where I leave it for now. Instead I pick up the small notebook paper with a list of tasks written in sloping cursive. There are only three things on the list.

Tabitha, on the other hand, makes her way around the desk to sit in her chair after taking off her light spring sweater and placing it on a hook. She leaves her scarf on though, the one that she was wearing when I met her yesterday.

"What's the first thing I wrote down for you to do? I can't remember."

I look back to the paper. "Memorizing all of the book sections."

"Right."

"I guess I'll start by just taking a look around?"

"That sounds smart enough, but first, would you pick one for me?" Without looking up from the book she now has opened, she points to a basket of records on the edge of her desk. "It can get so dull in here without something playing."

"Oh, sure." The tips of the crutches hit the tile harshly with each step I take towards the record bin, making me painfully aware of my every movement.

When I get to the edge of the counter I lean against it for support and start going through the music. After flipping through a few options, I come across one with a gray forest on the cover. The name is barely visible, faded with time. The mystery intrigues me.

"Good choice," Tabitha commends as she sneaks up behind me, takes the vinyl from my hands and places it in the machine to the right of us.

Soft piano starts off the first song and gradually a folk-like tune begins to play from the speaker. A mature woman's voice starts singing at some point as well, her words speak of different circumstances and what could be in another time.

Most of the workday has gone, only an hour left before the library closes. I can tell that Tabitha is surprised that I'm still here. I have completed everything on her to-do list and more. I have memorized pretty much all of the book sections, learned how to check books in and out, organized the back inventory, figured out how to open new library accounts, and cleaned all of the tables. Some of the tasks were hard in my condition, but I always managed to figure out a way to work around it.

"Will you be back tomorrow?" Tabitha asks as she stamps recently donated books with the library's seal.

"I have an appointment in the morning, but I plan to come in right afterwards."

"Perfect."

"Is there anything else that I can do?"

"No dear, why don't you head home?"

"Are you sure?"

"I'm positive."

"Okay, do you mind if I use the phone to call for my ride?" I gesture towards the corded phone on her desk.

"Of course."

I pull out the sticky note that I placed in my pocket earlier, knowing that I would forget the number of the driver Miles gave to me otherwise. I dial slowly in an attempt to prolong my departure. My feet might ache from standing most of the day, but I don't want to leave. Being here provides a nice change of scenery and a larger sense of purpose than what I felt at the diner the other day.

The driver pulls up to the house shortly after six. He helps me out and doesn't pull away until my key is in the door. I'm about to unlock it when Miles opens it instead.

"Close your eyes," he commands. "Please!"

"Have you been here all day?!"

"Someone had to be here to keep Bear company. Now seriously, close them." I do as he says as he guides me into the house before shutting the door. "Okay, now you can look."

When I open my eyes I discover that almost every project has been completed while I was away. The cabinets in the kitchen are painted eggshell white and feature the brass knobs that I fell in love with at the store. The backsplash is up and when I get to my bedroom, where I can see into the bathroom, I notice that the mirror and faucets have been replaced as well. No matter the room or the task Miles has managed to perfect everything that I wanted.

The only unfinished project is the living room walls, half painted with the sage green color I quickly decided on before leaving earlier. There's even a new pine shelf on the wall for extra storage that I did not ask for, but fits in rather well.

"It looks fantastic. Thank you, Miles."

"Sorry I didn't get the walls done in time, I wasn't expecting you for another hour."

"It's alright, I'll help you finish."

"Are you sure you're up for that?" He gazes from my legs to my eyes as if I might have forgotten.

"I've done pretty well on my feet all day, though I'm pretty sure I must have a mark on my underarms by now from the pressure."

"Maybe you can paint the lower area of the walls and I'll worry about the top. it's only the first coat so I'll even it out later."

"Sounds like a plan."

I drop the crutches to the floor and slowly lower myself to a sitting position as close to the baseboards as I can get. I take the extra paint roller and drag it through the tin a few times before steadily lifting it to the wall.

By the time I finish the first foot or so nearest me, I itch to stand. I place the roller in the plastic paint tray and use the wooden handle as leverage to help me up. Miles steps closer the second he realizes I'm up without any support, instinctively putting up his guard. I take a step, teetering like a toddler, and his arms hover around me protectively.

"Careful there soldier," he teases.

I give him a small appreciative smile before directing my attention back to my task. I focus all of my energy on planting my feet as I refresh the roller and put it to the wall. Each time I go up and down a panel I lean a little bit of weight into it to give my feet a break.

Once I'm done with one section I shuffle my feet over to the next, Miles's arms hovering back around me like a forcefield each time I do. At some point he ends up abandoning his own painting since apparently watching over me is a full time job... I realize the irony of that immediately.

I situate myself a final time, leaning into the corner of the room for support, and start painting again. Once he deems that I have sufficient enough aid, he steps a small space away and picks out a large, flat wash brush. He dips it in the container of green and continues to watch over as he fixes over a spot too high for me to reach.

"How was work?"

"Good. And speaking of, do you know how to access my bank information?"

"Of course. I'll get it to you tomorrow. Are you working again then?"

"Yes." I shuffle my feet back to the left, almost touching Miles. We're just about finished now.

"Hey, I almost forgot, I have a surprise for you."

"A surprise?" I put the roller face down in the paint and let the stick gently fall to the tarp.

"Yeah, it's just something small that I saw in the window of a store."

"What is it for?"

"To celebrate you getting a new job and for all the progress you've made with your walking this past week."

"Oh, that's so sweet." Luckily he walked away to retrieve the gift and can't see the rose blush that I am painfully aware is creeping across my cheeks for some reason.

I take slow and concentrated steps over to the couch where I collapse in exhaustion. That is the longest I have stood on my own so far. Eventually, Miles comes over with a medium-sized box wrapped in brown paper and twine. I scooch over to take up less space and he hands me the box in with a dramatic flourish.

"This is the first present that I will remember receiving." Even though the smile on my face is painfully large as this realization comes to me, the words I speak are terribly sad.

I pull at the thin, brown rope and rip the paper off with ease. The lid of the box flips off next, and underneath is the most beautiful pair of shoes I have ever seen. Simple, white, and only a two-inch heel to compliment my average height.

"Do you like them? I didn't know if the bow would be too much."

"No, they're perfect," I reassure as I toy with the

pristine ribbon on the toe.

"I'm glad to hear you say that because I actually got you something else."

"Something else? Miles, this has already been enough." He presents another, smaller box to me. I lift the lid slowly and sitting inside are two paper tickets. "What is this?"

"There's a charity gala being held two weekends from now in Cryoden. I figured with your track record, you'll definitely be able to dance by then, and I'm assuming you'll want to take full advantage."

"So me and you are going?"

"Well, you and whoever you would like to take."

I would like to take you, is what I want to say to him. But that would be inappropriate, wouldn't it?

"Thank you, this is wonderful. But who says I'll be ready to dance by then?"

"Are you kidding? I have no doubt that you will. I'll even prove it to you." Miles stands and holds his hand out to me.

"What is going on?"

"Just take my hand."

"Okay?" I tentatively place my hand in his and he pulls me up with more force than I expect. I practically fall into him.

"Sorry about that." He chuckles and leans me back up so I am supported by myself once more.

"Now will you tell me what we're doing?"

"We're practicing."

"Practicing what?"

"Dancing."

"But there's no music."

"There can be. Do you have a song preference?"

I think back to the one I heard earlier in the library. I can't remember the exact name so I ask to borrow Miles's phone and type some keywords into the search bar. Nothing familiar comes up. Then I try my favorite lyric, the one about pennies and pools. The song comes up. I press play and hand the phone back to Miles. He in turn places it on the coffee table with the volume up all the way.

"Perfect. Now place your hand here," he guides one of my hands behind his left shoulder and the other stays in his. "And I put my hand here," he continues as he puts his opposite hand on my hip. My breath catches as he does, and I'm suddenly aware of every movement I make. It's like when something cold unexpectedly touches your skin and it feels nice but it takes a minute for you to regulate the sensation.

The first chorus plays and my favorite lyric is sung into the air. How have thirty seconds already come and gone?

"If you need help moving just let me know and you can lean on me or stand on my feet or something."

I nod in acknowledgment and we start to sway, slowly turning in circles at a steady speed. This is fine, I can do this. The chorus and verses play and we dance along without a hitch for the next three minutes. I expect it to be over now, the dancing, since Miles has already proven his point. But another song of the same singer plays, this one with a faster tempo.

"Would you like to pick it up a bit?" He asks.

I can't believe I've done so much today. I have a feeling that I will really be paying for it tomorrow. But still, I say, "Sure."

This new song takes on the perspective of the singer as the onlooker of someone else's romance. As she narrates, I try to pay attention as best I can so I can see if it's on the same record Tabitha has tomorrow. I am so swept up in the allure of the story, the gifts, and the body so close to mine that it takes my thoughts off of my own stumbling feet. Then just like that, this song ends too.

The playlist continues, of course, randomizing yet another melody from the women's discography, but I am too consumed with fatigue to go on even though I want nothing more than to continue dancing. I think Miles can tell how torn I am because he praises me for all that I have done and helps me sit back on the couch with promises to dance again soon.

I will hold him to that.

Chapter Ten
Saturday, March 11th

I have barely seen Miles since my appointment on Tuesday. I was okay with it at first, and enjoyed my alone time for a bit as I tried writing again, but now it's going on day four with only twice-a-day quick phone call check-ins. It's starting to get a little lonely. It's just me, Bear, and my half-empty sheets of scribbled-on paper. Although, I've gone into work every day since Monday, so I guess I had Tabitha's company as well when she didn't prefer reading her book over having a conversation with me.

On my call with Miles this morning, before work, I asked him about the program I remembered him mentioning that connects volunteers up with Rebirth patients to help them socialize and make friends and shit. Miles seemed thrilled that I had brought this up and promised to get me information on some friend candidates from around town by tomorrow.

I was tempted to ask when he would cash in on his other promise of dance practice again, but I couldn't bring myself to. I wasn't even sure why I found myself wanting to or why the memory has been sneaking its way into my head on occasion.

And speaking of dancing, Miles was right. There is no way that I won't be able to regain one hundred percent mobility by next week when that charity ball comes around. I've made so much progress that at this morning's appointment, the first one I went to without Miles, Doctor Pierce said that we only have to meet monthly now. I have been practicing my balance and longevity all week by using the crutches instead of the chair anytime I can, and switching between strengthening each foot because I am determined to make today the first day that I don't use the chair at all.

Tabitha even let me close the library by myself tonight since I have become more mobile. She approached me an hour ago and claimed that she had to rush off somewhere, handed me the keys and told me not to fuck it up which is an honor because she treats the place as if it's her child and judging by the amount of different cat pictures on her desk it's probably her only.

Unfortunately, though, she left me with a box of old files to go through before I leave. I'm two-thirds of the way done when the bell on the door chimes. I check the clock on the wall behind me. It's 6:05.

"I'm so sorry, but unfortunately the library closes at six," I call out as I finish gathering papers together.

"Darn pregnancy brain, I totally lost track of the time." A woman, maybe a few years older than I, clutches her barely showing stomach as she breathes deeply. "Do you mind if I just sit for a moment?"

"Oh, of course. I apologize."

"For what? It's not you making my face break out."

I try to finish up with what I was previously doing, but her presence becomes harder to ignore as her breathing intensifies. Something is not quite right.

"How far along are you?" I ask in an attempt to distract her.

"I'm halfway through my second trimester." She catches my eye, seeming surprised for a moment, before looking back down at her stomach with adoration.

"Oh, how lovely." And then a silence settles in. I'm almost done now, only needing to clean up my mess, when the corded phone rings. I take up my crutches and make my way over to Tabitha's desk. "Hello?"

"Hey Em, it's Miles. I tried your house first but when no one picked up I figured that you would still be at the library."

I double-check the time hoping I am not mistaken. I'm not. We're not supposed to have our next check-in call for at least another fifty minutes.

"What's up?"

"I got those friend profiles that you asked for this morning, and I was wondering since you're still at work if you wanted to meet up at the diner to go over them."

"Oh yeah, sure."

I try to act nonchalant, but truthfully, I am very giddy at the offer. I know that it's literally his job to hang out and help me, but he really is my only friend right now, which no one needs to tell me is pathetic... I already know that it is.

"Perfect, I'll see you in ten?"

"Sounds good."

I hastily go back to the table for the files to bring over to Tabitha's desk and place each grouping in two seperate areas. One has a sticky note labeled "shred it," and the other says "keep." Then I grab my stuff from the back. I'm about to lock up when I remember the woman sitting in the chair off to the side.

"Are you alright to head back outside?" I feel bad for rushing her, but not bad enough to reschedule dinner with Miles.

"Oh, I think so. Thank you again."

"Of course. Do you live around here?"

"I do not, I'm just staying for a few weeks visiting family in a neighboring town," she clarifies as I show her out.

I lock the door with the key that Tabitha gave to me and wait until the woman isn't looking before hiding it in a small space between two bricks on the exterior wall, as I've seen Tabitha do every night this week.

"Well, it was nice meeting you."

"You too. I'm Seren by the way."

"Emily."

"Emily?" Seren repeats inquisitively.

If I had more time I would joke that tenty percent
of the population probably has my name and it's not that
interesting or, I could conjure up some story about how
Emily was the name of my grandmother's cousin who lived
in Altone and taught the poor to read during the First World
War. Maybe that's why I chose the name, because of some
grandmother I don't know anymore.

"I got us exactly what we had last time. I hope that
you don't mind," Miles announces the second that I sit down
across from him.

"That's fine."

"No chair this time?" Gloria the waitress queries as she
places a water glass and a straw in front of me.

"No chair ever again," I confirm.

"That's great dear. Can I get you anything else, or did
Miles pretty much cover it?"

"I'm all set, thanks."

"All right, well let me know if you change your mind,"
she instructs before going off to clean up some toddlers' mac
and cheese that fell on the floor.

Miles pulls a yellow folder out of his bag. "Here are
all the candidates signed up for the Rebirth friends program in
the area." He then pulls out a green folder. "And out of all of
those candidates, here are the ones recommended for you."

I take both of them from him and take my time to flip
through each stack. The options in the green folder are more
niche than the yellow, with a handful of publicists, reviewers,
and other professionals in the literary field with similar
interests to mine, but the pool is much smaller. What if I make
the wrong choice? I flip through them both once more, going
through slower and more thoroughly this time.

At some point, I pass a familiar face and flip back to
a page somewhere in the middle to be certain. It's Tabitha.

She's holding one of her cats in the picture. To the right of the page is a brief description of her life and some interests that she has listed. Books, tea, cats, plays, and crocheting. I bet that's how she got that red scarf she always wears. It also doesn't surprise me that she would want to take part in something like this.

"Find someone you like?"

"Kinda, my boss is in here," I explain while snapping the green folder shut and handing it back as he tries to peek at the picture over the table.

"You don't want this one?"

"No, I'll stick with the yellow."

"Okay."

Gloria comes back shortly with our food, and we direct our attention towards that for a while. I'm tempted to bring up the charity gala and see if he would be my plus one. I did some research on it, and the money from the tickets goes to distributing a vaccine for some disease spreading across Aelville.

I wipe the corners of my mouth so as to not embarrass myself. "Are you free next Saturday?"

He swallows, "I think so. Isn't that the night of the dance I got you tickets for?"

"It is!" I draw back a tad, wincing at my overexcitement. "I was actually wondering if you would be my plus one."

He stares at me. "I don't know if- maybe that's just not the best idea."

"Why not?" I try to keep the disappointment from my face but I can't help whatever emotion slips through my voice.

"I just don't know if that's appropriate, it's a fine line between mentor and friend."

Is he saying that he doesn't see me as a friend? I should've expected his professionalism but I didn't imagine how much it would sting. "Oh yeah, I get it. Sorry if I crossed that line by asking, you have a job to do, that's all."

"I'm sorry Emily, I don't mean to make it awkward or hurt your feelings."

"No, you haven't," I wave it off and try to put a smile back on my face.

"Maybe you could invite one of your friend contenders," he suggests while nodding towards the yellow folder now on the seat next to me.

"Yeah, maybe."

We both divert our attention back to our plates now except by the time Miles has finished I have only managed to take another bite or two. I ask for a to-go box the next time Gloria comes by, which happens to be when she drops off the check. I place my new card down on top of the bill but Miles slides his underneath.

"My treat."

"Thanks."

"Are you okay? You've seemed off since-"

"Yeah," I cut him off and hold up the yellow folder. "I've just been thinking about this."

"Oh, would you like help with making a decision?"

"No thanks."

Then he calls for a car.

When we started the drive home it was winsomely bright, the sun just dipping below the skyline, but by the time Miles was dropped off storm clouds overtook. Now as I step out of the car a light dusting of rain begins. It brings me back to the night that I lost power, when Miles stayed over.

The second I walk inside Bear jumps onto the arm of the couch to greet me. I run my hand from his head to his tail. In return, he nuzzles into me.

"Would you like some food?" I coax him over by picking up his bowls. I fill one with food and the other with water. He happily purs as he makes his way over.

While Bear is preoccupied I pull the blanket off of the couch to drape over myself and open up the yellow folder.

I flip past what must be twenty people within a thirty-mile
radius, mostly women. Only a few catch my attention.

The person that draws me in the most is a girl two
years younger than me named Ellie. She has frizzy red bangs
and a pretty smile. But it's really the fact that one of her listed
interests is dancing that convinces me she's the one. I make
my way towards the phone and dial the number listed at the
bottom of her page.

Chapter Eleven

Sunday, March 12th

I wait on a park bench next to pink tulips and under an elm tree. Two boxes of takeout from the diner are next to me. Ellie said that she would be here five minutes ago. I am trying to be patient but my nerves are getting the best of me. I decide to distract myself by identifying different types of birds, and by identifying, I mean taking note of their differences and assigning them fake names.

I haven't been to this part of New Cresthill yet, so there are many other sights to focus on like the view of the distant harbor I didn't know was nearby, the gazebo with a man playing soft music on his trumpet, and the handmade birdhouses that need to be refilled with seeds.

I take note of the sixth type of winged creature I've seen since sitting down and am about to think of a funny name for it when someone behind me speaks. I don't catch what is said.

I turn my head to face a doe-eyed girl with peach colored bangs. "Ellie?"

"Yes!"

"I'm Emily." I hold my hand out, but instead of taking it, she pulls me in for a hug. Her hair has been cut shorter since the picture in her profile was taken. It now sits just under her ears. "I like your skirt."

"Thank you." She twirls for me, the yellow and orange pattern blurring together. "I like your coat."

"Thanks." Today must be the first day I have worn something that isn't a variation of brown, black, or gray.

I got the feeling from her picture- where she was wearing a pink, crocheted tank top- that Ellie is the type of girl who likes colors. So, this morning before entering the park I picked out a white sweater with flowers embroidered into the neckline at a nearby shop. It's been extremely useful, considering the second I checked out, clouds gathered in front of the sun, dropping the temperature by at least five degrees.

Ellie travels into a spotlight of sun, basking in the glow. "I think we should set up camp here," she affirms before taking a green and white gingham patterned sheet out of her bag and laying it out.

The wind wrestles with her efforts, lifting the corners. I take the crutches propped against the bench, hobble the few steps over, and carefully lay one along the left side of the blanket and the other along the right.

Ellie stares up at me horrified. "I- I didn't realize that you had trouble walking. Don't you need those?"

"It's alright. At this point they are just for reassurance," I clarify.

"What happened? If you don't mind me asking." She lays out strawberries and a cake decorated with pink frosting. This of course reminds me of the food I brought.

"Just a complication from the surgeries I had after going through the Rebirth process. Would you mind grabbing those?" I point to the takeout containers.

"Oh yes, of course."

As she goes back to the bench I can't help but notice the way she moves with the grace of a princess. The wind fuels this illusion when a gust of air makes her flowing clothes dance with her.

"I actually have a somewhat personal question as well." She doesn't answer, instead tilting her head with curiosity as she sits back down. I take it as the go-ahead to continue with my inquiry. "Why did you sign up for the Rebirth friends program?"

"That's easy, because of my sister." Her posture becomes rigid as she sits back down, but still she tries to keep a smile in her eyes. Have I stepped too far too fast? "We didn't grow up under the best of circumstances, but she definitely got the sharper end of the stick. She tried years of therapy but the images in her head and the panic attacks from even certain smells sent her over the edge. I knew she wanted it all gone, but I didn't know just how bad until I found numerous web browsers open on a computer that she had forgotten to shut down while she went to the bathroom."

Any smart person that didn't want to be caught would have clicked out of open browsers before walking away but I don't bring up the idea to the girl that her sister might have wanted her to see what she did.

"Long story short, about a year ago I used all of my tip money and overtime pay to help her buy the cheapest way out of the life she was born into. I had to take out a loan to pay off the rest, but working since I was twelve helped for sure."

"Did she want you to contact her afterward to reconnect?"

"I didn't think it was a good idea. Amelia is too curious for her own good, and she's my weakness. She would only have to ask what happened to her in a certain way and I would give in, but the whole point of it was to get her away. I check up on her sometimes though from afar."

"How?"

It's clearly a touchy subject, but I crave the insight. Maybe my situation is the same and somebody is checking up on me in some way. Maybe through Miles if that's allowed. I've been trying to keep the questions inside because Ellie is right, there was a reason for doing this to myself. Clearly, it's better not to know. But now and then I can't help but let the oddity of my situation and the questions that come with it slip back into my consciousness.

Was I abused? Stalked? In the service? Maybe that's

the real reason I woke up with my legs as they were and blaming the operation was just an easy scapegoat. Although, I do know that all four countries' military powers haven't been used as much since we became a united front, therefore that's not likely. Unless I was of a lower service, meant to deal with more smaller criminals.

But if so, that would have been a side job because as Miles has told me, I am a writer. I have seen the pages upon pages of writing. I have flipped through the scripts with my old name deleted or crossed off in thick black marker. I am a writer. Or at least I was one. My efforts as of late have not been very fruitful. Maybe I'll head over to the library after this to try on the computer again. I have found it more effective than writing on paper since the mistakes are easier to correct, and there are a lot of mistakes.

"I keep in contact with her husband," Ellie finally answers. I didn't realize how long we had sat in silence until I was disrupted from my thoughts. "I reached out a few months after they got married. He was shocked at first, but we're close now. He's good to her."

"Thank you for sharing that." I reach out and lay a hand over hers.

She does the same, sandwiching mine in the middle as she squeezes. "Thank you for listening."

We spend the rest of the morning devouring our food and talking. She tells me more about her and her sister's childhood, how she plays guitar for her band, and lives with all of her bandmates in an apartment above the one bar in town.

I don't have much to provide to the conversation, so all I tell her about is Bear and my job. I also discover that I have a hidden talent for making bracelets out of dandelions. I teach Ellie how to make them as well once the conversation dwindles.

"I've had a lot of fun today. Thanks for choosing me." She smiles at me as I tie both ends of the thin dandelion stems together for the tenth time.

"Me too."

We throw away the trash and pick up our belongings, preparing to leave. I don't have any food left to carry, which makes it easier to walk with the crutches. Ellie, on the other hand, puts the leftover cake and berries in her bag to take back home.

I bring up my next location and suggest walking together, to which she gaily agrees so we start on our way, walking along the paved path toward town.

"There is something else that I meant to ask you about." We pass under the iron arch entryway to the park. A sign on a wood stake says goodbye to us as Ellie looks at me inquisitively. "I saw in your profile that you like to dance."

"Oh, I love to dance. My sister and I used to enter contests when we were younger."

"I'm glad to hear that because I have two tickets to a ball in Croyden for next Saturday and need someone to go with, if you would like to."

"Are you kidding? That sounds fantastic! I have to get a new dress. Oh my god we should go shopping together!" The excitement of my proposal has sent her talking at the pace of a jaguars run.

"I'm free tomorrow," I suggest.

"Great, Can I pick you up at noon?"

"Sure."

She then starts going off on a tangent about which dress colors compliment each skin tone, becoming too distracted to notice the glow radiating from my face.

"Today is your day off," Tabitha sternly reminds me, her arms teasingly folded the second I walk into the building.

"I was hoping to use the computer if it isn't being occupied." It isn't, so I make my way over to the back of the room. Tabitha follows after me.

"What for?"

"To write. I'm hoping to finally make some sort of

progress today.”

“Have you even thought of a concept?”

“Never a good one.”

“Well then, no wonder the backspace button is your best friend.”

“Ouch.” I power the computer on. The internal fan hums to life as the screen starts to load.

“Oh hush up, I know exactly what you need.”

“And what would that be?”

“Inspiration.” She hurries off into one of the many rows of books.

“Where are you going?” I call out after her.

When Tabitha disappears around the corner and I receive no answer I turn back to the computer and type in my password and username. The loading process unfortunately takes another minute and doesn’t finish until Tabitha comes back with a small book in her hands. She smugly tosses it on the table.

“Read it and let me know what you think,” she instructs before walking back behind her desk, humming happily to herself.

I’ve rarely seen her this giddy. Not that she’s typically a cynic but she does appear to water-down her emotions, at least in the week I have known her, which I’m aware isn’t long, but we’ve been around each other for eight hours a day most of the time.

“I don’t see you reading,” she lectures from afar. I roll my eyes.

I can’t remember the comfort and support of a real mom but, if mothering feels like anything, it is this. She reminds me to take lunch breaks and keeps up to date with my medical progress. Occasionally I’ll even get a random water glass shoved in my face and a stern reminder about staying hydrated.

Tabitha gives a slow clear of her throat with the obvious intent being to keep me focused. I make a dramatic gesture of picking up the book, to communicate that I have received the message, and turn my head to see a satisfied smile spread across her face as she places a record into the player.

It appears as if there once was ink on the cover, but years of reading and age have rubbed it clean off. The spine of the book is also too small for print, so instead the first page is where the title is. *The Two Houses Between The Bay.* I am given no author, summary, context, or forewarning as to what I am about to get into. I must simply read.

I flip to the first page and quickly discover that the story is not a novel at all, but really a script. Scene one: Exterior of house.

For an hour and a half the only muscles in my body that move are my hands and eyes. I devour all 13 scenes with a hunger I have never felt before, scanning each of the one hundred and fourteen pages to commit as much of them as I can to memory. The story is captivating and pulls me into a time when the world was just learning how to be one instead of separate.

"Thoughts?" Tabitha pulls up a chair to sit beside me.

"I love the way that they love each other. Their story is written with such anguish and pain. They help each other heal only to be taken away without explanation. How does someone write like this? It's quite a shame that the author didn't want to take credit for their work."

Tabitha shrugs. "I'm sure that there was good reason behind the decision."

I bite my lip, lost in thought. "What if I could- nevermind."

"Speak your mind, child."

"Do you think it's possible to get the rights for this play?"

"The rights?" She almost laughs, clearly perplexed at the question posed. "Now why would you want those?"

"People need to see this, to hear and feel it."

She thinks it over before taking the book from my hands and flipping through. "There's no copyright. Legally you don't need to ask permission."

This information only fuels my desire. "It could bring a lot of attention to the library if we held it here," I point out before rattling off ideas from poster graphics to audition dates. I stop when I notice Tabitha's reclusive body language. "Is everything okay?"

She takes a moment to herself before straightening her posture. "Listen, it's not that I don't like the idea but… why don't you consult your Rebirth mentor first?"

I'm stunned. Tabitha is the last person that I thought would hold me back from this. If anything I expected her to be going along with my crazy ideas, but even still I agree to consult Miles before moving forward.

Chapter Twelve
Monday, March 13th

I can't stop thinking about the story Tabitha lent to me yesterday. I know she meant for it to simply inspire me to write something myself, but it's done so much more.

I spend half of the night with Miles, trying to figure out logistics and attempting to do research on the play, but nothing comes up. It's as if the book doesn't exist anywhere else.

Around midnight I kick him out to concentrate on starting the first chapter of my own book, a medium of writing I don't believe past me got a chance to devel with. As of now, I am unsure of what I want to achieve with this book but I do know that I want its contents to be a secret to everyone but me. Until it is complete, I want to be the only one with knowledge of what I am putting to paper, that way there is less pressure.

I begin writing and don't allow myself to feel the cramp overtaking my muscles until the sun comes up behind the house. The seizing tension crawls up my left wrist as I grab the blanket off of the back of the couch to lay over me. I'll wash the smudge of ink off of my thumb when I wake but for now, I let sleep come.

The smell of bacon grease is strong in the air. I want to open my eyes to investigate why but they feel so heavy. Bear tries to help me up by shoving his bottom against my nose. I groan but comply by petting him, mostly because I know it's the only way to get him to stop.

"I made you breakfast," Miles whispers as the couch cushions move to adjust to his added weight. "Well really by now it's brunch considering it's just past noon."

"Noon?" I grumble.

"Yep, 12:02 to be exact." I can tell he checks his watch by the shuffle of fabric I hear. "Come on, knowing you, you probably haven't eaten since yesterday morning." He pats my leg twice to further rouse me before getting back up. "Plus you got a telephone call about a half an hour ago that you should probably return soon."

Who would have wanted to call me?

Oh, shit. Ellie. I bolt upright and dart for the phone. I move so fast that my still unsteady feet trip over themselves and I end up face-first into the wall. Thankfully my hands catch me.

I dial her number, which is still written on the back of my hand from the other day. Oh god, I must have had it written on me still when we hung out. I try to get over the embarrassment of knowing that as I peek out the window for her car. When I don't see it I sigh and slouch to the ground with the phone to my ear. I wrap the spiral cord around my finger as I wait for the ringing to end.

"Hello?"

"Ellie? it's Emily."

"Oh, hey! I was just about to leave."

"Speaking of, would you actually mind just giving me about another half hour to get ready?"

"Did you just wake up or something?" She laughs, she's telling a joke. Do I lie? "Okay, considering you haven't answered by now I'm going to take that as a yes so just call me when you're ready and I'll head out a little after that. Does that sound alright?"

"Yes, thank you and I'm sorry."

"There's no need to apologize, I'll see you soon!" I hang up the phone.

"Are you going to eat before you go?" Miles calls after me as I head towards the bedroom.

"I'll take it to go, thanks."

There's no dress store in all of town so Ellie insisted on driving the hour over to Croyden, which with traffic was almost an hour and a half. Luckily Ellie has her own car, or as she explained it, she has joint custody that she splits with her other three roommates/band members. They have assigned days of the week and today happens to be hers.

"I say just put the show on anyway. No one is going to be traveling to a barely existent town at the top of Accrington to sue you for a play that barely exists."

"I guess that's true."

We glide through the store as we talk. Ellie is on one side of the rack and I am on the other. We go down one of the rows, scouting out options for both ourselves and each other. Ellie has picked out at least six gowns for me, I am not a fan of any of them. I can't complain though when I have found only one for her.

I'm starting to think that I am just not that into dresses when I pass a light gold one and have to backtrack. I take the hanger off of the rack to observe the off the shoulder cut with ruffles and the boned corset. Suddenly I itch to get to a dressing room but restrain myself by picking out a few more options for Ellie before suggesting the idea.

A saleswoman shows us to the changing area and helps me with the corset of the gold dress before leaving. I admire in private now the way the fabric falls nicely around my hips, giving me a frame that previously wasn't there. The dress also does wonders for my chest, pushing it up dramatically. It's perfect.

"Ready to see option one?" Ellie calls out from the

room to my left. I confirm.

She sweeps her curtain to the side, the metal rings holding it in place make noise against the horizontal pole, before joining me in the communal space. She wears a spaghetti strap v-neck that shows off a tattoo on her right arm, a crescent moon. The dress is white lace and has a pattern of tiny suns running along the length of it. It almost looks like a wedding dress.

Ellie breaks the silence first. "Don't even bother trying on anything else. You have got to get that one."

"And you have to get that one," I repeat after her.

We head back into our respective rooms to change, leaving our discarded options behind as we were told to do, before checking out.

I'm about to get into Ellie's car parked out front when she suggests that we eat out before heading home. So we proceed to walk around Croyden's main street. The surrounding buildings are much larger than the ones back in New Cresthill and the roads much more adequate to fit two cars as opposed to the one way streets that I'm now used to.

Ellie spots a restaurant further down the block, claiming that she's heard good things about it. I agree to the suggestion so we make our way to the crosswalk and wait for our turn. Upon getting closer I realize that I recognize the name of the place all too well. Hartman's.

There's not much business currently with it being between lunch and diner hours, only three tables are taken.

"How may I help you ladies?" An older lady that resembles Miles in every way asks after popping up from behind a counter. She has a few menus in her hands.

"Ms. Hartman?" The words come out before I can stop them.

"Yes?" She furrows her brow in confusion but keeps the smile on her face. "Do I know you?"

"No. I know your son."

"Oh, you're a friend of Miles?" Her smile grows wider as I grapple for a response to this question. Luckily she doesn't allow me to struggle for long. "I apologize, I don't mean to pry. Are you looking for a table?"

"Yes, for two please."

"Right this way."

She places us in one of the only two window seats and promises to be back with water shortly. Ellie gives me a questioning look. I brush it off to insinuate the meaningless mention of a boy and avoid bringing up the fact that Miles is my mentor.

By the time Mrs. Hartman does come back she brings along with her a man. He has food stains on his shirt and crumbs stuck in his beard. "Here you ladies are," She says while setting down two waters. "This is my husband Mark."

He extends a hand out in greeting to both of us. "I'm Emily and this is Ellie."

"Nice to meet you two."

"You as well."

"How is Miles? You must tell him to visit more."

"He's good, busy with work but good."

"Yes, as always," his mom interjects sorrowfully.

"Do you live in the area?" Mr. Hartman asks.

"No, we're from New Cresthill."

"I think that's where Miles is currently," his mother mentions.

From the corner of my eye I can see that Ellie has now caught on. Thankfully I don't think that Mr. and Mrs. Hartman has. I would like to avoid the potential occurrence of an awkward conversation if possible.

"Well, we'll let you two eat in peace now, it was so nice meeting you."

"Same here Mrs. Hartman."

Miles's parents excuse themselves and shortly after the waitress comes over to take our order. Ellie and I each order an appetizer and small portion entrees to share. We make sure to order a variety too- a soup, salad, burger, and pasta dish. By the time we're done there's nothing on the plates but sauce and some inner workings of the burger.

"Would you like some dessert today?" The waitress asks as she clears our plates. "Our special this week is a key lime cheesecake."

Ellie and I both agree on the matter and decide to split the dessert. Between the white piped-on frosting, the key lime slice, and the zested skin of the fruit we devour the pie with ease.

The waitress then places the check on our table with a rehearsed speech of thanks and asking us to come again soon. Ellie snatches it up before I have the chance to check the price and pays the total plus tip in cash.

"I'll pay you back. How much was it?"

"Don't worry about it, plus I'm pretty sure that they gave us a discount."

"That was nice of them, and you."

"Of course. Now I hope you don't mind if we get going now, I have to get back for practice," Ellie says as we get up to leave.

"That's fine."

I wave a final goodbye to Miles's mom before heading out the door. She's occupied with restocking the bar but puts down some bottles of liquor to wave back.

"You should come and check us out sometime. We play at the bar in town every Thursday."

"I'd love to."

Chapter Thirteen

Tuesday, March 14th

The library is closed and the sun set about an hour ago. The printer in the back corner whizzes to life as it prints two dozen copies of fliers. I designed some for auditions and then separate ones for the show. For now, I only print the first set. It took forever to figure out how to use the design features on the computer software but it's better than anything I could have accomplished by hand. Last night I decided on the dates. Next Monday for auditions, which gives six days for word to spread on the matter, and three months from now for the show.

I stand to collect my copies but come face to face with Tabitha who is already holding the warm, fresh inked paper in her hands. "Don't make me start charging you missy."

"Employee discount?" I joke as she hands the paper to me.

She playfully rolls her eyes. "So you really want to do this huh?"

"Yes, I really do."

I log out, power off the computer, and grab my bag. I haven't been bringing the crutches out with me since yesterday and so far I have only had one minor fall when going through the backroom and that's only because stacks of books were in my way.

"Did you end up finding the author?"

"No," I confess slowly.

"That's too bad."

It's hard to see in the dark so I don't stray too far from the streetlights. I even hang a couple of posters on them. I stop in the diner too and ask to hang one on their bulletin board. I then do the same for a couple other shops.

Eventually, I round out my trip in town by hanging my second to last flier in Doctor Pierce's office. He makes a comment about how excited he is to see that I am without the crutches before I say my goodbyes and walk out.

I start down the walking path to the very outskirts of town where the local school lies. The building straddles the border between New Cresthill and the next town over which just so happens to be called Old Cresthill. Neither town has enough kids to make one full school so instead they used the opportunity to combine districts when both towns were established. Or at least that's what I saw on the website when I printed out the directions to the place.

"Emily?"

A door closes and a woman with a hand on her stomach comes down the steps of the nearest building. Her voice sounds somewhat familiar but I can't place just where I know it from. I can't make out her face either until she steps into the light that's illuminating the road.

"It's me, Seren, I stopped in the library the other day when you were closing."

Closed not closing, I want to correct her, but instead I smile and greet her properly. "Is this where you're staying?"

"Yeah, I have a nice room on the first floor all to myself. Well, me and this little one." She pats her belly to signify who she is reffering to. "Where are you off to?"

"The Cresthill school."

I know you're not supposed to tell strangers where you're going or what you're doing or you can end up being like that folktale about the girl with the red cape but Seren is no wolf. She's an innocent, pregnant woman visiting family.

"What for?" She continues questioning.

"I have to ask them for a favor and to hang this up." I hold up the last of my fliers for her to see.

"May I?"

"Sure."

I hand her the paper and she reads it over carefully, examining each detail. She seems intrigued. "I've never read the play, is there a role a pregnant lady could play? I'm not much for the stage usually but it sounds fun."

I think it over. "There's definitely someone that I could find for you to play."

"I just might stop by then."

"You should if you plan on being in the area for a while."

I can't help but grin from ear to ear. My first interested person. I tried to hint to Miles and Ellie that I would like for them to try out. Neither caught on. I understand if Miles doesn't considering he is so busy with work and this most likely does not fall under the umbrella of things that he has to do for me. But I really want Ellie to do it at least. I might ask again, more bluntly this time.

"Do you mind if I walk with you? I'm staying the night with my cousins so it's on the way."

I agree of course and we pick up a steady pace once more towards the school. We walk in silence until we see our destination in the distance then Seren starts on about something superficial regarding what life is like back home for her, which I guess based on descriptions is Alnerwick.

I wonder if that's where I was from considering our accents sound the same. It's impossible to tell based on dialect since everyone in grade school is required to learn all four of the official languages, therefore relying on accents is simply a safer bet to go off of.

By the time we approach the school the door is locked. I try jiggling the handle just in case but find no luck. I figured

that the building would be open this late because of after
school sports or drama club but no one is here. The only
indication of people are the lights on in the main hallway that
tricked me from a distance. However, I now realize they are
most likely on for security purposes.

"Shit," I curse under my breath as I rattle both door
handles once more for extra measure.

"What now?"

"Do you have a phone?"

She reaches in her handbag and pulls out the device to
hand to me. I graciously thank her before calling for a car. I
reassure her that she will get dropped off at her cousins too as
I hand the phone back.

"They actually canceled a few minutes ago," She
informs me. "One of the kids came down with a fever but we
were already so far into our walk and I didn't feel comfortable
turning back on my own, even if the crime rate here is close to
none. You can never be too careful, ya know?"

"That's rude to have canceled when you were already
on your way."

"He must have assumed that I was taking a car and
hadn't left yet."

"Still that's not right."

We balance between silence and the rhythm of
mundane conversation until a black car pulls up to the
school's roundabout where the buses must drop off. The driver
rolls the window down and to my surprise a very unhappy
Miles is behind the wheel. He removes the grumpy expression
from his face though once he realizes that we have company.

"Where's the usual driver?" I question.

"There were none currently available so I was sent.
Who's this?"

"This is Seren, I met her at the library the other day.
She was on the way to visit her family when we ran into each
other but they just canceled, could we give her a ride too?
She's just staying at the inn next to the cake shop."

Seren gives a small greeting wave to Miles who

gives a reluctant smile back. I note the oddity of his usual friendliness being absent but table the thought until our guest is not nearby.

"Sure."

The drive back home is completely silent, even after we drop off Seren. We don't speak until we pull into my driveway. "Would you like to explain what you were doing in the middle of nowhere late at night without telling anyone of your location?"

I can tell that he doesn't want to seem like a parent but can't help it. It's his job to keep track of me so that I don't become full of depression at the unknowingness of myself and jump off a cliff or something like that. I try to remind myself of this, but still, I am filled with rage. I don't have to tell him everything, even if he's right and I should have told someone where I was going. Instead I decide to flip this back onto him.

"Would you like to explain why you randomly ghosted me? Because one minute we're dancing and you're fixing the paint on my walls and the next you barely come around."

"Are you saying that I'm bad at my job? And what about you visiting my parents yesterday, huh? What was that? I call it overstepping."

I scoff at the accusation. "Ellie and I were in the area and she was the one that wanted to go. How is that overstepping? It's not like I went out of the way to find the place and track down your parents."

"You know what, I never should have told you about that anyway. That's on me for sharing personal details. I won't make that mistake again."

"If you shouldn't have told me then maybe you are bad at your job."

I get out of the car. I hear him get out too. He calls something out to me but it's too late, his words are killed by the slam of the door in his face.

Chapter Fourteen
Thursday, March 16th

I spent all of Wednesday held up in my room writing and ignoring calls from Miles. It is now Thursday evening and I am doing the same.

I'm still livid because of our fight. He pretty much accused me of stalking. But then again I did imply that he's bad at his job and he's not. He's actually really wonderful at it. Making people feel comfortable and needed is a skill that he excels at. And without him, I wouldn't have done half the stuff that I have in these almost three weeks. Instead, I would likely still be laying in bed, crying every hour with legs that only half worked. He inspired the need to carry on, to push past what I thought was capable of myself. The next time he calls I promise myself to answer.

Speaking of phone calls, I was able to get a hold of The Cresthill School yesterday as well and they agreed to let me use the auditorium for auditions and rehearsals on the weekends. I didn't ask them about renting it for performances though because I am still hoping that Tabitha will say yes to having the performances be in the library.

I abandon my writing once I notice the clock on the wall and the sun dimming to dusk outside the window. I head into the bedroom and rifle around the drawers of my dresser for a suitable outfit for tonight. Eventually I settle on a denim mini-skirt and a plain white tank top.

I leave the outfit thrown on the bed as I fix my appearance in the bathroom mirror. There's not much that I can do with my hair thanks to its length and I have yet to purchase any makeup since I haven't needed it until now so I keep my going out preparations simple before calling for a cab.

I double-check my appearance in the car's side mirror before it pulls away. In the reflection behind me Ellie tunes her guitar. She sits on the bumper of her van in the alleyway of the venue. The rest of the band passes by her to finish unloading their equipment out of the trunk.

When I get within an arm's length of reach she registers my presence and gives me an eager hug. "I'm so glad that you could make it, let me introduce you to everyone."

She slips the guitar off of her neck and leaves it to rest carefully against the side of the van before skipping around to the artist's entrance of the building, pulling me along with. There aren't many people inside yet but they're set doesn't start for another hour.

"This is our drum player, Scott," she introduces as she leads me up on stage. He shakes my hand. "And this is our keyboard player and band manager, Evan." Evan nods at me in acknowledgement before going back to talk to who I can only assume is the owner of the place based on the money in his hand. "And last but never the least Angie, short for Angelina."

Angie adjusts the height of the mic as we approach. She's the total opposite of Ellie with her tight clothing, heavy makeup and black, shaggy hair. "Nice to meet you."

"You too."

Angie finishes her task and puts a relaxed arm around Ellie. "Are you new to the area?"

"Yeah."

"Ya know Em is an artist too, she writes screenplays

and stuff," Ellie brags for me.

"Anything that I would know?"

"Probably not, they're all Alnerwick shows." Yet another fact backing up the hypothesis that I am from there. "But there's actually another project that I'm trying to start."

"And what's that?"

I pray that this plug works. "I'm putting on a play a couple of months from now. It's not very well known but it's something special. Auditions are next Monday if you want to just come and try it out."

"Sounds fun, I just might have to." She looks expectantly at Ellie.

"Well, if you're going to, I guess I have to as well, right?"

"Right," Angie confirms with a finger boop to Ellie's nose. "Anyways, it was nice meeting you but I got to finish setting up or Evan will give me shit." She holds her hand out for a fistbump, pulling away after letting our knuckles connect.

"So, we play from ten to eleven, then have a half-hour break before we go back on from eleven-thirty to midnight. The band and I usually get a few free drinks from fans during the break. If you want to stick around that long, I'll give you some of mine."

"They'll serve us alcohol? Cause I'm only twenty and aren't you nineteen?"

My question makes her laugh. "The only country with a drinking age of 21 is Alnerwick, the other three it's all 18."

"Right, I forgot." I must have never been out of my home country before since I didn't actually know that.

"Anyways I gotta go but have fun and mingle, more people will be here soon!" She gives me a tight squeeze and squeals as she skips back toward her guitar.

I take a seat at the bar while I wait for things to pick up and order something fancy-sounding but cheap. They have a small television in the corner, the first one I've seen since being here. It must be old because the screen glitches now and then and the color is decently faded. There's a sports game on that isn't very interesting but I direct my attention towards it until the music starts up.

The band is insane. It's mostly original works but they play some covers as well. When they introduce a song every now and then Angie will typically say which one of them wrote it and make a speech about the meaning behind it, the audience eats it up every time.

I've kept to my spot in the back by the bar and have been slowly sipping on my second drink, a beer, since the set started. I'm not a huge fan of the taste hence why after an hour it is still half full but I chug the rest down, squinting at the taste, before pushing my way to the front of the crowd.

I stay there for a song or two until Angie announces that they'll be back after their break. The crowd jokingly boo's in which she gives a dramatic and apologetic shrug of her shoulders. Evan and Scott go through the back to what I'm assuming is their dressing room while Ellie and Angie jump off of the two-foot stage to sandwich me in the middle. Together they lead me back to the bar.

"I am ready to have myself a drink," Angie groans as she lifts her head back to the ceiling.

There are only two available stools next to each other so Angie allows us to sit. She then taps on a man's shoulder and turns her voice into something sultry. It doesn't take much persuasion from there for the man and his friend to move to an already crowded, far table in the corner.

"Thank you, sir," she calls out flirtatiously after he leaves.

Ellie was right, within their half-hour break the two of them have chugged back at least a few free seltzers each. I on the other hand have been handed everything else since they still have to be somewhat conscious to continue singing. I have tried everything- vodka, tequila, rum. Some random man even handed me a flask of moonshine, which in hindsight wasn't the smartest idea to drink but Ellie and Angie said that I could trust him. All of it was disgusting to me but the cheers from the random bar attendants and the kindness of the offers were too motivating to turn down. The moment was thrilling.

"We gotta get back on stage now," Ellie yells to me louder than she needs to. "Are you good by yourself?"

"Yeah, I'm fine." I try to wave her off casually but something about what I do is funny because she bursts out into hysterical laughter.

"You're cute when you're tipsy." She cups my chin with her hand and pushes the skin of my cheeks close to my mouth.

"Ellie let's go," Evan calls via the mic as Angie climbs back onto the stage.

"Okay, I really got to go now but do me a favor and go say hi to that man who's been making eyes at you all night." She points to the end of the bar where we have indeed caught a man staring, except I'm not so sure it's at me. "Promise me you'll do it?"

"Okay, once you get back."

"No, promise now." She stomps her foot and crosses her arms like a child.

"Ellie!" Feedback comes through the speakers. She stays put.

"Okay, fine I promise to go over."

"I want to see you go over."

"Are you serious?"

"Completely." She narrows her eyes, begging me to try and test her.

"Okay, I'm going."

I raise my hands defensively and walk backwards toward the man, seeing how far I can get before she leaves. I alternate between looking at the floor behind me and at her. Unfortunately, she doesn't run back to the stage until I bump into the poor guy and his drink goes everywhere.

"I am so sorry." I gasp and grab a handful of napkins

from somewhere on the bar.

I place them along the edge of the tabletop to catch the liquid before it leaks onto the floor. The napkins do a good job of soaking up almost all of the spilled drink as the man laughs it off and begins to help.

I stop what I'm doing at that moment to observe him from a closer distance. Maybe it's the liquor coursing through me, infecting my judgment, but his laugh is like that of a siren, drawing me in. He has eyes of honey and strawberry hair much more subtle than that of Ellie's. And I want to kiss him, really kiss him.

Is this what alcohol does to you? I wonder if I ever had any in my past life or if I was too good for all of it. In the background the band picks up playing a fast-paced tune, Ellie's guitar taking the lead.

"How many drinks have you had?" The man asks politely. His words are magic, each one is a spell luring me further into desire.

"Only like five or six." I shrug my shoulders nonchalantly, trying to come across as less wasted than I actually am. "What about you?"

I go to put my elbow on the bartop but the residue from the liquid is still there and my arm slips off. He laughs even more now and takes my hand to help me onto the seat next to him. His fingers are warm but calloused.

"This is my fourth." He holds up a mixed drink and takes another sip before passing it to me. "You want a taste?"

I hesitate for a moment before picking the glass up and taking a generous sip. I don't know what it is but it's better than anything I've had tonight. "What is that?" I make sure to wipe my mouth before asking.

"A strawberry lemonade, you want the rest?"

Sober me would politely refuse but I can't help but aggressively nod at the offer and guard the drink as I gulp the rest down. Once I finish, rather quickly, he asks the bartender for two waters.

When the glasses come up they both get set in front of

him. I reach over to slide one of the drinks towards me just as he goes to do the same. Our hands touch and are together now, one on top of the other. We both look at each other, acknowledging what has just happened without moving away. Instead we do the opposite, simultaneously leaning closer, our noses almost touching.

Since the music started back up everyone now crowds around the stage once more, leaving me and this stranger at the far end of the bar in a dimly lit corner alone. If he actually were a siren this is when I would have thrown myself overboard to be taken with the waves.

"Can I kiss you?" He asks.

"Yes."

And then I throw myself overboard.

Chapter Fifteen

Friday, March 17th

I stretch my arms across the bed, feeling the cotton on my skin. But I bought linen sheets.

My eyes fly open and I sit up pin straight. It takes a minute to adjust to the sun streaming in from the open balcony door but once I do I take it all in, the studio apartment that is not mine. There are no photographs or other personalization decorations in the space that I can tie to its owner, it's all generic.

I throw the blankets on me to the side and walk towards the balcony. It isn't until I step outside that I realize I am not in the clothes I was wearing last night. Instead, I'm in an oversized band tee and sweatpants. I rub my arms to keep the chill away. The view overlooks the park that Ellie and I ate at the other day which answers at least part of the where am I question.

I sit in one of the two reclining chairs on the deck. I hug my knees to my chest and tip my chin up to the sky, letting what little piece of sun is out warm my face.

I don't know where I am. I don't know whose place this is but I know that I am at peace, which might be the most concerning part. Could it be that I have found contentment in the unknown? On second thought I realize that I am too curious for that to be likely.

I sit here for a while, occasionally opening my eyes to people watch below. I make up a story for some of them. The woman mowing the grass has children at home to support. She's gotten by just fine going from paycheck to paycheck on her own and that's what she wants to teach her kids as they grow, the power of hard work and resilience. And the older man warming up for a run is waiting for his son to join him as he always does on Friday mornings.

I can't help but notice that all of the stories I create for the little people below have the same theme and the one thing that I truly crave more than anything. I try to push this thought out of my mind and stick with my peace by continuing to play my game, forcing myself to become hypnotized within my own mind. It works because I don't notice at first when the man from the bar last night comes to sit beside me. Once I do register his arrival though my body does not feel alarmed by the stranger just as it did not last night.

"Good morning," he greets me as he hands over a brown bag. I open it and am filled with the pleasurable smell of morning pastries. There are two flaky, chocolate croissants and a bagel for each of us. "There's a caramel coffee with sugar and oat milk on the counter too if you want some."

"Thank you."

I draw my attention back to the park people as I pull out one of the bagels and strip it of its plastic wrap. I begin to eat as the woman on the mower powers it off to take a water break and the man waiting for his son begins his run alone, moving away from me.

"Your clothes are almost done in the dryer," The man informs. "I had to run them through two wash cycles to get the stains out otherwise I would have had them ready sooner."

Oh god, I remember what happened now. The making out, the running outside to throw up from the liquor and worst of all the crying. Fuck. "I am so sorry about last night."

"No need to apologize."

Another question rises within me. "Where did you sleep last night?"

"I wasn't that tired. I'm still on Alnerwick time which is six hours behind so really my brain is telling me that it's two in the morning right now, hence the need for coffee." He takes a sip from his to-go cup. The lid is popped off and steam wafts out the top. "I would have brought you to your house by the way but you were a bit too hysterical to get an address out of you. Every time I asked you just said that you didn't know. But I had the bartender let your friend know that I brought you back with me after her set."

Oh god, Ellie must be so worried. And I never came back home to Bear last night. "Can I borrow your phone?"

"Of course." He pulls out his cell and hands it to me. "I'll give you some privacy."

The ink used to write Ellies number has been scrubbed clean off of my hand by now so I'll have to remember to call her once I get back home. This leaves me with one other option, Miles. I know his number better since he's called the library frequently so I dial it as I debate the likelihood of him having sent a search and rescue team out for me last night. Ellie would have called him if she saw me walk out with the bar man, and even if she didn't I'm pretty sure he's legally obligated to check in on me every eight hours. The call rings through, luckily going to voicemail. I leave a brief message that I am alright, will be home soon and not to worry. Then I hang up.

"All set?"

"Yeah." I hand him back his phone and in return he gives me the iced coffee cup that he mentioned earlier. When I take a sip the flavor hits me, the sweetness of it all is just right. "This is good, where did you get it from?"

"The bakery below us," he explains.

He picks up the bag from where I left it on the glass side table and takes out the other bagel. We eat in silence until there is nothing but crumbs.

"I never found out your name last night," I pry.

"And I never found out yours."

"It's Emily, Emily Jane Weiss."

"Well Emily Jane, I'm Wren."

My body goes still and my throat hoarse as I try to say something, anything. "W-wren?"

"Yes?"

I can't believe what I'm hearing. I feel as if I might throw up again. Wren. The one connection I have to my past is in front of me. The one person that might be able to give me some answers, if he is the right person that is. But he's also dangerous, or he could be.

"Is there something wrong?"

"No." I need to buy myself time to figure out if he is who I hope and if so decode the reasoning for placing such a warning upon him when he has been nothing but kind to me so far. "What are your plans for today?"

The water below moves with rhythm, bending to adjust with the wind. We are the only ones on the lake. The rented canoe that we sit in has the initials of past riders scattered throughout its weathered body, etched or penned in with care.

I open the pizza box we brought with us, allowing it to cool into the open air, as Wren pulls out a pocket knife. Carefully he carves an uppercase E and R into the side, placing a dash between them. E-R. He does the same with the letter S. S-R. I almost ask about it but after noticing the look of mourning on his face I decide not to.

We left his place after my clothes were done in the dryer, stopping at my house to change into more suitable clothes, feed Bear and call Ellie. She let me in on the fact that she can no longer go to the ball in Cryoden this weekend due to a last minute family matter that she has to fly home for. She made up for it though by promising to be back for auditions on Monday and also informing me that she told Miles I had gone home with her last night, making me glad that I had kept my voicemail vague earlier.

We drove Wren's black pickup around this morning from my place to his, stopping to get the pizza in between.

The windows were rolled down, as a precaution of course, in case I had to make a quick escape but I figured if he was going to kill me he would have done so by now.

Our hands accidentally touched once or twice while taking turns rowing out here, it didn't feel like electricity like how people describe in movies but it felt normal, comfortable like it is simply right. Is it possible for my body to sense that I have known him in the past? Or maybe my head is just making it up, finding any excuse for me to believe what I want to.

"You okay?" He asks before blowing off a slice of still warm cheese pizza.

"Yeah, I'm just thinking."

"Me too." When I turn from the mountains to him he smiles. I return the kindness reflexively.

"What are you thinking about?"

"Home," he admits simply. "You?"

I could tell him the truth or I could take the opportunity to bring up a burning question. I settle on the question option and bring up the ball tomorrow night. I tell him how no one else I've asked is able to go and extend the offer out to him. He seems jovial at the invitation, insisting that I not let him forget to exchange contact information before departing each other today. I promise him that I won't as long as he promises to not ditch me too.

"Never," he swears.

His gaze begins to fill with intensity that I can't unpack right now so I change the subject and ask him where he's from. He tells me about his home in the southern part of Alnerwick and how he went to a university in the north where he's lived since. Then just when I think he is about to ask where home is for me he stops short.

"Your eyes. They're an interesting color in this light, not quite gold but not quite white either, almost like light sand."

On my ID my eyes are listed as grey- a bleak, colorless shade. It's hard to find beauty in something like this and yet he has. Is this when I should tell him that this is most likely not my natural color? If he is from my past then he would know this already.

"Have I overstepped?" He asks within the silence that I have created.

"No," I confirm.

"Good. So what's something that I should know about you?"

I think for a moment, trying to throw out any thought that doesn't pertain to what he is asking. "I have a cat, I work in a library and I'm trying to direct a play for the first time."

He seems rather impressed. "Are you putting on something that you wrote?"

"No, just something that inspired me."

He looks out to the lake. "Well, I'm in town for a bit and it sounds like fun. Mind if I try it out? That is if it hasn't started yet of course."

"It hasn't, auditions are at the Cresthill school at seven pm on Monday." Another detail catches my attention, something that I started to get curious about since the subject of home was brought up. "Why are you in town?"

"Visiting friends."

"For how long?"

"I'm not sure, it depends."

"On what?"

"However long it takes."

"Well what did you tell your job back home when you left?" I push.

"I said that I needed a temporary leave of absence. My uncle owns the clinic so it wasn't hard to get approved, he understood. If I plan to stay longer than a month then I'll get a job nearby until I go back, no big deal. Plus I've heard there's only one doctor in an hour radius from here for both pets and people so it seems like I could be put to good use if need be."

"You're a doctor?"

"Well, I'm currently studying to become a veterinarian. I completed my undergraduate degree in animal science last year," he clarifies.

"Do you have any pets?"

I lean over the boat to draw patterns in the water with my finger. After a moment I realize that it is his name that I spell over and over again. Each time the water takes it from me I rewrite it. I only stop when he brings up the name of his dog, due to the absurdity of the coincidence.

"You have a dog named Pig? I have a cat I named Bear," I reveal.

"You got a cat? I mean you have a cat?" He corrects himself.

"Yeah, if you came inside the house earlier you two could have met."

"You already want to introduce me to your cat?" He teases, faking awestruck admiration.

I don't say anything in response to his sarcasm. Instead, I mischievously cup water into my hand and flick it at him, getting drops of lake on his hair and clothes. It was more water than I intended. He stands up in shock as I stifle a laugh, the motion rocks the boat. I reach up to pull him back down but as I go to do so he grabs on to me and I get pushed overboard.

It happens fast but I anticipate the attack coming and have just enough time to hold my breath as I go under. I go further into the water than I thought I would and once I get over the shock I swim to the surface, debating if this was a vengeful or playful attack. Just as I break through the bone-chilling water the lake splits and absorbs another body, Wren, who splashes me in the process.

"What if I couldn't swim you jackass?" I yell at him as he bobs back up effortlessly. I tread water to stay afloat as I debate how to get back on the boat without it tipping.

"But you can." He jumped much further and has to swim over to me.

"That's not the point."

"What is the point?" He asks with a dopey grin on his face.

"The point is that I could have drowned if I didn't know how to swim." I instinctively cross my arms before remembering where I am.

"You have to admit though, the water is nice."

"No, the water is cold," I protest. I would never admit it out of principle but the water is in fact nice, despite the chill in the breeze. This does not overshadow the fear I felt while debating if this was a murder attempt though and the unbearably uncomfortable sensation I am currently experiencing from the jeans that now hug my legs too tight. But hey, at least I'm not dead. "Can you help me get back onto the boat?"

"Only if you can help me with something."

"What's that?"

The moment turns serious as he gently pulls my waist into his. I stop treading now and thread my hands around his neck for balance. He uses one hand to stay afloat for the both of us.

"I don't remember what it's like to be kissed," he whispers into my ear dramatically. "It's been so long."

"Are you serious?" Now I have the opportunity to fold my hands across my chest for real.

"Super serious. If you help me out maybe I could get you back onto the boat and only for the price of just one kiss."

"Just one?" I can't help the smile that plays at my lips, betraying me.

"That's all."

I can't believe that I am entertaining this. One part of me wants to stay in the water with him, to live in this moment a little while longer, but the other part of me is cold, wet and uncomfortable. The two sides compete for importance in my brain. I could push him off of me and try to get on the boat myself out of spite. Or I could just kiss the man that I have already kissed before. But what if the kiss isn't as good as last night when we were both a little intoxicated and bold?

"What's the verdict?"

I allow my body to choose for me and find myself

leaning in towards him, opening my mouth ever so slightly. He does the same, weaving a hand through my now slicked-back hair. I almost go through with it but just before our lips touch I pull back and reel one of my hands forward to produce a wave of water in Wren's direction. I then swim away vigorously, laughing with triumph.

I make it back to the boat while he's still wiping water from his eyes. I grab onto the side and try to climb up but with each attempt I slip back into the water. I must fail at least four times before Wren swims beside me and holds his linked together hands out to use as leverage to flip over. I land on the floor between the two wooden seats, just beside the barely eaten pizza, and quickly scramble out of the way upon Wren's instruction so that when he gets on the weight is somewhat distributed. I do so and he climbs back on. He then praises me for the successful fake-out before rowing us back to shore.

We both stall as Wren pulls up to my house. There is a moment where each of us clearly thinks about leaning in to connect the distance and complete what I didn't let happen at the lake but then I see Miles standing in the doorway of my house, hands in his pockets and staring respectfully at the ground. Wren follows my eyes.

"I should get going."

If he is the Wren that I am looking for then it is no big deal for me to mention my Rebirth counselor. But if he is not that Wren then I want to tell him about it when the time is right, when I can bring up the subject of me being a Rebirth patient and ask him if he is who I want him to be.

"Who's your friend?" I can tell that he tries to remain mutual with his tone, kind even, but the masked jealousy behind his eyes is still apparent which I guess is fair after I did just ask him on an outing that ended up being incredibly similar to a date, or it was a date, I'm not sure.

"I'll call you with the details about tomorrow," I confirm before hopping out of the truck and shutting the door without an answer to his question.

I tuck the receipt that I used to write Wren's number on the back of into my coat pocket as I head over to Miles. I mentally prepare myself for a lecture and another fight as Wren pulls out of the driveway.

Only after he leaves does Miles say, "I'm sorry. I didn't mean to lash out at you the other night. It's not fair of me to accuse you of something that I am guilty of myself"

It takes a moment for the shock of his words to wear off. That wasn't what I was expecting. "And I'm sorry for implying that you are bad at your job, I didn't mean that."

"You should have because I am bad at my job," he scoffs.

"What do you mean?"

"I've been doing this for four years, you're the 13th person I have mentored, and I have never had an issue balancing before and now all of a sudden I'm getting warnings."

"I'm still not quite following."

He sighs, not at me but rather at himself. "The reason I was absent last week isn't because I was with another patient, I'm actually not allowed to have more than one at a time." I knew it. "I was really gone because I had my yearly evaluation and there were some concerns that kept me there longer than I should have been. I never meant to miss your appointment but then they brought up some of the instances that I have reported about where my behavior blurred the line between mentor and friend. Luckily they gave me another chance to make it right."

"What do you mean reported about?" I have so many questions gnawing at my skull but this one begs to be asked the most.

"Part of my job is to keep a record of every conversation subject we have and every time we meet so that Rebirths headquarters can track your progress to determine when I am no longer needed," he explains.

"Oh."

I imagine his notes, typed out and professional. It disturbs me. The patient has acquired a new occupation today, one of the predicted outcomes. The patient has contacted me about arranging a meeting with a Rebirth friend today. The patient met with her chosen Rebirth friend, the occasion went well and they are now going on outings of their own accord. The patient and I danced around her living room.

Despite this eerie clause and the fact that Miles has gotten into trouble, the news makes me ever so hopeful as it confirms that Miles has also seen me the way that I have seen him or at least in the eyes of Rebirth. I didn't just make it up. The dance lessons, the wall painting, the personal dinners. I wonder how much other Rebirth counselors do for their patients, clearly not as much as Miles if this behavior is cause for concern.

"Don't worry about that though, from now on I will do everything by the textbook." Just as the meaning of what he has said starts to settle he picks up a brown box the size of my hand from the front step. "I almost forgot, I have something for you. Think of it as an early birthday or apology present."

I hesitate when taking it from him. "I can't keep accepting these."

"You can and you will. It's my last gesture of overstepping." I hold back a chuckle.

"When exactly is my birthday again?"

"October 9th."

"Over six months is a different type of early."

I can't help the laugh of astonishment that escapes me but it leaves rather quickly once I realize that by the time my birthday comes around he most likely will no longer be my mentor. He will have a new patient with a new birthday and new facts about them to learn. For some reason I don't want that.

"You need it and a birthday present is a good excuse," he reasons.

"I'll open it but only if you promise me you'll be here for my actual birthday."

"I promise I'll try."

"Good enough." I tear off the wrapping and stare at another brown box. "Do you have scissors?"

He pulls out a pocket knife and hands it to me. It reminds me of the one that Wren used earlier to carve our initials into the boat. Speaking of Wren, is he going to ask who was in the truck with me? I'm not sure what to tell him if he does.

I use the knife to cut the tape away from the box and pull up the cardboard tabs to reveal what's underneath. A phone and a charger.

"Wow, thank you."

"It's used but in great condition and this way you don't have an excuse to go on late-night walks in the middle of nowhere without alerting anyone or go home with strangers and also not tell anyone." He pauses to give me a dramatic look of concern. "Is this becoming a pattern?"

I can't help but blush at the confrontation of my actions and the confession that he saw through mine and Ellie's lies somehow. The big truck that dropped me off earlier was probably a good indicator of suspicion. I wonder if he assumes that something went on between Wren and I? Well, something did go on but nothing serious or more intimate than a kiss.

"Thank you and no this is not going to become a pattern," I confirm once I remember to respond. Unless it would delay Miles from leaving maybe… no, that's a horrible idea.

Chapter Sixteen
Saturday, March 18th

Ellie's flight got delayed so she picked me up this morning to shop for makeup at the drugstore, though I know that her underlying goal was to squeeze all of the gossip out of me until I am dry and she has absorbed all of my words like a sponge.

When we got back to my house she showed me everything- what brushes to apply with, in what order, how much of each product to use. By the end of our crash course I felt much more prepared for tonight. She even helped out by curling and pinning my hair into a fancy updo. When she finished I pulled some of the tighter strands out to feel more comfortable. She cringed at the sight.

Sadly she had to go shortly after that to catch her postponed flight and didn't have time to see the final product or help me into my dress, so I am forced to call Miles. He knocks on the front door a short time later and I let him in, leading him into my room.

"Is this what you needed help with?" His hands are in his pockets as he looks down at the dress splayed out on the bed.

"Yes," I admit. "I'm sorry if it crosses a line, I don't mean to get you in any more trouble. I just didn't know who else to call." How pathetically lonely I must sound. What a funny job it is to deal with pathetically lonely people.

"As long as you're comfortable then it's okay." He thinks it over a second longer as he looks at me warily. "Maybe I just won't mention this in today's report."

I nod in agreement. The dress has to get on somehow. The lacing in the back is too complicated to do myself even if my arms were long enough and contorted in that way.

"I'll turn around while you get undressed," He suggests.

He does so as I start to peel the clothes I'm wearing off of me. I then bunch up the fabric of the dress to toss over my head. It falls loosely over my slender and somewhat curveless body forcing me to hold it to my skin so it doesn't reveal more than it should as I announce to Miles that he can turn around now. When he does his eyes respectfully stay lowered, not rising further than where they need to be. He clears his throat and takes the lace ties into his hands, pulling until my chest enhances subtly without being too gradual.

"Is this alright?" He asks respectfully.

"That's perfect."

He quickly ties a neat bow with the thin strings and tucks them into the bodice, grazing the small of my back in the process. The touch makes me quiver but I disguise the reflex that my body inflicts on me by spinning in a small circle within what little room that I have.

"Would you like to dance?" I tease. "You promised that you would."

"When?" He takes my question seriously despite the joke that I tried to turn it into.

"Earlier this week." He sinks deep into thought for a moment before nodding in remembrance. "I was just joking though, we don't have to."

He holds his hand up to quell my protests. "A promise is a promise."

He then extends that hand out to me. I take it and we start to sway to invisible music. He relaxes into it the more that we move, I'm not sure if I can say the same.

"Do you want to try dancing in the heels that you're going to wear tonight?" He suggests.

"I hadn't thought about that."

I get down on my knees to pull the box out from under my bed. Miles stops me as it slides into the open, gesturing for me to sit. I do so as he flips the lid off of the packaging. He takes the first shoe in his hands, gracefully slipping it onto my foot. He then does the same with the other before helping me back up. I walk around myself to feel them out. Miles adjusts his grip based on my movement so that our hands can still stay connected.

"Ready for the final test?"

"I think so," I confirm.

We place our hands exactly where he showed me the other day and pick back up where we left off. This time Miles hums the tune of the song we first danced to, the one with the singer that I like, but as he finishes the second chorus my foot gets caught in a hole in the floorboards and I go toppling onto the bed, pulling Miles along with me. Luckily he catches himself before letting his full weight crash into me but he stays there, hovering above me for longer than he probably should. I don't want him to move. I'm not sure why.

Slowly I prop myself up on my elbows, leaning further towards him. It might just be my imagination but he seems to be getting closer too although I can't stop looking into his eyes long enough to discover the truth.

Then there's a knock at the door. We scramble off of the bed.

"Coming," I yell out to my guest. "Could you get that? I'll be right back." I then direct to Miles before hurrying into the bathroom and shutting the door.

I take a washcloth and lightly wet it before holding it to my forehead. I can hear Miles and Wren in the living room. I can't make out any words, only just enough noise for me to know that they are inside and conversing.

I can't hide here forever. The venue is an hour away and we have to get going. I check the mirror. My face is still flushed. Shit.

"Em, are you okay? I'm sorry for… that. It was an accident and our secret, remember?" Miles whispers through the door.

Right. An accident, our secret, no report of it happening.

I open the door.

The gala is being held in one of Croyden's largest hotels. There are fancy foods on fancy banquet tables and it seems that almost everyone else is somehow dressed more extravagantly than me which is funny because I was originally worried about being the overdressed one.

Wren fits right in, as if he was meant for the rich life. He doesn't know anyone here but he's charismatic and acts as if he does which is why I let him take the reins when talking to people, so that I can zone out.

I try to think about the library or the play but most of the time my mind brings my thoughts right back to Miles' of course cause there's nothing sexier than being on a second semi-probable date with one guy while thinking about another. But what if Wren didn't show up? Whatever would have happened would be off of the record.

"Are you alright dear?" Wren touches my arm to get my attention as he speaks in a posh accent. How long has he been doing that stupid voice for?

"Oh yes, just thinking." I copy his tone, going along with it.

"Honey I'm sure the dog is fine at home with the sitter but if you want to call then you can." Dog? Sitter? Honey? What is going on? He turns to the older couple he was talking to before. "She just gets so worried about him sometimes. They've become attached ever since we rescued him."

Now I get it, he's playing a bit. Has this been an all night occurrence? No matter, either way he's giving me a chance for escape that I plan on taking. "Yes, I think I might call the sitter. Excuse me." I seal the act with a kiss on Wren's cheek before making my way through the crowd.

My intuition takes me to the balcony, still lively but not as much so as inside. I turn the corner to find a dimly lit, isolated area and rest up against the brick wall there. Shortly after Wren comes to find me.

"You okay? You've seemed distracted all night."

"What do you mean?"

"I've been making up new stories about us each time we talk to someone new. We must have lived at least ten different lives in there that you didn't know about until only a moment ago." He laughs. I do not.

I have already lived a life that I have no recollection of, I do not want to live ten more. But I can't voice my discontent because I have been the one ignoring him all night, betraying him to take company with the thoughts running amuck in my head.

"I'm sorry, I was not aware of that."

"It's alright but I know how you can make it up to me." He moves closer until my back touches the wall.

"How?"

"You can kiss me."

"Fine but only if you answer a question for me."

"Wow, that was easy. Why couldn't you be so willing yesterday?" He teases. I give him a serious look and his comedy act sobers up real fast.

"I am a Rebirth patient," I confess. I wait for the shock to register on his face but it never comes.

"Okay," he says casually instead, waiting for me to go on.

"Well, the one thing that former me wanted to remember was a name."

A hint of amusement returns to his eyes. "What name?"

"Yours."

"So what's your question?" He tucks one of the hairs that I pulled out earlier behind my ear.

"Are you that Wren, the one that I knew before?"

"You have to pay up before I answer and it has to be a real kiss, not something quick so that you can get what you want faster."

"Okay," I answer back rather impatiently. I will never admit to him that that's quite literally what I would have done had he not said something.

Wren leans into me and I press further against the cold stone behind me. We both close our eyes and when our lips touch I don't taste the cheap mixed drinks that I had that night at the bar. This time there is champagne on his breath and a hint of mint. The kiss turns into multiple and the ocean waves from the other night come back to my stomach, except this time there will be no spill over or high tide.

We kiss for so long I almost forget my question to him, especially when he leaves my lips to travel along my cheek, then my ear, and eventually the neckline of my dress. He plays with the low fabric, pulling the material down more ever so slightly in the process but his lips stop when he reaches my collarbone as it is too low for him to reach without bending down or picking me up.

"My question," I breathlessly remind him.

"I'm sorry Emily, I am not who you are looking for."

Chapter Seventeen
Sunday, March 19th

I pull out the sides that I printed out for each character and lay them on the table as Tabitha brings over two chairs. I asked her to be my second set of ears for tonight during work, thankfully she agreed.

"Are you nervous?" Tabitha asks as she picks up one one of the monologues to read through.

"A little, is it noticeable? I want to seem like I know what I'm doing."

"Well if you want to appear that way then I suggest that you stop picking at your nails cause dear god girl you're going to bleed." She swats at my hands until I drop them to my side.

"What if no one shows up?"

"But someone did." She points to the door of the auditorium. The outline of a person can be seen through the frosted glass window.

I must start picking at my nails again because she demands that I go into a corner and take a few minutes to myself. I don't argue and head to the back left corner of the theater. The stage is completely lit. I wonder what it must feel like to be on a stage. I must have been on one at some point in my life before for a chorus concert or orchestra show maybe.

"Two minutes," Tabitha calls out to me as she checks

her watch.

I roll my neck, crack my knuckles and close my eyes. I am a casting director for some hot shot company, I tell myself. I know how to do my job. I have experience. This is not my first time. I can do this, as long as I keep up my pretend persona at least. Maybe pretending to be someone else isn't all that bad.

I head back to Tabitha as she invites the first person in the room. I am surprised to find that I do not know her so I shake her hand and she introduces themselves as Bianca. She then takes a side and we give her a moment to read it through before taking the stage.

From there I only recognize one of the next two people. Seren does okay and so does the other one who goes by James but it is not until Angie takes the stage that I am truly blown away. She laughs when she is supposed to, she shows emotions the way they were meant to be expressed and I can't take my eyes off of her. She commands the stage here just as she did that night at the bar with the script as her new music. Tabitha and I both clap when she's finished. Angie in response takes a dramatic bow before leaving. After her is Ellie who only stumbles over the words a few times, correcting herself instead of going with it but overall she doesn't do all that bad either.

Wren comes in last and walks over to the table to read over the sides before choosing the one for Raelyn's husband. It's a dramatic scene, the goodbye between him and his wife, but it is executed perfectly. It's almost as if you can feel him losing everything and though he doesn't have a scene partner right now I can just picture Angie weeping on command beside him. He's perfect and can't help but wink at me as he goes, making sure to do so when Tabitha becomes distracted scribbling something down in her fancy cursive.

Then we draft up a cast list. There's one more role leftover to fill, a minor one that appears in only a few scenes. But I'll have to scout out someone to play that character myself.

"Ready?" Tabitha asks as she picks up her purse.

"Almost, I just need another minute."

"I'll be waiting outside."

The second that the door closes behind her I move to sit in the front row. I imagine everyone dressed up in their knee-length dresses and short, curled hair like they jumped right from the pages of the script. The cliffside scenery will be painted and displayed in the background, looking like something out of a fairytale and everything will go perfectly.

"Am I too late to audition?" Miles asks as he walks out onto the stage from behind the curtain. I jump, startled by his intrusion.

"How did you get back there?"

"The door next to the auditorium. It's finally nice to meet Tabitha by the way."

"Wait, did you say that you wanted to audition?"

"Yeah, I didn't know how many people would show so I figured that I would show my support in case you need another person. And what's one more secret?"

"Are you sure? Because this is more than just dancing in my room. This would be rehearsals and commitment and a show."

"I know but I want to do it. Although on second thought maybe I can just get something small, that way there's a less likely chance of any of my superiors finding out."

I take a second to think it over. "How would you feel about getting the part of cop number 1?"

"That sounds low risk enough for me. I accept."

"Wonderful. Now let's hit the road before Tabitha gets cranky and cuts my pay," I joke as he makes his way off of the stage.

"She wouldn't do that, she seems like a wonderful lady."

"Oh, she is until you keep her waiting."

One of the Rebirth drivers drops Tabitha and Miles

off at their respective locations first. I'm not sure if Tabitha recognized the logo on the car but if she did she didn't say a word about it. She must have already assumed my situation from the scarcity of my background paperwork but this would have been a final confirmation. Previous jobs: unknown. References: none.

Miles is supposed to be coming over in a bit to help me design a website for the show, to gain some traction, but wanted to stop home first so I feed Bear and draft up a few layout and URL ideas on paper as I wait. By the time he gets here I have multiple drafts and numerous scribbled out or ripped up ideas. Bear has started to paw and play with my discarded scraps.

"It seems as if you could use my surprise right about now."

"What surprise?"

Miles pulls a bottle of champagne out from behind his back. The neck of the bottle has a ribbon tied around it. "I thought that we could celebrate the beginning of achieving your first dream in this new life."

I hadn't thought about that. "That's so sweet. But you seriously have got to stop with the gifts. I feel horrible that I never have anything to give back."

"You as you are is enough of a gift for me," he says as he heads into the kitchen.

I give myself a moment to feel his words with him turned away from me. When he comes back, with two glasses in hand, I force any leftover reaction away.

He places one cup in front of me and the other in front of himself as I unwrap the foil at the head of the bottle. He then untwists the wire cage and maneuvers the bottle around in his hand until it pops. I hold out my glass and he pours the bubbly, golden liquid inside. A drop spills onto the new carpet which Miles tells me he'll take care of. I assure him that it's not a big deal.

Once both glasses are topped off he takes a look at my ideas and I describe to him exactly how I want everything

to be designed. He reiterates to me, as he did multiple times
on the way home, that he only took one summer course for
website design and doesn't know all that much.

Despite his wariness, Miles proves to be a lot of help.
In the time it takes us to finish a glass and a half we buy a
domain, pick a name, and begin designing via the step-by-
step instructions that come along with the purchase. We agree
on the six-month subscription instead of the yearly one since
the production is only three months from now and I don't
see a use for the site after that. We do everything on Miles'
company tablet which is more advanced than the computer at
the library.

By the time we hit three glasses each the clock says
midnight, the bottle has nothing but a sip left in it, and the
website is done. There's a large section for the cast list with
the words "coming soon" right as you open the page and if
you scroll down there are descriptions of all of the characters
next to empty picture boxes with the same words. I take in
all of our hard work and triple-check for any imperfections
before hitting the publish button and closing out of the
program.

Chapter Eighteen
Saturday, March 25th

The alarm goes off on my bedside table, startling Bear who was formerly asleep. I, on the other hand, have been awake for hours because I am too pervaded with elation to waste my time with sleep. My head is full of ideas to execute. Only four more hours until my first rehearsal.

I printed out all of the scripts yesterday before leaving work and promised Tabitha that I would pay her back for the ink and paper or that she could take the cost out of my next paycheck. She just waved me off, claiming that the children's reading hour event that I set up this past week more than made up for it.

I throw the covers on my bed aside and go about my morning routine, making sure to put on a sweater over my t-shirt as the wind outside harasses my window panes. I even put some lip gloss on the way Renne did for me on the ship when someone knocks on the front door.

"One second!" I call out as I rub my lips together and hastily screw the cap of the tube back on. Then I go for the door.

"Happy first day of rehearsals." Wren holds out a dainty bouquet of slightly wilting daisies wrapped in newspaper.

"That's very kind of you. Where did you get these?"

I take the offering from him, bringing the flowers to my nose and letting the petals tickle my skin.

"The side of the road. I saw them and thought that you deserved something on this special morning. The newspaper is the only thing I had in my car to wrap them together.."

I blush at the sincerity and sweetness behind his gesture. "Thank you for thinking of me."

"Always."

He then asks me to breakfast. I agree of course as there's nothing bad about a free meal.

"So how was your week? I haven't seen or heard from you since auditions on Monday," Wren asks between bites of maple syrup-covered pancakes.

"It was fine, I pretty much just worked and wrote. You?"

"Good, I started a new job."

"So you decided to stay a while?"

"Well you see I have to because I got a part in this really cool show. You should come and see it."

I scrunch my nose up playfully and he laughs before going on to tell me all about his new job working in the mountains for a farmer. He primarily takes care of the horses but will occasionally do landscaping work or check on the other animals as well for extra pay.

Once this conversation topic dies down he starts up a new one by asking to read something of mine sometime. I shrug, unsure of what to say. I wonder if he would recognize my work if he saw it as he is from Alnerwick where all of my screenplays seem to take place.

"How about this, I'll take you to do something fun, something you've probably haven't tried yet in this life, if you let me read something that you've written," he barters.

"Where would we go?"

"It's a secret until you agree."

"But I hate secrets. And surprises for that matter." I

can't help but think back to everything Miles has gifted me throughout knowing each other and how much joy it has brought- the shoes, the tickets, the phone, the champagne. "Well, I guess what I really hate is when I know that a surprise is coming but not what it is because if it was truly a surprise then I wouldn't know anything about it at all," I revise. "If I know then it is just anticipation so really that is what I loathe."

"That makes sense."

"I'm glad that you think so. Now may I know this "surprise" that you have planned?"

"I want to take you horseback riding but only if I can read something of yours."

"Fine, I guess that you have yourself a deal." This is the kind of anticipation that I don't mind.

Wren and I are the first ones to arrive. We go in through the side door and straight into the auditorium via the key I was gifted by one of the staff members before audition day. Wren helps me to set up eight chairs in a circle. When he places the last one down I gently grab for his wrist, twisting it towards me to see the time on his watch. Fifteen minutes until rehearsal starts.

"That's the seventh time you've done that."

"Sorry."

He puts a hand on each of my shoulders and forces me to face him. "You will be okay." I nod to show that I've heard him and center myself by looking into his eyes.

"You won't just be okay, you will be the best damn director anyone has ever seen," Miles counters from behind me. I breathe a sigh of relief as he climbs the stairs to the stage. Maybe now that he's here I'll actually feel like I can do this.

"Hey, I'm Wren." He extends his hand out to Miles as he approaches.

Miles shoots me a questioning glance at the mention of

his name. "You're the one that dropped her off in the truck the other day."

"Yeah, and you're the one that was waiting at her door." His hands drops back to his side.

"Yeah."

I'm eternally grateful when Ellie and Angie walk in next, putting a stop to whatever layer of tension filtered into the conversation. The two introduce themselves to Wren and Miles and they strike up their own individual conversations, Angie with Wren and Ellie with Miles.

I take the opportunity to make a getaway, slipping behind the curtain and taking the remaining time before we start to shuffle around the prop room, looking for anything that could be of use. I find a few old telephones, parasols and other knick knacks lying around and set them off to the side in a box that I label with the production name as I was told to do when given my key to the school.

I make sure to keep an eye on the wall clock and head back to the auditorium once it's time to start. When I get there I can't help but observe everyone mingling for a moment. Angie is now talking with Miles, Ellie seems to be searching for something on the other side in the wings and the people playing Harry and his mistress are keeping to themselves in the corner. Wren on the other hand has disappeared and Seren must be running late. Either way, we should start now since I only have the space booked for two hours.

I correct my posture and step out of the shadows to introduce myself and thank everyone for coming. The chatter stops immediately and five of the seats become newly occupied as I grab the folder I brought with me to hand out the stapled scripts. Only once everyone has one do Seren and Wren walk in together.

"Sorry, I was just helping her find the bathroom," he explains.

"The baby has been pushing on my bladder all morning," she rubs her ever-growing stomach soothingly as she makes her way up the stage. Wren helps her into a chair.

"No worries, we just started."

I encourage everyone to introduce themselves before we start as I take my own seat between Ellie and Miles. Seren volunteers to go first, saying her full name and that she is playing the doctor. Ellie and Angie go after her and they both use the platform to promote their next gig before quickly adding in that they are playing Elena and Raelyn, the two main characters. After that duo it's Miles' turn who simply states that he is here to help out a friend by playing cop number one.

Wren raises his hand to go next. "My name is Wren, I'm originally from Accrington and I am playing Bill."

The girl to his right, who I now remember from auditions as Bianca is second to last. She asks everyone to call her by her nickname, Bee, and announces that she is playing the mistress. She has a collection of freckles dotting across her nose, right above her septum ring, and she twirls her platinum hair around her finger as she talks. She's just here to try something new and for her friend James who is playing Harry.

"Thank you everyone and I can't wait to get to know each other even better over these next few months. I want you to think of this stage as your escape or a safe haven where your outside problems can be put on hold for just a moment." I must have practiced this speech in the mirror at least twelve times last night. "I want us to leave all self-criticism and judgment at home and remind ourselves to have an open mind, keep focused, and enjoy our time here." I then instruct everyone to open to the first page of their scripts.

I read out the character, setting, and period descriptions before letting everyone else take it away. Voices bounce around the circle as characters alternate speaking and every now and then I interject with the action or set description to give a better picture of the scene. By the time we finish there is a half-hour left to spare so I take the time to start blocking the first scene. When our time finally does run up I thank everyone for coming once again, update them on tomorrow's rehearsal, and dismiss them like a teacher telling her students that they're permitted to head off to their buses.

Angie suggests a bonding dinner at the tavern in town as everyone gets their belongings together, even offering to pay for the first round of nachos. All except for Wren agree. He on the other hand moves away from everyone to answer a phone call.

"You coming?" Ellie asks as I watch Wren further disappear.

"Yeah I think so."

"Cool, do you need a ride?"

"That would be great actually."

"Mind if I tag along?" Miles interjects.

"Of course not, just meet us outside by the van when you guys are ready." She lightly bumps my side with her shoulder and a raise of her eyebrows. I put a tense smile on my face.

"You know I must say I am surprised that you are coming," I tell Miles after Ellie walks back over to Angie.

He shrugs and I don't push the conversation further in case he changes his mind and runs for the hills to abandon our new unspoken secret friendship policy. "Is he coming too?" He asks as Wren makes his way back towards the group of us.

"I'm not sure. Are you coming to the bar Wren?"

"As much as I would love to relive our little moment there I unfortunately can not. One of the horses at the barn is pregnant and is having close contractions."

"Okay well text me when you're done, we might still be there."

"Will do."

He leans over to kiss me on the forehead before picking his belongings up and heading for the door. Everything about the interaction is so public and yet so natural for him. I on the other hand feel embarrassed about the display, especially since it occurs in front of Miles.

The seven of us are packed into a small booth. Half-empty bowls of nachos and bread litter the table more and more as the night goes on. We play the type of icebreakers that teenagers pull out at sleepovers and pool parties: truth or dare, never have I ever, etc. Luckily there's no spin the bottle, at least not yet.

I'm sandwiched between Miles and the wall. We both try to give each other space but can only do so much. The next time the waiter comes around he orders something strong.

"You're up Emily," James projects over the noise and across the table. "Truth or dare."

"Dare."

"I dare you to call someone random and say that you miss them."

I confidently pull out my phone and open my contacts, which is when I remember that I only have five. Tabitha's home phone, Miles, Wren, Dr. Pierce and Ellie. I try to take a peek at the order they're in but I don't have the chance to before Bee puts her hands over my eyes. I don't know who I would pick even if I did know the order though, maybe Miles or Ellie since they're here and know the situation. I guess it doesn't matter that much cause I'll just explain the situation later to whoever I end up picking, I just really hope it's not Doctor Pierce.

"Pick somebody," James prompts.

I shield the phone against my body and hover over the five names before pressing my finger to the screen. The dial tone rings. Bee's hands still block my vision. Everyone holds their breath when the automated voice instructs me to leave a message.

"Hey," I pause. "I miss you."

Bee hangs up for me and removes her hands from in front of my eyes. "Beautiful work. Now it's your turn."

I take a sip of my water before scanning the group. They all stare back at me, waiting for my decision. Eventually, my eyes land on Angie. "Truth or dare?"

"Dare."

"I dare you to go flirt with one of the guys over there until you get one of their numbers." I point to a table of men who are playing darts against the back wall.

"Any preference in who?"

"Your choice."

She slips out of the booth and struts over to the boys, adjusting her bra before approaching one of the guys off to the side. This of course makes the others jealous and they swarm her like a pack of seagulls. We all watch, impressed. It doesn't take long until one of them goes to the bartender to ask for something. He makes his way back to Angie with a marker and tenderly takes her hand to write a string of numbers on her palm. She entertains them a bit longer before finding her way back to us. The boys watch as she leaves and make comments about the purple lace of her bra. It makes my eyes roll and my skin crawl, especially since they aren't being particularly quiet about it.

"The worst part is that guy had a wedding ring on." She slips back into the booth next to a sour looking Ellie. "Anyway it's my turn now. Miles, truth or dare?"

He's momentarily startled but still answers with, "Truth." Disappointed groans arise from the table. He is the first to pick this option.

"That's not what I was hoping for but I can work with that. What is your biggest secret?"

"My biggest secret?" He repeats.

Everyone is intrigued now but none more than I. Out of everyone at this table I know Miles the best and even I do not know all that much about him.

"You can just whisper it to Emily if you want since you guys are friends."

I can see the calculation behind his soft eyes as he thinks. Then he gently leans over. His breath tickles my ear as he whispers, "My greatest secret is the way I feel about you."

Chapter Nineteen
Sunday, March 26th

I was not drunk or dreaming. I heard what he said and snippets of what occurred afterward haunt me as Wren and I drive into the countryside. The radio is on but I don't recognize the song playing, though it does provide a nice background for the mountain scenery we drive through. The only clause is that the higher in altitude the truck gets, the more static there is that interrupts the radio. By the time we get to the top Wren just turns off the overbearing noise. Now we're forced to talk.

"Sorry, I couldn't join you last night."

"No worries."

He pulls the keys out of the ignition and the car goes silent as well. We are sitting in front of a small house with a front porch and all around us are animal pens. To our left are some sheep and a few cows and to the right of us is a chicken coop and a stable. It's not a large farm but it's got character.

"Let me introduce you to Levi and Wrangler." He gets out of the car and comes around to my side to help me out before leading me to the stables.

He pulls the doors to the barn open and sunlight streams in, illuminating two rows of horses, six in total. Levi and Wrangler's stalls are labeled with their names on fancy plaques. Levi is an all brown stallion and Wrangler has spots of white on his underbelly, which is how I plan to tell them apart.

"You will be riding on Levi and I will be on Wrangler," Wren instructs before opening their stall guards and coercing them out.

"But I'm not sure if I know how to ride a horse."

"We'll start off easy." He hands Levi's reins over to me. "Your sneakers and jeans are suitable for riding, however, you might be chilly in that t-shirt up here." I look down at the goosebumps on my arms. It was much warmer when I stepped outside this morning on a lower elevated terrain. "Here." Wren takes off his brown flannel and hands it over to me. Underneath he wears a gray, long-sleeve, thermal shirt.

"Thanks," I respond as I slip it on.

His flannel smells of cologne and dryer sheets. It makes me think of foggy mornings in bathrobes. I'm not sure why I think of this but it's comforting.

"Ready to go?"

"I guess."

Wren pulls a stool over to help me get on. It takes a moment to find my balance atop the animal but once I do I pet Levi's neck comfortingly as a way of thanking him for his patience.

Wren then climbs swiftly atop his own horse without help before directing Wrangler to be by my side. "I figured that we could do a loop around the sheep pen as a warm up before taking one of the trails. Does that sound okay to you?"

I nod so Wren makes a noise to alert the horses that we are moving. Wrangler takes the lead and Levi gets the sense to follow. Once we get to the sheep pen he ties Wrangler to a wooden fence post and comes over to help me guide Levi around. He instructs me on how to take control and be gentle at the same time. We practice veering in different directions and trotting until I am more comfortable.

Then Wren walks away and comes back with an apple that he picked from a nearby tree. He cleans it off on his shirt and lets the horse take half before giving the rest to Wrangler.

"Do you want to try the trail now?"

"Sure."

We make our way over to a corner of the property. A homemade, wooden sign on a tree states that we are about to enter the Somali trail. As we start down the path I get more comfortable. At some point I pick up more speed which puts me ahead of Wren and Wrangler.

"Wanna race?" I tease.

"I don't know if you're up for that just yet but I like the ambition."

Every second I ride feels like I am regaining an old muscle that hasn't been worked in a while. Maybe I did do this in a past life at least a few times or maybe this is the childhood sport that I picked up, the kind your parents put you into after you express the tiniest bit of interest and it becomes a fun fact in icebreakers on the first day of school. Oh, you played softball for eight years? I rode horses.

"Are you scared that you're going to lose?" I press on as my confidence rises.

"Oh please we both know that I would win Daisy."

I pull back on the reins to stop the horse. He does the same. "Whose Daisy?"

"No one, just a stupid nickname. Sorry."

"It's fine, it was just so random. But anyway, we should race."

"Emily, no."

"Okay fine then chase me instead."

I flick the reins and Levi takes off. We start at a trot but after another encouraging flick we pick up a steady run. I'm not sure if Wren and Wrangler are following.

I travel through the trees so fast that the world around me blurs into colors of blue and green. I have yet to feel so alive and adventurous. With the wind tangling my hair into a matted mess and the pounding of my heart syncing with Levi's steps I almost totally forget about last night. Almost.

I hear Wren yell something in the distance but I'm too busy feeling to listen and too caught up in my freedom to

care. He'll catch up to me if he wants. I know he can. But then
he whistles and the horse starts to slow before coming to a
dead stop in front of an overgrowth of bushes. I casually jump
off as Wren approaches.

"What were you thinking?" Wren gets off of Wrangler
as well to inspect me for scrapes and other injuries.

"I was thinking that I wanted to have a little fun," I
retaliate with.

He holds my face now between his hands, lifting
my chin to look at my neck. "Did you even realize that you
veered off of the path at some point?"

"I did?"

"Yes." He pulls me close to him and wraps his arms
around me. I hug him back. "Next time if you want to run
please do it in one of the fields and not on an unreliable
mountain, okay?"

"I'm sorry, I didn't mean to make you worry."

"It's okay, as long as you're safe." He pulls away and
surveys the land around us. A mountainscape peaks out over
a grouping of bushes. "This is a pretty spot, or it would be
at least if these were gone." He swipes at the overgrowth,
trying to push it aside to better see the view across from us.
A waterfall, no more than twelve feet tall, and a mini lake
reveals itself.

"We should go down there," I suggest giddily.

Wren ties the horses to nearby trees, both with plenty
of grass at their bases, and holds out his hand for me to take.
Together we trudge down the decline, making sure to be
careful with our footing so that we don't slip. Once we get
back on flat terrain we look out over another drop. Below us
is a field of flowers, reflecting a multitude of colors. I want to
pick some but the only way down there is to jump.

Wren seems excited by this outcome and begins
to strip down into just his blue boxers, leaving him very
exposed. I know it's rude to stare but I can't seem to turn
my head away and he never asks me to. He backs up to get
a running start, flipping mid-air and breaking into the water

below. When his head pops back up he yells up at me to come down too.

I take off his flannel and my t-shirt first, leaving them in a pile on the grass with my sneakers and jeans. I am left in just a cream bra and baby pink underwear, wishing nothing more than to have matched the two undergarments this morning.

Before I can think too much about it I also take a running head start to jump off of the rocks, plugging my nose and tucking my legs to my chest on the way down. The water swallows me and I discover that it's deeper than I thought it would be. When I come up for air I look around for Wren who is nowhere to be found despite me having just seen his feet treading under the water. I call out his name. I receive no response so I call it out again.

"Gotcha!" He yells as he grabs me from behind, pulling me close to his bare chest.

I scream playfully, splashing water in his face and squirming until he lets me go. I try to seek solace from the shore but don't make it far on my own before Wren sweeps me off of my feet bridal style and carries me the rest of the way.

He kneels to delicately lay me in a bed of flowers before falling on his back next to me. We let out the rest of our giggles before coming to a comfortable silence. The clouds change above us. Our breathing aligns. The breeze is softer now, more gracious on our bare skin. The sun even basks us in warmth now and then. I close my eyes and take it all in.

Then the light becomes darker behind my eyelids. Wren is propped up on an elbow, leaning over me now. We steal glances at each other's lips and we both know what is coming next. The kiss starts light but quickly grows deeper, hotter, heavier. He makes his way down to my neck and I savor each time his lips linger on my skin. Our bodies move, doing a dance that feels as if it has been done countless times before. His fingers move over the crease where my leg and hip connect and he plays with the band on my bottoms, slipping his finger under.

I want to stay in the moment with Wren but it reminds me of Miles and last night. Us arguing in the back alley of the pub, his hands on my stomach, his tongue twisting with mine. Well, that last part is an almost and an almost that can't seem to stop nagging at me. Would it have been so bad if it did happen just once? No, I can't keep thinking of that. I want right now to be about me and Wren not me and Miles. I push him out of my head.

I splay my fingers across the dirt and between the flowers as he kisses where his hands just were. "Can I?" He whispers against the light fabric as he looks up at me. I nod.

His hands tug at the sides of my underwear gently until it comes loose and is pulled to my ankles. He opens my legs and the air chills me in areas it previously didn't. I wait for more contact to come but nothing does. I open my eyes to find Wren staring down at me with a sly grin.

"You haven't held up your end of the deal yet."

"What? What deal?" Is this really the time he is choosing to do this?

"The one that we made in the diner."

"Oh that. Yeah," I mutter as I lean forward to kiss him again. He pulls away.

"When?"

"Later."

I wrap an arm around his neck and kiss him as we fall back onto the cushioned grass. He allows this for a moment before grabbing my hips and rolling me over so that I sit on top of him.

"When?" He casually puts his arms behind his head as he awaits an answer.

I let out a frustrated groan. "Once we get back to the car."

"What did you bring me to read?"

"It's an episode from a television show," I disclose.

"What's it called?"

"The show or the episode?"

"The episode."

"The Second Denial."

"That's one of my favorites. It's from that post-apocalyptic show, right? It's the episode where she has to go within the enemy's base and save her best friend from her sister and then in the end he kisses her and it's revealed that they had feelings for each other all along and then the sister gets jealous and declares war."

I stare blankly back at him. "How did you-?"

"I watch a lot of TV," he explains with a shrug.

"Still you just recalled the entire plot of the episode by simply hearing the name of it. Do you want to read something else that you're not so familiar with?"

"That's alright, I just wanted to know what you would bring me." He props himself up on his elbows and smiles innocently at me until something else catches his attention. "I think I hear your phone ringing."

I get off of him and listen closely,over the breeze and sound of running water. The alarm I set on my phone is in fact going off, the one alerting us that it is time to head back for rehearsal.

I retrieve my underwear and make a disapproving noise. "So genius, how do we get back up?"

Wren eventually discovers an exit by swimming behind the falling water, a rope ladder leads us back up. It presses into my hands in an odd way and I scrape my legs a few times on some rocks but were able to get back to where we left our clothes.

I'm doing the final button on my jeans when one of the horses lets out a loud cry. Wren immediately goes running up the hill, leaving his boots behind. I grab both of our shoes and dash after him.

"What happened?" I call out as I break through the leaf barrier.

Levi prances around aimlessly as Wren tries to calm

him down. I'm not sure how much good it will do but I untie
Wrangler and pull him away so that he doesn't piggyback
off of his friend. But just as Wren succeeds in settling Levi,
whatever creature is hiding under the leaves comes this way,
startling Wrangler as well. The horse in my hands bucks and
gets ready to run. The momentum of the animal causes me
to fall to the forest floor as his legs come up for an attack on
what I now see is a snake. I try to move away from the chaos
but I can't.

I feel time slow as Wren falls to the ground to help me.
Blood drips into my hands. Then the world goes black.

I can't see clearly but I hear cheering. It's hot, I know
it is but I can't feel it. Somebody walks towards me. I'm in
a summer dress and I'm watching the horses. A girl is riding
right now but the sun is strong so I can't see her face. The boy
walking towards me says something but it's muffled. Then it
all disappears.

My eyes flutter open. I can tell now that this is the real
world, whatever I just experienced was not. I try to speak
but my jaw feels screwed shut so I just end up grumbling.
Someone talks back to me but I don't understand.

I am placed in the back of a car that is not Wren's
truck as he doesn't have a back seat. I begin to panic until the
person that gets in the driver's seat turns to check on me.

"It's okay Em, we're going to go see Doctor Pierce.
Wren will meet us there," Miles reassures.

I fall asleep peacefully.

Chapter Twenty
Yesterday

I become consumed with nausea. I can't tell if I'm going to pass out or throw up, maybe both. One second I am digesting his words and the next I am ready to regurgitate my food back onto the table.

I slowly pick over everything in my head as I feel his eyes casting fleeting glances at me, no doubt trying to read what I'm thinking or maybe even take it back. He can't.

Maybe I just zoned out and daydreamed what I wanted to hear when in reality he told me that he accidentally killed his cat when he was younger or that he used to egg his neighbor's house every Halloween and gaslit them into thinking otherwise until they went insane. I probably just heard a projection of my own thoughts. But do I feel that way about him?

I make sure to wait a turn or two before excusing myself and pushing past the door to make a run for it around the side of the building where Ellie and Angie's band was unloading their equipment last week. I press a hand up against the wall for balance and close my eyes to settle my stomach as I continue processing the past few minutes.

He confessed his attraction to me and I actually wanted him to. So, why am I so uneasy now that it is done? And since when have I started feeling the same for him?

"You alright?" Miles asks as he squats down next to me.

I swallow a mouthful of bile. "I'm just peachy," I reply with an undertone of anger.

"Actually you look more gray to me right now," he teases as he presses the back of his hand to my forehead.

I push his hand off of me and pace away from the wall. "Why would you say that? I mean I wanted you to say it but I also- I don't know. You can't, you shouldn't have." I give up on my words and turn away to face the red, weathered brick.

"I know."

"You know?" I almost screech at him.

"Yes. I know I shouldn't have said that just as I know I shouldn't have shared personal information about myself or that we shouldn't have been dancing let alone even that close to each other. There are lots of things that I know I'm not supposed to do with you. But I want to break every rule with you. And for you."

"What about your job? And your reputation? Aren't you worried about that at all?"

"Worried?" He practically laughs, now starting to get worked up as well. "I'm absolutely petrified but not about my job, I love it but I can always find another one. I'm worried about you."

"Me?" I scoff.

"Yes, you. You scare me beyond belief. You have been able to persevere through hardships that no one should face and any self-doubt or loathing you had along the way you eliminated faster than anyone I have ever seen. You approach this new life not with bitterness but with hope and your outlook on everything comes from one of compassion."

I didn't know he felt this way. Is this how I am perceived by everyone or just by him? It is certainly not how I view myself that's for sure. Either way, it eases my anger a bit.

"I am only the way I am because of your guidance." This reality settles back over me. "Which is exactly your job."

"This is true, it is my job to help you. However, half of the things I do for you are out of my jurisdiction."

"What do you mean?"

He sighs and looks around as if the sky will be able to give him the words that he is looking for. "The purpose of a Rebirth mentor is to take a backseat ride in our client's lives. I am not usually as active or present with my other assignments as I have been with you. My job description is to provide guidance and that is what I have done by giving you job options and providing you with friend candidates such as Ellie. Think of me as your 24/7 on-call life coach," he explains with gentleness. "But when you wanted that living room wall painted I should have called a painter. And when the faucet in your sink broke I would have called a plumber. Or when you were still in the wheelchair and not quite a comfortable height to cook yet so I made you food all of those nights, I was supposed to have called in food services. Most of what I have done for you has surpassed my job description but I did it because I wanted you to be happy and I wanted that as quickly as possible. That's all I've ever wanted."

I had no idea. I turn back towards him. His glasses are crooked. I itch to reach out and fix them for him.

"Are you happy?" He asks me.

I think back to all that I have achieved, especially with his help. My job, my friends, the house, the play. "Yes."

"Then I have accomplished my heart's true passion."

My face flushes and my stomach feels funny but not how it did before when I thought that I might throw up. This feeling is different. It is my turn to respond but I can't seem to form any words. Instead I walk closer to him. He tenses. I've never seen him like this before, it's cute.

He wears plain clothes for once- khakis and a white button-up rolled to his elbows, as casual as this man will probably ever get. I play with one of the buttons on his shirt and watch as his chest stops moving, his breath hitching. I place my other hand over his heart to feel the rhythmic beat and use the button I'm playing with as leverage to pull him closer. He stumbles into me, accidentally pushing us against the brick wall of the alley. Thankfully he catches himself. One of his arms is by my ear now and the other reaches up to trace my lips. I watch his eyes. I want to kiss him. But I must know something first.

"What happens if you are caught?" I whisper.

It takes him a moment to process the question. "If the extent of my actions are discovered then I will be brought in front of the ethics committee, likely sued by Rebirth for every penny I have or will ever earn and potentially criminally charged."

"For what?!" I pull away from him, aghast. How can he be so crass about the matter?

"For damaging the company's image and integrity."

"Screw integrity, that's insane!"

"And risky," he reminds me.

"The more secrets we vow to keep the worse the situation. We can't keep doing shit like this."

"I know."

I start to pace. Miles places a hand over mine to stop me from picking at my nails. "Would there be any consequences if I wasn't your client anymore?"

"If anything is done after our professional relationship is over then I can not be punished as I wouldn't be breaking any contracts nor causing any headlines to be made. Although I could still be brought in front of the ethics board where I would most likely lose my job."

"That seems complicated."

"And messy," he once again adds.

"Well I don't want you to get into any trouble."

"I know."

"So we have to stop."

"Can we?"

Chapter Twenty One
Wednesday, March 29th

I lean over the sink in the library bathroom to change the bandaid on my forehead. The small cover only sits over the direct wound, the rest of the injury spreads across the top left of my head in the form of a bruise.

Dr.Pierce put me on bed rest for the past three days in case I received a concussion from the kick so, besides eating primarily ice cream and playing with Bear, all I've done is sleep. I tried writing but it usually resulted in a headache that started at the base of my skull and worked its way forward. I haven't even allowed any visitors, despite Miles's knocks and Wren's phone calls. Anytime I think of the two of them it makes the headaches worse. I just want some time alone.

"Are you alright in there?" Tabitha knocks gently on the bathroom door as I gather up the scraps of my bandaid to toss in the trash.

I open the thing barricading us and greet her with a smile. "All good."

"Wonderful because we're going to be closing for a bit."

"We are? Why?"

She takes me by the arm and leads me over to the front desk where she grabs the keys and her scarf. "Do you like mimosas?"

We sit outside of a restaurant in Old Cresthill, at an umbrella-covered table, with mimosas in front of us. Tabitha encourages me to take my first sip so I raise the glass to my lips. Her's is already a quarter of the way gone with a dark red lipstick stain imprinted on the side.

The first taste goes down my throat then the second. It's citrusy and light with juice. "It's good," I conclude.

"I'm not much of a drinker but my best friend used to love them so sometimes I'll come here and have one in memory of her."

"Is she-"

"Dead? No, but she might as well be." I'm not sure how to take this. "Anyway, how's your head doing?"

"It's fine. I still have some headaches but all the rest and extra painkillers Dr. Pierce recommended have helped."

"Good. And how have play rehearsals been so far?"

"The first one went pretty well. The second one though had to be postponed to today. I'm lucky that the school allowed me to move it to a weekday. Did you want to come and watch?"

She waves away the offer respectfully and fiddles with her scarf, adjusting the fit to be looser around her neck. I don't realize the intrusion or duration of my stare until she asks if everything is alright. I decide to be honest.

"I was just wondering why you wear that all of the time. I rarely see you go without it."

She flushes and puts her hand back to it before deciding to pull the garment off slowly and lifting her neck. A scar runs from the base of her ear to her collarbone. It seemed to have healed many years ago but you can still tell the brutality of the injury.

"What happened?"

I do not gasp or flinch as she runs her hand down the line. She can't see it for herself at this moment but she seems to know its exact path down her body. "A boating accident when I was young. At first, I covered it up with makeup or light shawls in the summer months but as the fall drew near every year I would always find that it was easier to hide with scarves."

"But why do you always wear the same one?"

"Because somebody special gave this to me," she explains as she bundles the red cloth into her hands and falls captive to a daydream.

I'm about to inquire further but our food arrives.

It's fifteen minutes before rehearsal starts when I find the auditorium door propped open, causing me to stop in my tracks. Typically it's locked. The room beyond sits in darkness. No one should be here yet. Maybe somebody turned the lights off but forgot to shut the door earlier. Yeah, that sounds probable.

I make my way into the room feeling around the wall for the switch. I flip it and am immediately overstimulated when eight people jump out at me, creating a cacophony of noise.

"How are you feeling?"

"Doing alright?"

"Sorry about what happened to you."

Once I overcome my confusion I become a revolving door of thank you's and yes's, and I'm fine now. Everyone is here, including the janitor. The only person that I don't see is Wren.

"Okay everybody let's give her some space," Miles calls out to the group.

The sight of him causes all of the feelings from the other day to come rushing back. Maybe I can use this brain injury to my advantage and say that I don't remember our confrontation. Fight? I like confrontation better. Would that be an awful thing to do or a relief to us both? Maybe it is possible for us to reset.

Miles steps aside and everyone parts to give me space which is when I see Wren at the foot of the stage with a bouquet of white and purple tulips. He walks closer to me as everyone watches us. It's like a scene straight from a movie.

"I'm sorry, I never meant for you to get hurt." He holds out the flowers for me to take. Twine wraps around the stems to hold the bouquet together.

I thank him. "And thank you to everyone else as well for your compassion and understanding. I'm okay and would really like to get back to working on this project so can we get Angie and Wren on stage please to start page one?"

We end rehearsal by sharing a small cake with the words 'feel better soon' piped onto it with frosting. We get up to the scene where Raelyn, or Angie, takes her boat across the bay to see Elena, Ellie's character, and falls overboard. It reminds me of the story that Tabitha told at lunch, which might be why she likes this play but if it were me I would not want to be reminded of something so traumatic in this way.

"Can I talk to you real quick?" Miles asks politely, placing his half-eaten cake on the table next to him.

"Sure. Is everything okay?"

He guides me to a private corner shaded by the rising auditorium seats. "I had another meeting this morning regarding your case."

"Oh, and?"

"And they think that based on your stats and the information that I have been providing that you will no longer need a mentor after next month."

I've read up on Rebirth during my spare time in the library which is how I know that this is not normal. Typically mentors are with their patients for a little over four months on average. "But it's only been a month," I protest.

"Yes but you have been able to excel far beyond what was predicted for you at this time."

I give myself a moment to take this in. "So what will

happen to you once you're off of my case?"

"Me? I will get some time off and then head to wherever I am assigned to be next."

"You'll leave?"

"I'll leave," he confirms. I knew that this would be coming but didn't expect it to be so soon. It feels as if I have just swallowed a tennis ball that blocks my vocal cords from producing any type of sound. "In the meantime, I just want to make sure, are we still friends?"

I refuse to put him in any danger so I nod my head yes. "Just friends," I painfully force out. He stuffs his hands in his pockets and smiles meekly at me. Then something else comes to mind. "Should I recast your part?"

"I'm not sure yet, maybe give it a bit more time."

"Well if we're already partially fibbing your reports then I could always fake a depressive episode so that you stay in town longer," I half joke. We laugh and then let the silence consume us. Someone behind me calls my name but I don't want to leave our little space to reveal myself so I think of a new topic to strike up. "Thank you for the cake by the way, I know it was your idea."

"No it wasn't," he denies, shrugging off my compliment.

"Food is one of your love languages." I know that I have won with this selling point.

I can tell that it means something to him that I noticed when his face goes soft and he can't look at me for too long without having to look away. When his head comes back up after his brief intermission with the ground we are closer now and I see that the limbal rings of his eye have a hint of amber. Did I step closer or did he? Either way my knees go weak and my mind turns on autopilot mode, eliminating everything from my head except the goal of what I want my body to do.

I close my eyes to let instinct, or programming, take over as I lean towards him and press my lips to his. At first the kiss is awkward and stiff but once he registers what is happening he relaxes into it and puts a hand on my face with care just as he did the other day before I allowed reality to spoil our moment. He uses the leverage to bring me in even closer, causing my feet to stumble. He catches the weight of me and we kiss until our lips start to chap.

When we finally pull away, remembering where we are, I touch my fingers to my lips to savor what is now defunct. "I couldn't have you leave without doing that at least once. Think of it as a parting gift."

"Am I allowed to regift your present?" He questions.

I pretend to think it over. "I'll allow it."

Miles grabs my waist to pull me in for a second round but just before our lips touch something falls to the ground and a faraway figure darts out of sight.

"Do you think they saw us?" Miles jumps back, the worry visible on his face.

"Give it a few seconds before following after me," I instruct before slipping out of the shadows to follow after the person.

People have started to pack up on the other side of the room and are mostly consumed with their own lives to pay any attention to mine. Someone slips out the door, the only one near Miles and I. I run after them.

"Wait!" I call out, pushing open one of the double doors to the auditorium.

The hall is deserted and the mystery person is gone. The only thing around is a get well soon card on the floor in front of me. I pick it up to open it.

Someone you love has a secret. I'll tell you what it is. -S

Chapter Twenty-Two
Thursday March 30th

I stop by the inn that I remember bumping into Seren at. The keeper at the front desk informs me that she used the phone to call a driver early this morning. Because of this I get no closure as to what this secret she supposedly knows is nor persuade her to keep what happened between Miles and I a secret.

I try to distract my nerves throughout the workday by keeping myself as busy as possible. It works and once closing time hits Tabitha takes off to a doctor's appointment, leaving me with the task of closing up alone. I decide to take the opportunity to surprise Tabitha.

I have had an idea floating around my head for a while now that instead of using money to buy tickets for the play, people could instead bring new or gently used books as a gift upon entry as I have noticed that a lot of the stock we have here is outdated, falling apart or both. I haven't pitched the idea yet and I'm still not sure if Tabitha is totally on board to have the play performed here so I think that a little extra surprise cleaning would definitely put me into Tabitha's good graces more than I already am.

I go into the cleaning closet and pull out anything and everything I might need from window washing spray to floor waxer. I want every spot of this place to shine even if it smells like chemicals. So I scrub, wipe, and mop every square inch of the building until there is not a single sign of age in the rustic library, except for the cobwebs in the corners of the ceiling that are too tall for any chair or normal ladder to reach. And even when all that is done I push on to do more.

The clock on the wall reads a half-hour past my usually departing time when I turn the handle on the closet in the hallway to take on the task of organizing it. It's the only door I haven't needed to open yet but I've heard Tabitha mention that she wants to get around to decluttering it soon. Upon opening the door I audibly gasp. Every inch of the four-by-four room is riddled with painting supplies and mural paper. I wonder if she would let me use all of this for the set.

"Why are you still here?"

I jump in fright, bumping into some of the unopened paint cans. Wren helps me up. "Why are you here?" I throw back at him.

"I drove by your house but all of the lights were off so I figured that you would be here still."

"Did you need something?" I start to go on with my prior task of decluttering the closet by pulling everything out of it. Wren jumps in to help.

"I was just wondering if you wanted to go on another date, maybe one that you didn't get hurt on this time. "

"Oh, well what were you thinking of doing?"

"Gee what am I on trial or something?" He jokes. "Just trust me, it's a surprise." I want to remind him that I hate these kinds of surprises but don't want to spoil any effort he might have put into his act of kindness.

"Fine, but we have to finish organizing this closet first."

Wren puts the car in park once we pull into the parking lot of an ice cream parlor in Old Cresthill. A small statue of an upside down ice cream cone is displayed on the roof, clearly labeling the building. It's one of those places where you order and pick up at the window and for a Thursday night it is busy.

He asks me to find us an open seat as he gets in line. I'm not sure what he plans on ordering but considering a milkshake and convenience store ice pop is the closest thing I've had to ice cream in this life I'm not particularly picky.

It takes a while for me to find a spot, as most of the picnic table seating is being taken, but I sit in the only empty area just as Wren gets to the front of the line. I people-watch to pass the time as he waits for our order to be made. At one table a mother ignores her child who tries to do cartwheels to get her attention and at another a couple breaks up or at least is very much on the brink of doing so. Their untouched ice cream melts in their cups.

Then I see an older couple tucked away in a corner to themselves. They are the only ones I notice who don't seem to have some sort of fragmented or broken element to them. The man feeds the woman a spoonful of colorful ice cream. A drop lands in her lap and he tenderly dabs at it with a napkin. They have wedding bands on their fingers and wrinkles that tell a story of their past.

Someone in this world must have cleaned up my messes at some point and had stories about me to tell. Suddenly I envy everyone here despite them being broken or fragmented because at least they have families to be with and can remember crucial details about themselves such as their favorite ice cream flavor.

"I got six different kinds so you can really taste a variety and best determine which ones you like," Wren explains as he swings his legs over and through the wooden bench. His small gesture puts a smile on my face. "There's the basics: strawberry, chocolate and vanilla. And then there are some random ones: cotton candy, birthday cake, and peanut butter cup. So which one first?"

He hands me a spoon. I observe my options and end up choosing the most colorful one first. I'm not sure if it's accurate to the sugar-spun dessert since I can't remember if I have had that either but the cream melts on my tongue and the flavor dissolves into my mouth tastefully. Wren asks me what I think of it, I reply between bites. He then urges me to try the birthday cake flavor next, claiming that it's his favorite. I lick the remnants of cotton candy off of my spoon and dip it into the one that Wren suggested, biting down on some sprinkles upon bringing it to my lips. I determine that I like the cotton candy more much to Wren's dismay.

"Okay fine, now try the peanut butter cup," he prompts.

I taste that one next as well as the regular flavors before coming to the conclusion that nothing beats the cotton candy. When I'm done Wren asks me to rank them in order of most to least liked. I do so but have trouble figuring out if chocolate or strawberry should be in last place.

"What do you think?"

"I think that neither should be up for last and that you're crazy," he exclaims as he holds a spoonful of brown ice cream out to me. I scrunch up my face and stick out my tongue like a young child when their parents force them to eat a vegetable. Then I take the utensil from him and guide it into his mouth. He smiles and accepts the offer before getting serious once more, "I still think that you should try a few more bites before making up your mind about something like this."

I scoop another hefty chunk of chocolate and lick it clean off of the spoon. I pretend to think some more before letting him down. He deflates. At first I take his reaction as a joke but when he doesn't let up I realize that he might feel some actual disappointment, though I'm unsure why my dislike of chocolate flavored ice cream is being taken with such severity. Neither of us verbalize our feelings on the tone switch.

Darkness has officially covered the sky as we pull into the farm I can't remember leaving from the other day. Stars scatter over the countryside like a splattering of paint on a canvas. I thought that he was going to drop me off at home but didn't question it either when we turned onto the road that leads up the mountain.

"I think it's too soon for a re-do with the horses," I put out there.

"We are not going to ride the horses again." He gets out of the car and comes around to the other side to help me out.

"Will there be any traumatic injuries at all this time?"

"Not if you wear this." He grabs something from the open back of his truck and hands it to me, a helmet.

I put it on as Wren jogs over to the front porch of the house. He comes back towards me with a bicycle on either side of him. One is a rusted silver and the other a golden yellow.

"We're going on a bike ride?"

"Yeah." He's suddenly giddy with all the excitement of a child. I'm not sure that I feel the same but I'm glad that his mood has shifted.

"And what if I don't know how to ride a bike?"

"Then I will help you learn just as I did with the horses."

He gives me the yellow bike, holding it steady for me to get on, before showing me how to balance and steer. I follow his instructions to a t but never make it more than a few yards before stumbling and having to put my feet back on the dirt. A few trials in he decides it best to hold on to my waist, tilting me one way or the other to keep me upright and steady. With his promise of support, I gain a better understanding and start picking up pace. I'm going fast now, Wren running beside me. I look at him and laugh at the thrill only to realize that he isn't there anymore, he let go. I panic and swerve into a bush. Wren runs over, unclipping the helmet and holding my head close to his chest.

"Are you all right?"

I reassure him that I am, even standing and brushing off my jeans to prove it. Then I take the helmet back from him, resecuring it to my head, and pull the bike up. I get on it myself this time, rejecting his offer to help, and start pedaling. I swerve a bit but I'm steady. And once I stay upright for a sufficient amount of time Wren gets on his own bike to start riding next to me.

The feel of the handles under my grip, the wheels underfoot, and the wind in my hair cause me to become stuck in my head and suddenly I am no longer here with Wren anymore. Instead, I am racing against the setting sun and there's a boy next to me and someone calling out from behind. We're in a neighborhood. Everything around us is a blur including the faces of the people I am riding with. The boy and I laugh. I think we're running from something or someone.

"Watch out!" The boy on the bike yells to me in warning.

No, wait. That was Wren and it was real. My daydream ends as I swerve away from a tree and pull back on the pedals to break. Wren runs over to check me again for injuries as I stare into the horizon at the stars in the sky. It felt so vivid, so real. And then I realize why.

It wasn't a daydream, it was a memory.

Chapter Twenty-Three
Friday, March 31st

I decided to walk home from work today, which would have been nice if the sky didn't release a torrential downpour while I'm still two minutes away from my front door.

I'm forced to strip off all of my clothing directly upon entering the house, leaving everything in a pile on the floor. My left sock gets stuck on my heel and I hop to pull it off as I make my way to the bathroom, turn the shower on, and get inside. The instant heat warms my bones and I enjoy the temperature until my fingers turn pruny and my skin turns red.

When I get out, Bear waits for me, curled atop my towel. I pick him up and move him to the floor before wrapping myself up and pulling my wet hair into a clip. I head into the bedroom and put on blue-lined pajama pants and an oversized crewneck before brushing out my hair.

I spend the rest of the evening listening to the rain and adding to my writing. I haven't thought of an ending for the story I am creating but I have a feeling that I am over halfway through. It takes a while to get through a page or two since I handwrite everything but once I know what I want to say I do not stop until my hand cramps an unbearable amount.

My next spending purchase should definitely be a car or computer. Except I need to learn to drive before investing in the first one. I should get a hold of Miles to see how I would go about learning to do so. As of a week ago I would have assumed that it was him that would teach me but now I understand that he would recruit the outside help of another specialized in that field to do so.

I give him a call. It goes to voicemail and he doesn't get back to me until an hour later when I am making a pathetic dinner that I have almost burnt two and a half times now.

I put the wooden spoon in my mouth and reach across the counter to grab for my phone. "Hey, Emily." The absence of the nickname he gave me makes my stomach drop.

"Ey,"

"Huh?"

I take the spoon out of my mouth and lay it on a kitchen towel as I should have done the first time. "Sorry, I meant hey."

"Oh, well I got your voicemail and checked in with the nearest driving school. It's in Croyden and they are booked full with lessons for the next two weeks."

"That's okay, did you put my name down for them to reach me or be put on a waiting list?"

"I did. But I was thinking and I can also put in a request to teach you myself which would only take a few hours to get an answer back on. Would that be okay with you or would you rather wait for the official driving school?"

"Aren't you worried about your superiors becoming suspicious?"

"They shouldn't be if I explain that you have an eagerness to learn and want to take some more initiative and control back in your life."

"Okay, then yeah that's okay with me I guess."

"Perfect, I'll put in the request now, and should get an answer by the morning. If they approve the proposal does after rehearsal sound good for practice? Maybe you could even drive us home."

"I can't afterwards, Wren and I are hanging out, but I'm free beforehand."

He's quiet for a moment. "Okay, i'll pick you up tomorrow morning then."

"Perfect."

When we hang up I feel uneasy and horrible for mentioning Wren. The feeling only intensifies when I look at the food I am making and remember everything that he has done for me.

I give up and turn the oven off, leaving the pot to rot on the stove top, before sinking to the floor. I lean my back against the kitchen cabinets, taking in the loneliness that surrounds me, while resting my head against my arm.

I'm in a small town in a country I likely did not grow up in with people that I met mere weeks ago and I am jealous. Jealous of those who live near their childhood best friends or with their college sweethearts. But most of all, I envy those who have a family or even people that miss their family because at least they have a family to miss. I, on the other hand, long after the idea of a family. I have no mom or dad to phone when I have big feelings. No brothers or sisters to give advice to. No aunts or uncles, nieces or nephews, or even cousins to meet up with when they happen to be in the area.

It's just me. Me and Bear.

Chapter Twenty-Four
Saturday, April 1st

Miles has me flip through the user manual before quizzing me on what all of the dash emoticons mean. "In two of the countries you have to be at least eighteen to obtain a license. However here and in Alnerwick the minimum age requirement is sixteen," he explains as he turns the car on. The engine sputters to life.

"Did I have a license before?"

"You did but it is not viable in this country."

I nod in acknowledgment as he points out the pedals and their functions. Miles tells me to gently step on each. I put pressure on the gas first, so light that we don't move more than an inch.

"Press down harder," he instructs.

I put more weight into it and the car shoots forward, forcing me to stomp on the brake in fear. He encourages me patiently to try again so I put an intermediate amount of weight onto the pedal this time and we move forward at a steady pace.

"Good, now try turning the wheel."

Slowly I put one hand over the other just as one of the instructional videos Miles showed me this morning displayed. The car turns around a corner. We do a full lap before he suggests trying to park.

"The hope is that your instincts will kick in at some point and take over. You can erase the memory from your brain but not your muscles."

I successfully pull into and back out of a parking space. Miles provides me with encouragement throughout. The first time I put my turn signal on I was labeled 'the greatest driver to ever grace the roads,' which is most definitely overkill.

"You're a natural. Have those instincts kicked in yet?"

"I'm not sure." I do feel confident in what I'm doing but it still feels like a shock to my body. "Maybe if I try driving around other cars on an actual road instead of the school parking lot."

"Are you ready for that?"

I check the analog clock on Miles's wrist. I have ten more minutes before I plan on tracking Seren down before rehearsal. "We'll see."

When I pull onto the main road no one is around. I start slow on the straight strip before increasing to thirty and then forty miles per hour.

We're about a mile out from our departing location when I see a car coming up in the distance on the opposite side. It looks like a truck similar to Wren's so I slow back down. My window is rolled down and so is theirs. I'm about to give a friendly wave when someone in the passenger seat catches me off guard. It's Seren. He's too focused on saying something to her to notice me. She looks angry.

My momentary lapse in focus causes me to swerve the car for a second and slam on the brakes. I close my eyes on instinct.

When I open them I'm in a driveway.

A man is working on the underbelly of a car. His feet stick out and now and again he rolls out from underneath as the girl next to me holds out a bottle of water for him. Their faces are warped but the voices I can hear clearly.

"It's almost done girls, then you two can go to the mall."

Someone on a bike rolls up then. It's the boy from the last memory but slightly older and the bike he's on is not like the one from before. This time the boy is riding a motorcycle. His face is still blurry, as is everybody else's. He calls out to somebody and at first I think it's the girl next to me but instead it is me walking towards him.

"Emily! Are you okay?"

Miles hands are in front of me, holding me back so that my chest wouldn't slam into the steering wheel. I mutter a sincere but pathetic apology as I try to wrap my head around what just went down.

"What happened? You were doing great."

"Is it possible to regain memories?" I stare out at the open road, afraid to look anywhere else.

"What?"

I repeat myself and Miles asks me to clarify. "At first, I thought they were dreams or hallucinations from the concussion but I think they're memories. I can't make out everything around me but-. "

"How many have you had?"

"Three in this past week. One right after the horse kicked me, another when I was riding a bike the other day, and one just now."

He allows this to soak in. "It's not common but it can happen, especially with something like a concussion to trigger it. A Rebirth doctor might be able to prescribe you medication to make the memories stop."

"And what if I don't want them to stop?"

I have kept my curiosities at bay for so long. Squashed every fiber of wonder because I wanted to trust myself, that this was for the best as I have been told. But all of the memories I have seen are positive. Would it be so bad to know why I put myself in this position? I wouldn't have the experiences associated with the words so I couldn't feel what I must have before right?

"We can talk about it more later. Did you want to head back now? Rehearsal will be starting soon."

"Yeah."

Upon approaching the building I tell Miles that I need a moment to myself and to go in without me. He's hesitant to do so but eventually goes, which is when I track the smoke lingering in the air to the side of the building, exactly where I saw Seren go after getting out of Wren's truck.

She leans up against the wall with a cigarette in her hand but once she sees me she puts it out. I'm sure I've never been a mother or pregnant, based on the medical history that I glanced at the last time I was in Doctor Pierce's office, but I'm pretty sure smoking while with child isn't necessarily healthy.

She goes to speak but I hold a hand in the air to cut her off. "Just answer one question for me." She raises her eyebrows and tilts her head but keeps her silence so I got on, "who is it that's keeping this secret from me?"

"You don't want to just know what the secret is?"

"No, I want to give them a chance to tell me themselves."

She scoffs and fishes a stick of gum out of her purse. She unwraps it and begins to chew as she stares out. The longer she chews the more I get annoyed. Eventually, she takes the wad of gum out of her mouth and sticks it to the brick.

"Wren," she whispers into my ear as she walks past me to go inside.

Rehearsal goes by slowly with Seren being cold towards me all of a sudden and me being cold towards Wren. He will get one chance to confess and then I will go back to Seren.

In the group setting she acts sweet and caring, even helping to braid Bee's hair. In passing though is when she holds an ill attitude towards me for something I still know nothing about. It must be something to do with me that affects her if she is treating me this way. But didn't she and Wren meet for the first time the other day?

We get through the rest of act one today, ending with the death of Wren's character, Bill. It's an emotional closing to a rehearsal and there are many stage directions to be noted but eventually we get through it.

The second that I announce the end of rehearsal Wren jumps off of the stage to approach me. "Are we still on for our date tonight Miss Director?" He kisses me on the cheek and I pull away. "Are you okay?"

"Yeah. I'll see you at seven tonight." I give him a fake smile, grab the rest of my things, and call out a goodbye to everybody before heading over to Miles.

He offers to let me drive home. I accept.

I pull into the driveway rather harshly but overall the ride has been pretty smooth and I kept with the speed limit somewhat well. Miles continues with his over-praising, of course, as I turn the car off and invite him inside. I can tell he is wary so I clarify that it is for help with something which seems to ease him and he agrees to come in.

When we get inside I head towards the dining room table and show Miles the paper bag of seeds and gardening tools that I stopped to get the other day after work. I hold it out to him as an offering. He takes it and peers inside as I dash off for the bedroom.

"I'll be right back, I'm just going to change."

"And what about me? This is a nice shirt," he calls after me once the door is closed.

"Take it off, I won't look," I yell back to him. This is a lie, I will probably look.

I hastily change into some jeans and a t-shirt that

I don't care to get dirt on before heading back out to him. Surprisingly he has taken my advice and his shirt is in fact off. In response I dramatically shield my eyes from him once I notice but very obviously peak through my fingers. He laughs it off and the two of us go around back to start digging.

"I want to plant the first one where I found Bear and I was thinking of a pretty flower like a lily or a rose."

Miles pulls out both options for me as we settle into the dirt. He holds each one behind his back and has me blindly pick after shuffling them between hands. I end up choosing the lilies. We then each dig a certain number of spots and drop the tiny seeds inside before picking another section of the yard to put the roses and tulips. We also plant the daffodils, azalea and baby's breath.

All of this takes about an hour and I don't realize how late it's gotten until Ellie's van pulls into the driveway. I had entirely forgotten her offer to help me get ready for my date with Wren.

"I'll clean everything up, you go," Miles offers.

I thank him and run around to the front of the house. I am pleasantly surprised to see Angie here too.

"She's a fashion god Emily, I promise. Wait, why are you outside?"

"And dirty..." They both stare at my jeans with the dirt stains.

I open my mouth to answer when Miles comes back around the side of the house as well with the bag of gardening tools in his hand and still shirtless. Fuck, I had been doing so good at not looking but now I regret not doing so sooner.

"Hey Miles," Ellie greets, slightly frazzled. He flushes but nods politely to the group of us.

"Hey everyone, I just have to grab something from inside and then I'll be on my way." He sidesteps past the two of them to let himself in.

"What the fuck?"

"You better spill," the girls take the opportunity to interject while he's inside.

A moment later Miles walks back past the three of us, his shirt now on. He says his goodbyes. Angie lingers around him and waves flirtatiously as he walks to his car, thankfully Ellie pulls her inside.

Once we get settled inside Angie asks to see what I'm wearing tonight. I lead them into my room to show them the outfit splayed out on my bed.

"It looks like something my grandma would wear. Do you mind if I-?" She doesn't finish her sentence and instead points to my drawers to communicate the rest of her sentence.

I give her the go ahead and she stuffs the sweater and jeans that I had picked out to the bottom of the drawer before digging around more and pulling out a tight floral dress that I haven't gotten around to wearing yet.

"Don't you think it will be a little chilly for that? The date is outside."

She ignores me, tossing the dress towards me before crouching down to choose from my four pairs of shoes. "These are perfect." She holds up the heels that Miles gave me.

"No," I protest, grabbing them politely from her hands and laying them back on the floor where they were. "I'll wear the boots. I don't want to ruin those."

"Are you sure?" Angie and Ellie both make distasteful faces, clearly disagreeing with my decision. I don't budge.

The shoes bring me back to the night of the dance. If Miles went with me instead, would we have kissed or confessed how we felt sooner? No, I need to stop this line of thinking immediately. I shouldn't diminish my time with Wren just because I could have done it with Miles.

Ellie and Angie lounge around on the couch, playing with Bear, as I get dressed. When I'm done I gather all of the makeup up and bring it out into the living space. The girls get excited at the sight and start grabbing for things to touch up my face with. Angie dabs a cream base around my forehead as Ellie applies a light layer of something sparkly to my eyelids. I try to keep one eye open to catch the color but she lectures me to close both otherwise something about creasing, I think.

"I have a question," Angie directs to me as she moves to my cheeks now with the makeup brush. I give her the go ahead. "Are you dating Wren or Miles? Because I can't tell if you have a thing for Miles or if you two are just friends. Or is it like a one-sided feelings type of scenario and now you are dating Wren to get over him?"

"I was wondering the same," Ellie sheepishly admits. "I see the way you are with both of them and the way they are with you. The two of them feel something for you but the affection is different."

"How so?"

"Well one of them, Wren, loves you as if he's known you forever. He smiles more when you're around and dotes after you. But Miles is the opposite. Whenever you're around he's on his guard, always looking out for potential threats to your happiness or health," Ellie explains.

"Is that bad?"

Angie puts a hand on mine. "No, it's not bad. They just love you in their own ways."

"Love is a strong word," I fend off. "And to answer your question, it's complicated. It didn't used to be with Wren but now it is or it could be. And it always has been difficult with Miles. We can't necessarily be together but I can never stop thinking about him and what could be for us." Surprisingly this confession slips out easier than I thought it would.

"Why can't you and Miles be together?" Angie pries further as she digs through the makeup pile for something.

"His job."

Before they can ask for further clarification the loud exhaust of a truck pulls into earshot and a car door slams firmly shut. Angie abandons looking for whatever it was that she was in need of to grab the handful of makeup, running to toss it onto my bed.

"I'll get the door and you finish up," she suggests.

Ellie agrees and pulls me into my bedroom, slamming

the door in cadence to when Wren knocks. Casual greetings and small talk occur in my living room after the door is answered. Meanwhile, Ellie sits me down and rubs a brush over the pink compact powder in her hands, generously stroking it against my cheeks afterwards.

"Now blink and blink and look left. Okay now look right," she coaches me along as she rubs something black against my eyelashes. "Okay, are you ready?"

"I think so."

"Good, get your shoes on." She pats my leg and packs the makeup back into the plastic bag I had it stored in.

I put on socks and my black boots as Ellie hands me a purse. But it is not my purse, it is her much nicer one. She shakes her head and shushes me as if to dismiss my future protests before pushing me out of the bedroom.

I practically stumble into Wren but he holds me steady, looking me over after he helps me stand upright. "You look incredible. I know that's a cliche line but it's true."

"I think it's sweet," Ellie interjects. When she realizes she's said this aloud she blushes and makes a discreet exit with Angie out the front door, waving goodbye discreetly.

"Shall we go too?" Wren suggests, holding out his elbow for me.

"Yes, but I'm driving," I authorize, holding my head high and looping my arm into his.

"Oh, yeah?"

"Yes, I learned this morning and need to practice." I ruffle the spot under Bear's chin as we pass to say goodbye. He holds the front door open for me.

"Only this morning? Maybe it's not such a good idea then."

"It's too bad that you don't really have a choice considering I have the keys."

"No, you don't."

"Yes, I do."

I dangle the keys in front of my face to show him that they are no longer in the back pocket I just stole them from.

He playfully attempts to grab them back from me but I pull
them out of reach and run towards the car.

We've been driving for almost a half hour by the time
I veer off of the main road as Wren instructs, pulling onto
a winding dirt road off to the side. It reminds me of the one
we've taken to get to Wren's client's farm except instead of
rapidly inclining this one stays stagnantly flat. There's a forest
surrounding it but once we come through a clearing a small,
nearly empty field is revealed. No one is here but us. He tells
me to park anywhere so once we hit the middle of the field I
shift the gear to P, locking the wheels in place.

"That wasn't that bad."

"Thank you, now would you like to tell me what we're
doing here?"

"Oh, right. We're going to watch a movie, a classic
musical about a girl taken by a tornado into an alternate realm
with witches and wizards and talking animals and such."

"We're going to watch a movie? Here?" I look around
and can't help but laugh. There is no television in sight and
even if there was there must not be service for miles. Wren
seems completely serious though.

"Yes, right here," he confirms. "The screen will be set
up over there and people will show up then once it gets dark
in about an hour the movie will start."

I still think he's messing with me until two cars pull up
to ours at that moment and start pulling equipment out of their
trunks. Wren excuses himself to go help and I watch them put
up a large sheet that they string between two trees. A third
truck shows up then and they unhitch a small trailer full of
frozen treats and popcorn. And finally as Wren said other cars
show up in droves until the field is packed with at least a few
rows of vehicles.

In all of the rushing around I have had no private time
to speak to Wren and I couldn't very well bring up the secret
in the car because I had to focus on driving. He has kissed my

cheek a few times in passing and checked on my wellbeing but that's the extent of our interactions since we got here.

"All of this work will be worth it once the movie comes on," he promises while coming to check on me for the sixth time.

I finally get the chance to ask if there is anything I can help with and he assigns me the task of setting up the back of his truck for us before rushing off once more. I open the to-go bag he packed and pull out pillows, a comforter and throw blankets. I lay them out accordingly, taking my time with it to prolong my boredom from setting in again.

By the time the movie starts the sun has gone down and a soft breeze has made the air grow cold. Everyone has settled in with their snacks and one of Wren's friends has to run to the nearest convenience store for more.

I'm leaning against the side of the truck when he finds me in the sea of people and cars. He pulls down the hatch in the back and helps me to climb inside before doing so as well. He compliments the setup upon seeing it and I do the same in regards to the movie.

The first musical number is already ending when he shows me the candy that he bought for us and I hum the tune of the song as we split a bag of sour gummy worms. I haven't seen any films since being in New Cresthill so this really feels like a treat to me. I guess Wren's secret can wait just a bit longer.

Our stash of snacks runs out near the end of the movie and Wren excuses himself during the final few minutes to start packing up. I make myself busy by folding up the blankets that we used. When I'm done the booth in the middle is almost completely broken down and packed away. Any other leftover popcorn or candy is being handed out to children.

"Did you enjoy the movie?" Wren asks once we sit in the front of the car. He turns on the engine, making sure to put the heat on as high as it can go and turning the vents to face me.

"I did," I answer honestly. "Did you?"

"I seem to have a different opinion on it every time I watch."

"And how many times have you watched this movie?"

"It used to be my roommate's favorite so a lot."

We sit there for a minute before moving and watch the train wreck that is people trying to get out of here. The line moves slowly, inching forward every minute or so. I'm out to bring up the topic of his secret but then Wren puts the car into drive and we head back onto the road with ease. He turns the radio on, which ironically plays one of the songs from the movie, and puts a hand on my lower leg. Then we head back towards home.

I have to say something about it now or I fear that I never will. No more excuses. "I have a question and I'm asking you to be one hundred percent honest with me."

"Okay, what is it?"

I take a shaky deep breath, preparing myself for anything. "Are you hiding something from me?"

He's stunned. "What do you mean?"

"What do you mean what do I mean? Are you hiding something from me?"

He shifts in his seat and removes his hand from its previous resting position. "Can we talk about this when we get to your house? Please."

"No, I want to talk about this now."

"I don't think that we should."

"Well, I don't really give a shit what you think right now. What is it that you're hiding from me? Clearly it's something."

He pulls the car to the side of the road. We can't be more than two minutes out from the field with another thirty minutes until we would arrive at home. I can't sit in silence again for that long with this question nagging at me.

"It's all very complicated Emily but I think that I could better explain if I show you something instead."

"But it does have something to do with me doesn't it?"

"Yes."

I expected this to be the answer but it still makes my cheeks burn and my knuckles white. "Okay, where is this thing that you want to show me?"

"At my place. I could drop it off tomorrow if you would like." I can tell that his nerves are getting the better of him.

"No, I want to see it now."

"Okay."

He turns the music up higher to quiet our conversation and we drive to his place in silence.

Chapter Twenty-Five
Sunday, April 2nd

The dashboard of Wren's truck says that it's 12:03 am. When he left it was 11:49 pm. I become restless waiting and take the keys out of the car. The hum of the engine settles, I do not. I step out, lock it, then head up the two flights of stairs to the top floor. I knock on the door that I remember being his. No answer.

"Wren? You've been gone for over ten minutes." I whisper yell to not wake the neighbors. No answer follows. "Wren?!" I try again more urgently. Still nothing. I put my ear to the door to listen for any activity. I think I catch something. I lean closer. Faint, stifled sobs. Concerned, I turn the door handle and allow myself in. "Wren?"

It's dark but I can see the outlines of two figures on the floor. One is lying down and the other is crouched over the first. I turn on the light. The woman jumps up, startled, and reveals the scene behind her. Wren is on the floor, a knife sticking out of his stomach. He tries to reach out to me but the woman steps between us. She wipes the tears from her face and when her hands pull away I see that it is Seren.

"It was an accident," she claims.

A noise of fear escapes me and I clap my hands over my mouth to keep from screaming. That will do him no good. I have to stay calm. "We need to get him help, what happened? Why were you here?" This is not how I thought the night would go.

I step around Seren to get to Wren. She doesn't fight me on it, even backing out of my way. I fall to my knees beside him. Any secrets kept from me don't matter right now.

I use one hand to pull out my phone and the other I place on the side of his face for comfort. Both are shaking. He's cold and pale and I attempt to dial an emergency number but accidentally drop the phone.

"Th-"

"Hold on Wren." I go to grab for the phone but Seren's foot kicks it out of reach. "What are you doing? I need to get him help!"

"You can't."

"What do you mean I can't?"

"I-I stabbed him," she explains between gasps of crying.

"Yes, which is exactly why I need to get him some help!"

"This wasn't part of the plan." She puts her hands to her ears and squeezes, trying to block everything out. I don't have time to deal with this psychosis right now.

I go to grab for the phone again but she stomps on my hand, sending excruciating pain shooting up my arm and white and black spots that look like television static fill my vision. I bite back a cry as I observe the injury. Three of my fingers are already swollen and throb with pain.

"What is your fucking problem?!"

"You are my problem!" Whatever trace of panic Seren just experienced is replaced with anger now. "I fell in love with him first."

"What are you talking about?"

Wren tries to say something again. I hear him try to form the words but a coughing fit ensues instead. I put my hand on his chest to feel for his heartbeat.

"We knew each other before, back when your face looked like mine and your name was Selina."

"Selina?" I test out the name letting it slowly slip off of my tongue. Something starts arising to the forefront of my memory but I push it away, not allowing myself to focus on it right now.

She grabs another kitchen knife, tracing the outline of the blade with her finger. "I met Wren the summer going into middle school when I started riding horses at the barn his parents own. We would hangout after hours sometimes in the stables and he would allow me free practice time even though he could have gotten in trouble." She walks towards Wren. His eyes are closed, likely having passed out from pain, but I can feel his heartbeat. The knife is still in him, keeping him from bleeding out. "But that all changed when he met you. I didn't get it and I still don't because you look exactly like me, or at least you did at the time, I mean we were fucking twins so what did he love so much about you that he didn't see in me?!"

"T-twins?" I stutter out.

My head spins as I process this information. I put my hand on the floor to ground myself and scream as the pain in my fingers comes forth like a crashing wave, a reminder of what has just happened. The nausea of it all has me holding back the popcorn I consumed earlier.

"Listen to my fucking story!" Seren yells at me after snapping in my face to bring my attention back to her.

"I'm listening!" I scream back. Wren stirs. Tears slip down my face.

"Good. Anyways, I partied my way through high school and then my first year of college, until I was kicked out, all to try to forget what you stole from me. And while I was in pain you and Wren had been together for four fucking years and lived in a fancy apartment where you got to work from home writing your stupid fucking stories while he was going to college. And then when the time came for him to go on to veterinary school he asked you to move with him across the country." Wren's eyes flutter and his mouth moves like a puppet. No sound comes out. "And you were a fucking fool

because you said no, which caused a big fight of course. He
left, you cried and the two of you broke it off, which is when
I swooped in," she gestures to her stomach. "But the next day
he said that he only slept with me because he thought that I
was you, which is when I realized that as long as you were a
possibility he would always want you. So I went back home
and thought of every way to get rid of you which is when I
realized that I could just become you," she remarks manically.

"What do you mean?"

She stalls, dragging the blade gently across her belly to
remind me of the armor that she has- her baby. I could attack
her and get to the phone but then I fear pushing the blade into
her stomach which is probably what she wants, to make it
look like I was trying to kill both her, Wren and their baby for
some insane reason.

"What do you mean?" I scream at her again, hopfully
loud enough for the neighbors to wake up and call some type
of emergency personnel to disrupt this fuck show.

"It wasn't you that signed up for Rebirth Selina. It was
me. I instructed them to take me, or really you, in the middle
of the night from your apartment, peacefully by injecting a
drug that would make you drowsy. Then they carried you off
and into your new life. I used the savings that Mom and Dad
left for me in their will to do so. Then after you were gone I
took yours."

"You stole my identity?!"

She shrugs her shoulders nonchalantly as if the act
did not take much effort. "Only for a day. Four months of
meeting and planning with Rebirth all to get one day with
Wren thinking that I was you. I used the baby as my in since
I know how highly he values family. But once he got past the
euphoria of the fake you coming back to him he realized that
the timing of the pregnancy didn't align with the last time he
had slept with you meaning it was either not his or it was not
you. He demanded a paternity test and during our fight I let
slip what I had done to you. He immediately got on a plane
and this baby became the end of us."

I'm seethingly angry now. It was never my decision to be here like I've been led to believe. I turn to Wren, taking it all in. We were in a relationship before, that's why everything came so naturally to him. He had kissed and touched and loved me a million times prior. This was his secret, this is what he was keeping from me. He really is the Wren from my past.

"Of course I had to follow after him, to try to convince him to come home and accept that what's done is done. But that didn't work and instead he tried to get you to fall in love with him all over again so I decided to kill you myself because no one would suspect the pregnant girl."

I look up at her and draw back when I notice the tip of the blade in front of my nose. "So that stab wound was meant for me wasn't it?"

"Now she gets it," Seren lulls as she backs me into the side of the couch. I have to use my one good hand to help me move away. "Because even with your new face and your new hair he still loves you and he hates me even more so."

"But didn't you see me with Miles? Surely that would change your mind," I say in an attempt to persuade her that I feel nothing for Wren.

"What are you talking about?" She must not have seen us kiss like we thought.

Behind Seren I watch as Wren points to the phone that was kicked towards the kitchen. I'm not sure what he's trying to communicate until I look at the phone again and realize that it did call someone before I lost it. I'm not sure who. I just need to hold on and so does he until whoever it is sends help. I quickly look away from the device hoping that I didn't draw her attention to it.

"So what is the plan now, Seren? Because you got the supposed love of your life bleeding out on the floor over there and you won't let him get help."

This realization settles back upon her. She's lost and doesn't know what to do. But I know exactly how to make her think she's back on track while also helping Wren.

"What if you erased his memory instead? I'll stay here and I promise that I will never bother the two of you."

Wren makes a noise of disapproval from behind me. He tries to speak again but the pain prevents him from doing so. I don't know how he's still with us.

"How would I get him to agree to that?"

"You can advocate that he needs it and is delusional thinking that we were together. Tell the doctors that he has a history of mental health issues and frequently forgets who his girlfriend and future child are. I'll advocate for it too."

"That's not a bad idea. There have been a few cases that Rebirth has taken on because of familial wishes."

"Exactly, but we need him alive for that plan." I'm glad that she is too delusional right now to see through the plot holes in the plan I just proposed.

"Okay."

She pulls the knife away from my face so it is not as minacious as before but she still holds it out to me as a warning that she can get close again or even cut if she needs to.

I make my way back towards him and slip my good arm underneath his back. He's in and out of consciousness again as I struggle to pull him up. And after a few tries I lower him gently back to the floor, accepting that there is not much I can do in terms of mobility. So instead of getting him out of here I have to find a way to get Seren to leave without causing damage to the unborn infant in her uterus.

I sneak a glance at the phone in the distance. Whoever was on it has hung up. I hope they are getting us help.

"The j-journal," Wren forces out. "It's in my dresser."

"Stop talking, you'll make it worse."

"It tells you everything."

"That doesn't matter right now."

"Stop talking!" Seren screams at us, shoving the knife to my throat this time. "The next time you say a word I leave a mark." To prove her threat she holds my head still and pushes the blade against my skin until droplets of blood fall onto the floor below. Wren watches in horror and I bite my lip to keep from crying. "So are you going to open your mouth again?" She taunts.

"N-no." The blade presses in further and I can't help but cry out.

"You're not a very good listener Selina."

Then everything seems to move in slow motion as Wren pulls the knife from his torso and stabs Seren in the lower leg. She doesn't drop the knife but she pulls it far enough away for me to slip out of her grasp. I go to Wren's side as blood oozes from his wound faster than I can keep track of. I put pressure on it to help it stop but it doesn't do much.

"Why would you do that, you idiot!" The tears are falling faster now, blurring my vision. I swipe them away vigorously.

"She was h-hurting you."

He smiles and pats around his stomach until he finds my hand. He squeezes tightly for a moment before he closes his eyes and lets his muscles relax.

"Wren?" I shake him, hoping he'll reach consciousness again. "Wren?!" I press my ear to his chest. His heartbeat is faint, practically gone.

My body shakes from the pain, blood and adrenaline. My hands don't feel like my own and it overwhelms me as I attempt to wipe them off on my clothes, which only sends me further into hysterics when the dampness soaks through the fabric to my skin. I hyperventilate until the world around me spins and goes on mute. I can't think or focus on anything other than Wren's lifeless face in front of me and the blood that was once inside of him now all over me.

Someone yells my name in the distance. My second name, not the first. I could get up and run to them for help if my legs felt like working but they don't. I hear my name for a second time but my bones still feel like noodles. I'll wait it out until whoever it is finds me. For now, I curl up into a ball and rock myself in an attempt to self-soothe.

Eventually, someone kicks the door in but only after a cold foreign object pierces my skin, burying itself into my flesh.

Chapter Twenty-Six

I'm arguing with someone. I don't know who or what it's about. We're young though and in a shared bedroom wearing pajamas. The other girl slaps me in the face and to retaliate, I push her.

Two older figures come in. The woman pulls the girl out while the man stays to comfort me. He strokes my hair and I can almost hear the words he whispers to me.

There are boxes all around me now. One half of the room from before stays intact while the other is packed away. Somebody helps me carry the boxes down the hall, the boy, I can see his face now. It's Wren.

Now we're sitting on a couch, kissing. In the background a movie plays. We've gotten to my favorite scene so I push him away to intently watch the next few minutes, commenting on a detail that I've brought up a million times. He says something and then teases me by kneeling on the hardwood floor as if he were proposing. At the last second he fixes his pant leg and I tackle him to the ground, laughing as his lips kiss my neck over and over again.

Chapter Twenty-Seven
Tuesday, April 4th

Something is clamped onto my pointer finger and a rhythmic beep echoes throughout the room. The lights are dimmed. A needle is in my right, non-damaged, hand and the cord attached to it connects to a saline drip. My other hand has a brace on it that wraps around three of my fingers and goes up to my wrist. A tube is also stuck down my throat and once I become aware of its existence I start gagging, choking on the plastic.

The noise must alert a nearby nurse because a button on the outside of the room is pushed and the mechanical doors slide open. Somebody rushes inside, calling for a doctor as she checks my stats on a screen. She tells me to relax and disconnects the drip for a moment to insert something else into the tube connected to my wrist. I try to fight the drowsiness that comes over me instantly like a tidal wave but the anesthetic surrounds my blood and overtakes me.

The tube previously in my throat is gone now but the brace on my left hand stays. Miles is here now. He's talking to a doctor on the other side of the door. I've been observing them for a while. They don't realize that I am awake.

After the doctor leaves the police also approach Miles.

I watch this interaction too. The clock on the wall ticks, officially making it eight am as he shakes both of their hands and steps into my room.

Once Miles sees that I am awake he summons a doctor and comes over to my side. I reach out for him and swallow to force bile through my mouth, coating it so that it becomes easier to speak. He laces his fingers through mine.

"W-wren?"

His face falls. It tells me everything that I need to know. "The police will talk to you about that soon but let's worry about you right now, okay?"

I don't want to worry about me right now. I want to know where Seren is and tell them what she did to me and Wren. But I don't have the strength to protest or scream so I stay silent. Miles squeezes my hand, letting it go only when the doctor comes in.

He shows me x-rays of my hand that display three fractured fingers and informs me that I will need to keep a brace on at all times for the next few weeks. He then shows Miles how to take care of the stab wound on my back, notifying him that the dressing has to be changed at least once a day. Luckily the knife avoided any major organs or arteries. He then goes through a standard check-up- listening to my heartbeat, shining a light into my mouth, taking my blood pressure, etc. Before leaving to ruin or save the life of his next patient he gives me extra pain medication, wishes me a full recovery and instructs his staff to move me out of the ICU.

I ask Miles for the date as the staff rolls me into the elevator. He holds onto the railing of my bed as if his life depends on it and tells me that it is Tuesday. I accept this answer but it leaves me with even more untamed resentment than I had before as I have now lost almost two more days of my life on top of the years of memories Seren has already stolen from me.

The elevator opens to reveal a glass hallway connecting two halves of the hospital. The staff start to push me across as I notice a large industrial dock in the distance with a ship next to it, similar to the one I woke up on, in fact it might very well be the same one. I'm tempted to ask if we can stop so that I can continue inspecting my suspicions but just as I open my mouth the cityscape is replaced with a white hallway once more.

"We're in Croyden," Miles leans down to confirm to me.

I am wheeled into a new room on the sixth floor of the hospital. My new room is similar to my last except instead of a large sliding glass door there is a smaller wooden one that provides more privacy. I also now have a connected bathroom.

The nurses that transported me re-fluff my pillows and turn the television on before leaving. I turn it off the second they exit. Miles tries to fill the space by telling me that the police will be back in a few hours to take my statement and give an update. I can't wait that long for answers though.

I look to the window, shielding my face from Miles. "Is he dead?" My throat is dry and my stomach holds nothing but air and regret. My body already knows the answer. I just need to hear the confirmation.

"Like I said, the police will be here soon to explain everything."

I slam my fist on the tray table next to me. "Yes or no?!"

The clock ticks, the lights hum, the monitor beeps and the people outside the window go on with their lives. But not Wren because Miles says yes and time is no longer measured by the round device on the wall but instead by the number of sobs that rack my body uncontrollably, growing greater and gradually more intense. I don't bother hiding the grief. I let it take me, neglecting the pain that builds in my ribcage from the spasms of my panic attack.

Miles climbs onto the bed and pulls me into his chest, stroking my hair in an attempt at soothing. I hold onto his arms for support, accidentally digging my nails into his skin in fear that he will leave too. I cry for Wren and I cry for a past me that had her life stolen. I go on like this until my voice begins to go and my muscles become tired of the tension they hold. I release the built up heartache and give way to sleep, still wrapped in Miles's makeshift security blanket.

I stare at the ceiling to keep busy, pretending I'm a small fly trying to find a way out. The windows and doors are closed so those won't work. The vents might.

A young nurse interrupts my make believe by announcing the arrival of two police officers, one man and one woman. They both introduce themselves but their names slip in one ear and out the other. The nurse leaves then and the man shuts the door behind her. I'm not sure where Miles ran off to but I wish he would come back already.

Both officers shake my hand. I try to sit up so as to not appear as weak as I feel but my effort backfires when an excruciating pain shoots up my spine. Upon witnessing my struggle the woman cop comes to my side and uses the remote on the frame to raise the bed for me. I thank her and begin to give my statement, starting from the day I met Wren and working my way up to when I passed out two days ago. Once I finish they ask why we were at his apartment in the first place. I provide the reasoning by informing them that he was grabbing something to give to me. They then inquire about what that item was, which is when I recall Wren whispering something about a journal in a dresser. They make note of it.

Miles comes back from wherever the hell he was just as we wrap up. He politely introduces himself as my Rebirth counselor, apologizing for not being here sooner, and takes a seat in the plastic chair next to me. I forgive him for his absence once he explains that he was checking up on Bear and grabbing me clothes from home.

Before the officers can leave I plead to know what happened to Seren. I'm indifferent on how to feel about her now that I know that we are siblings. I want to hate her for everything that she has done but a part of me can not put this to rest until I know my part in the story. Did I ever egg her on to act out of jealousy? Or maybe our parents set us up to compete with each other from an early age.

The female officer explains that Seren was hospitalized after the incident to check on the fetus and treat the wound in her leg, the one that I inflicted upon her in an act of self defense. She then goes on to inform me that the injury is mild and that she was brought into court for arraignment on the same day. The judge put her on house arrest with constant surveillance until the trial starts on Friday. I am unsure of how to reply to this news so I nod and thank the officers for their time and information.

They are halfway out the door when the man turns back around, "By the way I wouldn't worry too much about the outcome of your court case with your sister considering your counselor here recorded most of her confession."

I look at Miles. He avoids my eyes. It was him that I had accidentally called. "I tried to stay on for as long as I could once I clocked what was going on but I had to hang up eventually to call for an ambulance," he explains.

I grab for his hand. He willingly obliges despite the officer's presence in the room. "Thank you," I whisper. He gives a weak but affirmative smile in response. Then I let go and turn my attention back to the others. "Did she plead guilty?"

"She should've," he scoffs. "Her lawyer is trying to claim temporary insanity because of her pregnancy hormones."

My jaw tenses at this news. "That's insane! I mean after everything she won't even take accountability for her actions?!"

"On the bright side her chances of winning are practically zero."

I turn away from the two of them and look to the window, hoping that it will provide me with some sort of solace. "There is no bright side."

My fists clench and my heart picks up speed, aiding

my rage by pushing angry blood throughout my veins. My sister stole my identity, rid me of everything that made me who I was, killed my ex-boyfriend and then tried to kill me. How can there ever be any good found from that?

Miles pipes in once he notices the switch in my body language and ushers the two of them out, making sure to thank them for their time once more before closing the door. He comes back over to me once they're gone and runs his hands along my arms until my muscles relax and my body gives way to his touch. Once he gauges that I am okay enough he takes a seat in the chair across from me and starts to update me on where everything is in terms of my relationship with Rebirth.

"The company is providing you with a lawyer for your case against Seren, all expenses paid of course. You'll meet with her soon to go over everything you need to know for court in a few days. And in regard to the negligent part that Rebirth played in what happened to you, they hope to settle. The amount is unknown as of this current moment but your lawyer will have more information on that for you."

"And what about you?"

He seems momentarily stunned that I have asked about him. "Well even though you were never meant to be a patient of this company my superiors think that it would be best to continue following through with our arrangement, at least until a verdict is reached in court. They want me to help you heal and guide you on where you could go from here. But if you want some alone time at any point just say so and I'll be out of your hair so long as I don't deem you a danger to yourself or others."

"The last thing I want to be right now is alone," I confess.

"Okay. Why don't we do something then to get your mind off of everything that's going on?"

"Like what?"

He puts the knuckle of his pointer finger to his lips as he thinks. I can tell when he has successfully come up with something when his eyes light up and his lips press together. Without saying anything he runs out of the room to talk to one of the nurses at the desk across the hall. She searches around the space and in some of the drawers for something and when she finds what she's looking for she hands it over to him. I'm too far away to see what it is and he shields it from my sight when he comes back. I start to become impatient at the anticipation he's building and give him a look that communicates this right before he reveals his treasure, a pack of playing cards.

We play for hours, even poaching an intern during her break to join us for a bit. It does well to pass the time and distract my mind, especially when one of us teaches the other a new game or alternative rule.

I'm just about to win our rematch of cribbage for the second time when Miles gets a call from Ellie, which reminds him of the fact that he has been holding onto my cell phone. He digs it out of his bag and encourages me to call her back myself.

I hold the power button until the screen lights up and click on her contact, or at least I try to but my finger slips and instead it is Wren's name staring back at me. I immediately hang up but it is too late. My brain falls into panic mode as if I've just been jumpscared by Wren's ghost. When the call screen goes away our last sent text messages are revealed. I scan over our words with clenched teeth and sorrow. I was so cold to him right before he died. Seren had just told me that it was him who was keeping a secret from me, a secret that was not supposed to come out the way that it did, and I shut him out.

I don't delete our messages but I do decide it best to clear them out from my view and follow through with my original task, to call Ellie. She picks up on the first ring and gives her condolences before pouring her heart out to me about how my experience has changed her and the way that she plans to live her life. I appreciate her sharing the new perspective she's gained and I know that her intentions are good but the execution leaves a sour taste in my mouth. The only thing that makes up for it is the fact that she has vowed to take care of Bear while I'm away. I thank her for doing so and shortly after fake the arrival of my doctor to get off the phone.

When I finally hang up I feel spent and it must be obvious because Miles suggests going for a walk to the cafeteria to try to rejuvenate my spirit. I agree because he seems so optimistic about this plan working but I make it clear that I will not be using another wheelchair.

Miles helps me to stand, put on a robe and get into a pair of slippers before guiding me out of the room. We walk around a bit for practice, my IV bag trailing along with me, before entering the elevator and descending to the first floor where Miles says the cafeteria is.

The doors open and we're let out directly across from the cafe. Upon entering the open room I sit down at the closest table and discreetly massage the muscles in my legs. Miles asks me what I would like from the menu. I tell him to pick something that he thinks I'll enjoy. Then he goes off to order and waits by the pickup area until the food is finished. When he comes back he places a bowl of soup in front of me and opens a package of chips for himself.

"I'll pay you back," I promise.

"No, don't worry about it. All of your expenses are covered by Rebirth until the settlement goes through."

"Oh, really?"

I raise my eyebrows and grin mischievously at Miles before sending him back up to the counter with a list of demands. He comes back carrying a tray covered in all flavors of pudding, cake, and jello. On the side are even two variations of brownies, one with hot fudge and sprinkles drizzled on top and the other with nuts baked within it. The aroma and sight of all the different desserts turn people's heads and even though I haven't started my meal yet I push it away to make room for the actual main course.

We both sample a small bite of each item before setting up a rating system that will create a fair balance for who gets the rest of what. My top choice is the lemon meringue cake, Miles's is the vanilla pudding. Our second choices are the same though, the green jello, so I pull the trauma card and he lets me have it without complaints.

By the time we sort through the last four options we're both full so we auction off the last of the desserts to the mediocre crowd in the dining hall with a mock bid session. Everyone involved seems to get a kick out of it, especially the exhausted mother with three kids who gets the majority of our primarily untouched leftovers. The children fight over who gets what as we hand off our last piece of cake to an elderly woman.

"Do you want to go outside?" Miles suggests just as I was beginning to think that we would have to go back to the room now.

"I would love to."

The sun paints my face with light as I walk through the door that Miles holds open for me. Shrubs and perfectly cut bushes line a stone walkway and a fountain sits in the middle of the arboretum area with a few benches surrounding it. They all have memorial plaques on the top of the backrests.

We travel to the middle of the garden and sit on one of the benches, this one dedicated to Mr. and Mrs.Capachae. I push the intrusive wonder of how these people died out of my mind and close my eyes, tilting my head up to the sky to listen intently to the birds feeding on something in the nearby trees.

"May I ask a question?" Miles requests, disrupting my peace.

"Of course."

"Would you prefer for me to refer to you as Selina or Emily?"

I take a moment to think and consult the sky for an

answer. When I look back at Miles I have to squint. He sits with his back to the sun, an angelic halo forming around him in result.

"Well, on one hand Emily is the name that my wicked sister has gifted to me but on the other hand I have no idea who Selina is. She's practically dead now or at most a stranger because anything that made me her is unknown to me, except for the occasional flashbacks."

"So you prefer to still be called Emily?"

"It's impossible for me to go back to being who I once was so despite the dark history of my name I am going to have to say yes."

He nods, accepting my answer respectfully. "It's odd that she kept your surname the same. She never mentioned that she had the same one?"

"No, it never came up. Although I do recall her putting the name 'Greer' on her audition form which must be a middle name or something."

Miles considers this possibility, the thinking evident across his face. I wonder how he now sees me behind the opal-like shine of his eyes. Is it any different than before now that the mystery of who I am is gone?

"Today kinda reminds me of the first day that we met," Miles acknowledges. "You're starting new again, in a way, except this time we're viewing a different atmosphere of nature and you know a lot more now about who you are."

"Plus my legs work," I add.

"This is true." The laugh that follows his commentary cures my every worry more than any medicine ever could.

I feel moved to lay my head on his shoulder and without a second thought I do so. His chest hitches, drawing in a sharp intake of air as my ear makes contact with his shirt. Then his breathing resumes its normal cadence. The change is so slight and quick that the EKG machine back in the room might not have even picked it up but I did.

Eventually he too leans his head over to rest on mine and I swear our breath aligns. But then I think too much about

it and we fall out of rhythm.
    "We can start again too."

Chapter Twenty-Eight
Wednesday, April 5th

In the early hours of the morning when sleep does not come I do something stupid. I take the pulse oximeter off of my finger, grab my phone and tiptoe past Miles, somehow asleep on the tiny couch next to me.

When I make it to the bathroom I lock myself inside, turning the dial ploddingly to make the least amount of noise. Then I call Wren. I know that he will never pick up or hear my message but I just need to talk to him in a way.

The dial tone rings out over and over again, echoing against the empty hospital walls. I press the base of the phone against my stomach in an attempt to quiet the noise. Then the automated message plays followed by the beep of the recorder. I try to compose myself as best I can but I can tell that my voice is about to start shaking because my hand grips the phone and my skin starts to turn red as a result.

"Hi, Wren."

I was right, my voice is shaky. I hang up. Calling is pointless. I won't hear his voice telling me that the past few days have all just been some scary nightmare. This is real.

I wish that I had more pieces of my life from before, to remember him better. My heart and body mourn him appropriately, aching as if a vital organ has been ripped from me and now I must relearn how to live without it. My head however can't seem to figure out exactly why I am taking his death as hard as I am since I only have access to the memories of us from the past few weeks to go off of. But we lived a whole life before. We grew up together, went through pivotal growing moments with each other, probably had the same friends. Once upon a time our lives were heavily intersected.

Maybe I could invoke more memories in some way but I'm not sure how to. They have just come to me so far. I wish that I had confided in Wren about them. Maybe he would have told me about everything sooner and then we wouldn't be where we are.

I feel an onslaught of panic the more my brain plays the what if game so I try to clear my head and take some deep breaths. My efforts prove to be fruitless though and my thoughts only build upon each other brick by brick until I have become a large wall of terror and dread. I can't hold it back anymore. I let the panic come, curling my knees to my chest and hyperventilating, dropping the phone to the floor in the process. I claw at the ground for support but everything around me spins anyway. My vision is then further incapacitated by the tears that start to sting the corners of my eyes.

I must be making a great deal of noise because I have woken up Miles who now bangs on the door, threatening to kick it in if I don't open it immediately. So with my good hand I reach up to undo the lock while maintaining my seated position on the cold tiled floor. He bursts in as if he was about to ram into the door anyway and the second he comes in I am wrapped in a hug. I grab onto his arms and breathe in the smell of him. It somewhat helps bring me out of my psychosis but not entirely.

"Let's get you back to bed."

He picks me up like a bride on her wedding night and carries me back to the bed. I wrap my arms around his neck and lay my head on his chest. He sets me down on the left side and lays behind me, pulling the covers up to my chin and tucking the edges of the thin blanket underneath us. His hands then run up and down my right arm to further soothe me and gradually my cries turn to sniffles and the sniffles into light snores.

Miles holds off my visitors until the early afternoon, allowing me to sleep in and take some time for myself. I've been warned of and have approved my upcoming itinerary of guests for the day starting heavy with Wren's parents.

Miles has briefed me on the basics that I should know but don't anymore. I soak up every detail, highly interested in the man who was still such a stranger in many ways.

Wren is adopted, with one parent from Altone and the other from Aelville. The couple were best friends with his biological mom who they met in university. She passed away due to complications in childbirth and never disclosed who the father was nor did she ever want anybody to know. Wren's maternal grandparents would have taken the child but were awfully poor and could not give Wren the life he deserved so they agreed to have visitation rights and signed over full custody to Wren's parents instead. Miles also claims that they cared for me and highly approved of our relationship which puts at least some of my nerves at ease.

I'm having an internal battle on what outfit to choose for the day when a nurse walks in to change the bandage on my back. I let her work in silence at first but then get curious and ask if she's heard anything about my situation or upcoming trial. She hasn't, which tells me that Rebirth is doing a good job to keep this scandal under wraps. If they didn't then thousands of people would question the credibility of the business. It also brings into question if this has ever happened before without the general public knowing.

"I like the white sweater with the cuffed jeans," the nurse informs me as she ties my gown back up.

I thank her for the opinion before she leaves and head into the bathroom to change. When I come out Miles is sitting on the couch waiting for me. He announces that the couple is in the lobby. I tidy up the room as best I can as he goes to the lobby to escort them up.

In an attempt to look casual I sit on the couch and use the remote to turn the television on. I bring up the program for the evening and use the search bar to type in the name of the movie that Wren took me to see, the one about a girl trying to get to a city to meet up with a wizard. One hit comes up. I click on the channel and find that it's halfway through the movie already.

Miles gently knocks at the door to alert me of their presence. The heads-up gives me enough time to stand up straight and brush off my sweater. "Emily, this is Mr. and Mrs. Rivera."

I hold my hand out for them to shake but the woman takes the opportunity to run over and embrace me, fresh tears in her eyes. Her husband then follows her example. They smell of expensive perfume and cologne and Mrs. Rivera's pearls dig into my shoulder. I stay stiff as the hug goes on, unsure of where to put my hands. Eventually they pull back.

"It's so nice to see you again dear," Mrs. Rivera greets as she holds onto my arm.

Her smile is wide and makes the creases around her eyes more profound. She must have lived a happy life. Her hair is pulled back and her skirt and tights are perfectly pressed to her body. Mr. Rivera on the other hand has a more disheveled look. His tie is loose and one of his shoes is untied. Neither of them look like Wren, which I shouldn't have expected since he's adopted but a part of me hoped that maybe they still resembled him anyway.

"She changed so much of you," Mr. Rivera whispers regretfully. His wife gives him a warning look. Based on Seren's features I have a good understanding of what has been changed but I want to see what he has noticed so I ask. "Well, for starters your eyes used to be a deep brown instead of gray and you always had these beautiful, natural, black curls ever since we've known you and when you were a child you refused to let anyone cut it so at one point your hair was to your waist." He smiles at the memory.

I run my fingers through my hair until the top of my chest where it falls from my hands. I see a glimpse of the light brown color. It has grown a bit in the month or so since it was chopped to my shoulders but it's still nowhere near as long as he's describing it to have been.

The eye detail catches me off guard though. The ability to permanently change the color of an eye is terrifying yet fascinating. It leads me to wonder if it could be undone.

"What else?" I find myself asking.

"Your face structure," Mrs. Rivera chimes in with. "Your nose used to be less upturned and your lips more full,"

I suddenly feel out of place despite having asked for this information. I've never cared much for my looks in this life so I'm not sure why I do now. I sit back on the couch, defeated.

"Would you like some space?" Miles asks, jumping to the rescue. He's on edge, ready to round up the couple for me if need be.

"It's okay. I want to hear this. No, I need to hear this." He backs up. I continue with my questions, "What was I like? My personality, I mean."

Mrs. Rivera comes to sit next to me. She lays a hand on my leg. "You my dear were incredibly driven and headstrong. Wren loved that about you and so did we."

"What else?" I need more.

"You had a comfortable upbringing and many friends growing up."

"Do they ever wonder about me?"

"They do," Mr. Rivera adds as he sits on my opposite side. "Or at least from what I hear. If you want I can give you their names, the ones I can remember at least. I'm sure that they would love to hear from you."

I smile at him. "Yes please." And then a more solemn question comes to mind. "Are my parents really dead by the way? Seren mentioned that they are but I was hoping that maybe she had lied about that to get a rise out of me."

"Sadly she was telling the truth about that."

"Oh, okay."

Mrs. Rivera looks up and blinks an excessive amount to keep the water in her eyes from spilling over and taking the makeup off of her lashes. "I think that I might need a slight distraction for a minute." She searches for something else in the room to discuss when her eyes find the television, I can tell by the way the pixels reflect back in her corneas. "I love this movie."

I turn my head to look where she is. "It's the last thing I watched with Wren, one of the only things I've watched in this life actually."

"He showed you this movie?"

"Yeah, why?"

"It was your favorite and even the theme of your sixteenth birthday party. You and Wren made homemade party hats and food for the occasion."

Mrs. Rivera pulls out a small video camera from her bag as proof. She plays one of the videos and points me out as the one in the middle wearing a sparkly blue dress. People sing to me and when they're done I blow out the candles on the cake in front of me, everyone claps. The couple directly behind my chair smiles down on me before wrapping me in a group hug. Their love for both me and each other is radiant.

The second the clip is over I ask to watch it again. We do and this time I pause the twenty second treasure each time a new face comes into frame and ask for information on each individual. We get through half of the people when I notice that one of the girls sitting down in the corner is Seren with a scowl on her face.

"Why is no one celebrating her? It's her birthday too."

Mrs. Rivera sighs. "From what I remember she was very upset that the two of you had to have a joint party and had such a temper tantrum about it. You came over that day right after fighting with her, crying about how she left the house. A few days later she came back, bragging about how she spent the weekend getting drunk at college parties and sleeping on the floor of random dormitories three hours away so as punishment your parents didn't let her participate in the party at all which I found to be rather fair. She's always had such destructive behavior that girl I just never thought that she would go this far."

I put a comforting hand on her shoulder and give her a second to work through her emotions before picking back up with the crash course of my family members. She gladly accepts the distraction and continues providing me with descriptions of my aunts and uncles, cousins, and friends. Once we tire out this activity the three of us then watch the rest of the movie on the couch together until the credits roll.

Miles must have slipped out of the room at some point during our reunion. I don't notice this until he pops back in to announce the arrival of more guests and ask me for a ballpark estimate of when they can come in so that he can relay my answer back to them.

"We should probably head out now anyway," Mr. Rivera announces just as I'm about to ask for a few more minutes with them. Mrs. Rivera agrees with her husband.

"It was nice meeting you, or seeing you again I guess."

"Yes you too dear."

The two of them take turns saying goodbye to me. My interaction with Mr. Rivera is brief. Mrs. Rivera on the other hand stalls by fixing my hair and wishing me well more than once. I finally think she's about to head out when her face lights up with remembrance. Wordlessly she digs around in her purse until she pulls out an envelope to give to me. I make sure to thank the two of them for everything- the insight they've provided, the truth, the video and whatever it is that I have just been handed.

"Anytime," she whispers into my ear as she pulls me back into another hug. "I'm Jia by the way and my husband's name is Amaro. It completely slipped my mind to re-introduce ourselves until just now."

"What beautiful names," I compliment as she pulls away.

"Thank you."

They each say one last goodbye before leaving with Miles for the lobby and it isn't until after they're long gone that I remember what Jia gave to me. I open the envelope meticulously and pull out an invitation for Wren's funeral. It's on Sunday in Alnerwick. I can't go. I will likely have to be here for court and I'm not sure if I could even afford the flight.

I sit back on the couch as the next movie starts up on the television. I don't have long before more people occupy my hospital room so I take the time to myself to go over everything that I have learned from Jia and Amaro's visit. I do so by reciting the information of my cousins, aunts, and uncles under my breath until Miles knocks on my door again.

I get up to answer this time and upon doing so discover Bianca, James, Ellie, Angie, and of course, Miles balancing a massive sheet cake in their hands. They all yell some sort of greeting as I let them in. The cake is set on the one small tray table connected to my bed, the ends hang off but it is balanced enough so that it doesn't fall. I don't know what it is about these people giving me cakes when I'm injured but if it continues this way I might gain a few extra pounds.

The mood in the room is a mix of somber, confusion and relief. There's no writing on the cake and the scene I picture in my head of a disagreement ensuing between the group about what to write almost makes me laugh. 'We're sorry that your sister took all your memories, literally stabbed you in the back and killed your ex boyfriend.'

Thankfully we get through the process of cutting and distributing the dessert without anyone bringing up the subject of Wren or Seren and I would like to keep it that way. Instead we simply catch up as a group and celebrate my, so far, well recovery. The only mention of them is when I announce that the show will be temporarily suspended until further notice. Everyone agrees with this decision.

After an hour or so the chatter has dimmed and a third of the cake is gone. Slowly my guests begin to head for home,

Bianca and James first and then Angie to bring the car around. Miles and Ellie stay back with me and put themselves on clean-up duty. He's almost done collecting the plates to toss in the trash when he gets a phone call though and steps out into the hallway to take it.

"How are you doing?" Ellie asks, taking advantage of our alone time. She sits by my side on the bed.

"As best I can be for someone in my situation I guess."

She looks to the open door where Miles is engrossed in what must be a frustrating call judging by his body language. "We should talk."

"What about?"

"Miles. He's your counselor, how long have you had feelings for him?"

I'm caught off guard by this confrontation and at first I try to deny it but she gives me a look and I give in. "I'm not sure."

This is a lie. I know exactly when. It was the night he took me to the bottom of the ship to see the ocean and told me about the wildlife he knew of. I know it is or was him just doing his job by trying to make me feel comfortable and getting me to trust him but my mind took his kindness and his heart and lusted after it, especially the more he hung around. I would never share this though because I know how pathetic it must seem. I take that back, I know how pathetic it is. I am just glad that he has at least somewhat similar feelings to mine because at least I haven't been delusional alone.

"Have you acted on your feelings?" I leave room for silence, allowing her to fill in the blank. "Emily, what did you do?"

I sort out a quick timeline of events in my head before reviewing at rapid-fire speed. "Well at first there was almost a kiss but then there wasn't. That's when we decided to just forget everything and I was going to throw all of my efforts into trying to build something with Wren. It was a perfect distraction and worked until it didn't because it wasn't long before we were right back where we started, only worse because we did end up kissing this time and Seren almost saw but I guess she didn't. And that's when she told me that someone was hiding a secret from me aka this whole mess."

Ellie takes it all in, thinking over everything that I have just said. She goes to speak but clamps her mouth back shut and looks to the door. I follow her gaze to see Miles putting his phone in his pocket and walking back into the room, ceasing any further discussion on the topic.

Chapter Twenty-Nine
Thursday, April 6th

I wake with the sun and roll onto my opposite side, pulling the thin covers over my head to block out the light slipping underneath the shade. Before the blanket goes over my nose though I see Miles asleep on the couch. I can't help but feel at ease.

Ellie and I continued our conversation from yesterday over the phone most of the night while Miles was off doing something somewhere in town, I didn't ask. We discussed ethics and went over what would happen if it came out that we have had some sort of relationship and we came to the conclusion that what Miles told me behind the pub is true. He would be fired, sued and likely have to pay a large fine for breach of contract. He could also go to jail. After doing the research though I realized that that part is not as likely thank god. Plus everything has changed now. I might no longer be his patient.

Rebirth has appointed me a personal attorney free of cost, due to their error, that Miles has been in close contact with since the incident. I am supposed to meet with her tomorrow to go over everything about the trial and how it will work as well as reaching an agreement about any further compensation from the company for their mistake.

An alarm goes off. It gets snoozed. Miles groans,

there's a shuffling of feet and then I hear the bathroom door shut. When he comes out I pretend to be asleep. He "rouses" me by pulling the blanket out of my hands ever so slightly and brushing hair off of my forehead, tucking it behind my ear. I mumble a measly good morning so that he knows I am awake.

"Tabitha will be here shortly," he announces. "I'll stay until she gets here but then I plan to head out and make sure that our hotel room is all set for when you are discharged."

I agree to this plan and take my time sitting up to add to the illusion that I have just awoken. He turns on the light and gathers up his belongings as I pick out an outfit and head into the bathroom to change.

"Sorry that I couldn't make it here before today," Tabitha apologizes as she settles onto the couch in my room.

"That's alright."

"With you gone there's just been me again and It seems that I have forgotten how to function without your help. You've made me soft."

"I should be back to work soon," I reassure her.

"That is lovely news but please don't rush your recovery." I promise her that I won't. "Oh, here you are by the way."

Tabitha hands me a basket with a blue ribbon tied on the handle. I pull it closer to look inside. There's strawberry jam and blueberry jelly with wooden spoons taped to the jars, a red knitted scarf identical to the one she's currently wearing, and small candies inside.

"How thoughtful, thank you."

"You deserve every bit of kindness given to you, especially with what you have had to endure." She pauses, clearly thinking of how to word what she is about to say next. "When I met you a little over a month ago you were re-learning how to walk again, completely unsure of who you are and now you have flourished into someone inspiring and worthy of admiration. I have seen you persevere before and I know that you can do it again."

Her words feel like a mother giving praise to her daughter and the thought of that invokes deep emotions to stir within me. "Thank you, Tabitha."

She puts her hand on my cheek soothingly and offers me a warm smile. When she pulls her away the corners of her mouth drop. Something is wrong.

"I know that you are still recovering my dear but I must ask for your help."

"Of course, what do you need?"

"I am in search of some of your brilliant ideas as the town has been cutting the funds down the past few months for the library and I remember how much traffic your last event generated."

I perk up at the mention of my plans and relay out all of my ideas to Tabitha starting off with the postponed play I plan on showcasing at the library. She officially agrees to this and we go on to discuss having annual Sunday storytelling days for children with guest readers and snacks as well as partnering up with the Cresthill School to host a Summer Reading Camp where each day of the week is themed after a different children's book.

"We can even do an adult version too!" I exclaim suddenly as the doctor walks in.

He hands me a clipboard with discharge paperwork and follows up once more on my care plan, making sure that I understand each extensive step on how to take care of my hand and back. When he leaves I skim through the numerous pages that I have to sign.

Tabitha helps me to pack and while doing so insists that I tell the world about what happened to me. "It's important for people to hear your story," she claims. This sticks with me long after she leaves and the paperwork has been filed. Her words fill me with an itching urge to create and add on to my writing.

The nurse that's been taking care of me the past few days comes to check on me one last time before I leave. She changes the dressing on my back and hands me a sheet of care instructions for extra measure. I make sure to thank her.

"Ready?" Miles asks, standing in the doorway with my duffle bag.

"Absolutely."

Rebirth has booked us two adjoining rooms at a luxurious hotel in the center of Croyden. Our rooms have mini kitchens, large bathrooms, open balconies, and king-sized beds.

Once we get settled in, the first thing that I do is shower the smell of hospital off of me. I try to wash my hair too but the pressure of the shower head stings my wound and almost soaks the bandage on my back so once I'm done with my body I wrap myself in a towel, plug the drain in the sink and improvise.

By the time I get out my stomach is begging for food. I quickly put on brown pants and one of the patterned sweaters in my bag before knocking on the door that connects our two rooms to discuss the topic of going out.

He comes in and when I suggest going to his parent's restaurant he immediately shoots the idea down. I play the pity card as I remove the towel wrapped around my head. My slightly tangled hair falls and I begin to brush it while he re-thinks. It could just be my imagination but I swear my hair is curlier than it usually is when I get out of the shower. Eventually Miles gives in and I silently celebrate my victory.

My hair is still damp by the time we get into a line that goes around the corner of the building. The air is chilly and makes my teeth chatter, even with the sweater. The sun peeks out between buildings and behind clouds now and again but not often enough to provide warmth.

"Are you sure that you want to wait?" Miles asks after two minutes of looking from me to his watch.

226

"I don't mind." This is not the answer that he wanted.

We wait in silence, moving forth with the line ever so slowly once tables open up. Some pairings or families walk right in to take their reservations, my stomach is most jealous of them.

After twenty minutes we make it under the awning at the front and after thirty we get inside. Heat surrounds us the second that the door opens, warming up any exposed skin. We stand for a few minutes longer until the host spots Miles, which is made known by the shocked look on his face and the quick phone call that he places. We're only two parties away now but any advancement forward would greatly benefit me and my ever-growing hunger.

Once he gets off of the phone the man informs us to step out of line. Miles's mom makes her way over to us shortly after we do so. She has flour on her cheek and a drop of something red on her blouse but other than that she is the epitome of perfection. She hugs Miles first of course but then greets me as well by grabbing my hands and giving them a light squeeze.

"Thank you for bringing him home," she whispers.

She drops my hands and heads back to the host's station to grab menus before showing us to a private table in a back room. We're not the only ones around but we sure are separated from everyone else. Miles's mother places the menus in front of us on the tabletop. He doesn't bother to open it.

"I'm going to get my husband but in the meantime would you two like anything to drink besides water?" We both decline and she disappears into the crowd. A waitress comes over right after to give us our water.

"How long has it been since you've been here?" I ask, twirling my straw around the glass.

"A year or so."

"Why?"

Any hope I have of getting an answer though is squashed when his mom comes back over, accompanied by

his dad. The disbelief on his face turns to shock. Miles stands
to greet his father, it starts with a simple handshake and then
he gets pulled into a hug. They both smile upon contact.
He greets me as well, the same way his wife did but with
increased care once he notices the cast.

"If you have some time, do you want to join us?" I
offer.

His mom hesitates for a moment and Miles seems
taken off guard. His father on the other hand does not hesitate
to grab two nearby chairs and make space at our table for
them.

When the waitress comes back again she asks us what
appetizers or meals we would like to order. Miles and I give
our answer but his parents just wave the question away. She
leaves us then to sit in our silence. I make it my mission to
break it.

"So how long have you two owned this place?"

"Well I helped my parents to renovate the restaurant
when I was young after the second world war but they
officially passed it down to me when they retired about fifteen
years ago. I was just a child but I would come here every day
after school to help clean up the debris from past warfare,"
Mr. Hartman narrates.

"Wow, what a beautiful story."

"Thank you. Is there anything that you are passionate
about?"

"I like to write and I've recently found a love for
directing. Your son is actually in the show I'm working on
right now." I bump my shoulder lightly into his.

"Is that so? When and where will it be taking place?
My wife and I would love to see it." She nods along in
pleasant agreement.

"It's actually on a temporary hold right now because
we just lost a cast member," Miles jumps in to say.

"Oh, I'm sorry to hear that. I hate when someone quits
halfway through a project, it's so very selfish of them," Mrs.
Hartman says. I wince and look at Miles. We share a look of

unspoken agreement to just go along with this version of the story so that we don't have to explain the real one. "How did you hurt your arm?"

"Horseback riding," I lie.

From here on out Miles and I do a good job of keeping his parents talking, neither of us in the mood any longer to discuss our own lives. Eventually, food is brought to our table and his parents dismiss themselves to go back to work.

Miles ordered a lemon chicken concoction and I ordered a truffle sandwich with a side salad. We each devour our respective plates and then order dessert. It shows up rather quickly, a raspberry tart topped with homemade cream. I give Miles the first bite from my spoon and then finish off the rest with ease. The ability to do so makes me very glad that my broken fingers aren't on my dominant hand as that would greatly impact my dexterity and the ability to get the delectable dessert into my mouth.

Miles's parents don't let us pay the bill but he does throw a stack of cash on the table for a tip. I once again promise to pay him back and he waves me off but I really doubt that dining out is included in the expenses that Rebirth is paying for. Either way I don't push the subject any further.

We say goodbye to his parents and head the three blocks back to the hotel. On the way, Miles gives me suggestions of activities to do in the area to keep me relaxed and busy before tomorrow. He starts with the hotel amenities and once he mentions the word 'pool' I stop him and beg him to swim with me once we get back. He of course refuses and I once again pull the injury card which ends up backfiring as it only ends up reminding him that I am not allowed to swim. I then vow to stay in the shallow end though and beg until he once again gives in. Miles- 0, Emily- 2. I would feel bad about the manipulation but based on his smile I can tell that it wasn't much of a fight in the first place.

He opens one of the doors to the lobby for me and we head over to the elevator as it lets people out. We hop on now that it's empty and press the button that will take us up to the twenty-second floor. The doors close and the elevator rises. I decide to take the opportunity to debrief.

"Why haven't you visited your parents in so long?"

He stares at the numbers, watching them go up. When they don't do so fast enough he finally answers, "I was supposed to work for them and train to take over the restaurant in a few years but I couldn't."

"Why not?"

"Because I was an idiot and a coward. I didn't want to ruin what my grandparents built and what my parents turned it into."

"So you left?"

"No, I just never showed up. I got a job with Rebirth which gave me the perfect excuse to run and stay away. I would still visit at first but every time I did I would feel more and more guilty about it so then I just stopped. It was cruel luck that you happened to pick somewhere so close to my home."

"Seren did that, not me," I remind him.

He cringes when he realizes his mistake. "Right, sorry."

The elevator opens. Neither of us move. "Well for the record I don't think that it's possible for you to fuck it up. It's like you have a superpower to just naturally fix everything and somebody like that can't possibly do what you're so worried about."

The elevator doors go to close, not sensing any movement. He puts his hand between the metal, holding it open. "I appreciate that."

He gestures for me to pass and once I do he follows after me. The elevator closes and we each go to our respective rooms to change. When I search my bag I come across a single bathing suit, a blue and white one-piece with ruching at the top of the chest. I pull it on along with my sweater and wait outside Miles's room for him like we agreed upon earlier.

He must be on a phone call, I know because I can hear parts of the muffled conversation through the door. Still I wait for him to finish, eventually having to lean against the wall for support. I make sure to put the pressure on my shoulder in comparison to my back though. When he finally comes out he apologizes for leaving me waiting and we head for the pool.

It's indoors and smaller than I would have imagined but even still I kick off my sneakers, the only shoes with me at the moment, with excitement and take off my sweater. A few kids are splashing around with floaties in the shallow end and two parents are busy arguing by the vending machines.

Miles takes off his shirt and dives into the deepest section of the pool, splashing water onto my legs. It's cold and reminds me of the lake where Wren and I went canoeing.

"Are you coming in?" He calls up to me.

"Yeah."

I push memories of Wren out of my mind for the moment and try to regain my excitement by making my way to the shallow end, on the opposite side of where the kids are playing. I slowly dip my feet in first before gradually lowering the rest of my body into the water. Luckily, Miles had the good sense to stop at the front desk and ask for a plastic bag and industrial tape to wrap up my arm so that I can keep the brace on without it getting wet.

He swims over to me and as soon as his head resurfaces he splashes a handful of water at me. I cough up what got in my mouth and splash him back. We swim, or more so attempt to run through the water, attacking and defending, mimicking a joyful battlefield. At one point Miles lifts me by the waist and pulls me partially underwater with him. I would scream in pain at some of our roughhousing but I'm too busy giggling and being enamored by Miles's physical touch to call for a cease fire. He's careful though to avoid my areas of injury and stays alert for when I get too low into the water.

The kids across from us don't stay long, hurrying out with their angry parents soon after we arrive. They leave in such a rush that they forget some of their pool toys. We borrow them to play games with each other as if we are their age. Which mostly means I throw rubber sharks in random directions with my good arm while timing Miles to see how long it takes for him to get to them. It feels nice to act young and as if nothing else in the world matters except for plastic pool toys and how far they can be thrown especially when joy has been so rare lately, though never with him.

"Ready to head back?" He asks after an hour or so. "I need a shower and we need to change your bandage now that it's likely soaked." He lifts himself out of the water and onto the pool deck.

"Sure." Luckily the backing of my bathing suit has shielded the gauze and medical tape from coming free from my skin but it most certainly should get changed tonight.

I use the ladder to get up and make my way over to the chairs that we dumped our stuff onto upon arriving. Miles hands me one of the hotel towels before drying himself off with one. He ruffles it through his hair, wipes off his chest and arms and then ties it around his waist. When he looks at me I pull my gaze away and act as if I have been busy doing the same instead of staring at him. Then we head out, back to the elevator, and up to our rooms.

I take my second shower of the day to rid myself of chlorine, making sure to leave the plastic bag on until I'm done. I rub shampoo and conditioner through my tangles and use a packaged hotel razor to shave what has grown on my legs since being in the hospital. When I get out I put my hair in a clip and knock on Miles's door so that he can help me re-dress the wound on my back.

He comes over with the medical materials, setting them on the bedside table before sitting himself on the edge of the bed. I am still wrapped in a towel which he instructs me to lower. I bring the terry cloth material just below my shoulder blades which allows him to rub a cream on my back with a q-tip before taping on some gauze.

"You're all set."

He cleans up the leftover garbage, throwing out the scraps in the bathroom. Meanwhile, I drop my towel to the floor to dress in the comfortable clothes that I picked out

for myself before getting in the shower. I just barely get
my undergarments on though when Miles walks back into
the room. He closes his eyes upon seeing me and starts to
insistently apologize for the intrusion. I grab the towel from
the floor to cover myself back up as he starts to feel around
the space for the door that will bring him back to his room.
When he is unsuccessful he opens his eyes ever so slightly
and lowers his gaze to the floor.

"To your left," I help instruct.

He moves that way and bumps into the bedside table.
I can't help but laugh, he does too which causes him to
instinctively lock eyes with me. Slowly the laughing dwindles
and his pupils dilate as he steps closer to me. I follow his
lead and we move towards each other as if we're being drawn
in by a tornado, you know it's going to cause a disaster but
you can't help getting pulled in. Once there are mere inches
between us I drop my dinky towel to the floor.

We're nose to nose now. The heat of his breath coats
my skin. I want to feel what it is like to kiss him without
the fear of any onlookers so I close my eyes, giving him the
power. I made a move last time, now it is his turn, that is if
he wants to keep playing our game. I can feel him leaning
in, hesitating. I can smell the soap from his shower. And just
when I think it will never come it does. The kiss starts slowly
but rapidly builds, tumbleweeding into something more
passionate until his hand travels to my upper leg and I jump to
wrap my legs around his torso.

He climbs onto the bed that way and places me gently
below him, shedding his shirt in between kisses that stray to
my neck. Every touch between us is gentle but hungry, every
breath shallow and begging for more of each other's air.
The buildup and anticipation of each other has only left us
desperate.

His chest is more defined than I had imagined and I
hadn't realized in the pool with all of the movement but he
has a tattoo of a snake that runs from his bicep to his forearm,
wrapping around the back of his elbow. When my eyes travel

back up to his I notice him looking me over as well, taking me in in a way that he hasn't before as he grazes his hands along my sides, tickling my skin. My back raises because of it and then I seem to be frozen under his stare as if he is Medusa. He takes the opportunity to slip his fingers under the lace of my underwear, pulling them down my legs and throwing them to the floor. He takes his pants off as well and kisses his way back up my legs, alternating between both. He stops at the space between my thighs, just under my belly button, gently kissing there as well. I bite my lip and my breathing becomes more uneven.

"Is this okay?" He asks, moving back up to my neck.

"Y-yes," I force out between labored breaths.

"Did you know that you have a birthmark right here?" He asks, pointing to the bone that connects my hip to my leg. "It's shaped like a heart." He moves his finger to outline it.

"I didn't know," I confess.

He sits up to turn the lamp on the bedside table off. We can still see each other because of the partially closed curtains but most of my visibility is gone. He traces the shape of my body with his hands until they reach my chest where he stalls by playing with the strap of my bra. He continues kissing me as he tugs it down my shoulder, first the left then the right. I lift my back so that he can undo the clasp. Once he does he flings it across the room and takes in everything that was previously hidden from his view.

"Are you sure?" He asks once more.

I wrap my arms around his neck. "I want you."

The second I speak those three words into the air he pulls the blankets over us and slips off what remainder of clothing he still has on. I barely have time to process before my breath is taken away from the movement he makes. I grab onto his arms in reflex and any noise made is stifled by his hand. He reacts as well but it's much quieter.

"Shhh" he whispers into my ear as he plays with my hair.

We both melt into each other, settling into a steady

rhythm. Once I get used to the feeling he removes his hands and uses them in other ways. We go on like this for a good while until we're exhausted and fall asleep, my chest pressed against his.

When I wake it's dark outside. I feel around the sheets for Miles. He's gone.

Chapter Thirty
Friday, April 7th

The sun's not up yet but once it's a semi-respectable hour I knock on the door between our two rooms. There's no answer. I try again hoping that he is simply deep in sleep. Still no answer so I turn the handle, letting myself in, and feel around for the light switch. He's definitely not here but I check the bathroom for extra measure. Where has he gone? I figured it was just back to his room after last night.

I rush to my phone and try to call him, more than once. Each time I hear the dial tone end, asking me to leave a message, my heart cracks just a little bit more. After the fourth or fifth time my blood starts to boil. I throw the phone to the ground. This makes no sense but I have no time to mope around or let my imagination wonder about possibilities. I have to get ready to meet with my lawyer so I force myself to get up and pick one of the respectable outfits that Miles had grabbed from the house for me- tights, a long skirt and a black top. Hopefully, the darker colors will convey the message that I am trying to go for, that I am mourning the life and person stolen from me.

I input the courthouses address into my phone and follow the directions it provides for me, stopping for coffee on the way. The walk isn't long and I get to watch the sunrise between buildings.

My destination is in the center of town, across from city hall. Many people populate around the area, getting ready to start a day at work. They look like me with their modest outfits and caffeine to get them through the next eight hours.

Upon entering I sign in at the front desk. An officer directs me to a room shortly after and closes the door behind me. I am alone, but only for a moment because an older brunette woman in a pencil skirt and glasses walks out from an adjoining room holding a book in her hands. She sits on the edge of her desk and extends her hand for me to shake, introducing herself as Sussannah Warren.

"I am the attorney that Rebirth has hired to represent you and I thought that I would start out by letting you know that we are on your side and we will make this right."

I want to question her about any ulterior motives and ask if this is all actually because they want to help or if the company just want to save their own ass but I believe I already know the answer to that so instead I say nothing and she goes on to explain the agenda for today. Opening statements start at eight then we present evidence and witnesses first and following that Seren and her lawyer will do the same. Each side will also get the opportunity to cross examine any witnesses.

"Today the goal is to show the court all of the damage that Seren has done and hope that the jury makes the right choice with the evidence that they will be provided with. And once this case is settled I will then help you discuss and finalize any settlement with Rebirth," she explains. I nod so she knows that I understand.

We then go over the night of the attack so that she can cross reference the statement I made to the police and make sure that what I'm saying tracks. When we're done she shows me around the currently empty courtroom, explaining where everyone will be and their roles. Then we head back to her office where she instructs her assistant to order breakfast for us.

As we eat I ask who she plans to call to the stand. She

provides me with a list of names, some that I don't recognize. Miles is on the list though.

"What happens if someone doesn't show up today?" I dare to ask.

"Everyone on that list has been subpoenaed so if they don't show then they will be held in contempt of court which would mean they would be subject to a fine, jail sentence or both."

Well now I really hope that Miles' disappearance has to do with some fluke event that he forgot to mention.

I spot Wren's parents in the crowd and wave to them upon entering the courtroom. They wave back, Jia even blows me a kiss. When I turn away to continue walking to my spot I see Seren fuming at the interaction. It's the first time I've seen her since I blacked out. She's still pregnant as ever but now wears a fun little ankle bracelet.

Opening statements run smoothly. Sussanah has a solid argument as to why Seren should be guilty despite her pregnancy and most of the jury seem to respond more to my pity story than hers.

I am up first to take the stand. I am sworn in and told to take a seat. I tell the court my story, recalling as much as I can. Sussanah asks some follow-up questions to fill in any blanks that I had left out. I filter enough emotion into my voice to appeal to the court without losing control of myself. Unplanned tears even slip down my cheeks when I tell of Wren speaking to me for the last time. Mr. Rivera has to escort Jia out at this point. The jury takes note of it, I can tell. Seren's lawyer on the other hand has no further questions for me so I am sent back to my seat.

Sussanah then calls Miles to the stand. No one in the room comes forth. She calls for him again. This time a side door opens and he is escorted to the stand by an officer. He is not in handcuffs but I can tell that the man with him is not there for his protection. He is sworn in and sits down without making eye contact with me. I want to call to him, ask him where it is that he went and what it is that he's doing. I almost do.

"Mr. Hartman, can you recall everything that you remember about the night your client, Miss Weiss, called you?"

Miles runs through everything that he heard on the phone, why he had to hang up and how he drove to Wren's place after tracking me via an implanted Rebirth chip in the back of my neck. He then goes on to explain that it is there for extreme circumstances and how it goes inactive after a few months.

A chill runs through my body as I listen to this new information and I tenderly touch the back of my neck, feeling around for any sign of the microchip. Sure enough at the nape of my skull is a small, raised scar- still in the process of healing.

I tune back into the trial as Sussanah is giving the jury and the people of the court content warnings. I'm not sure what the warnings are for though until static fills the room and I hear my own voice crying out for someone to help. The recording is loud, as I'm sure it's intended to be. I look over to Seren's reaction, she is still scowling. If I didn't call Miles then she might have gotten away with trying to pin this on me.

The recording doesn't go on for very long but in that time you hear everything, including Seren's confession. At the end it goes silent and cuts out. I know what would have come next though, his death.

Memories flash back to me stronger than ever and not just of that night but of every night with Wren. Every outing, makeout, and memorable time of our lives together comes back to me. I am remembering a million moments at once and they won't slow or stop. They run through my mind, fighting for attention, throughout the cross-examination making it hard to focus and it isn't until Sussanah calls for a quick recess that I notice Miles leaving the room.

"Where did he go?" I ask Sussanah as she goes through

her belongings. "I need to speak with him."

"That is not possible at the moment."

"Why not?" I push back.

"Because he is being detained."

"Detained? By who and for what?"

"Weren't you listening?" The blank expression on my face causes her to sigh and exhale some of her frustration as people file out of the courtroom to take advantage of the break. She signals for me to follow her and together we head back to her office. When she closes the door she continues, "Mr. Hartman is being questioned by Rebirth for his relationship to you, which by the way I really wish that you had disclosed to me."

"What are you talking about?" My heart races as my mind tries to process what's going on.

"Seren saw the two of you kiss and he admitted to initiating it so her lawyer is trying to use that to discredit him as a witness, claiming that he is too infatuated with you to be credible though I don't think that a little crush will be effective enough to win let alone draw enough attention away from the real matter at hand."

He said that he initiated? But I was the one to have done so. It is just like him to lie and take all of the blame just as much as it is just like Seren to have actually seen us that day in the auditorium and play dumb until the perfect time came around to pull out this hat trick. Either way one thing is clear, I must talk to Miles.

"When will I be able to speak with him?"

"That is not up to me. Now are there any more secrets that I should know about?"

I'm about to shake my head no but stop myself. "Maybe." She looks at me with an irritated raise of her eyebrows until I go on. "It's just that after my head injury I started to get some of my memories back. They were all hazy and there weren't many but in there just now I think that I got them all back, or at least a good amount of them. I'm not sure."

She thinks this over before holding up a finger and excusing herself. When she comes back she gestures for me to stand. Recess is over.

When we return to court Wren's parents are back and Sussanah calls up her next witness, a man named Sawyer Bonavich. He is sworn in and sits down. Sussanah then asks him to introduce himself to the court.

"My name is Sawyer Bonavich and I was Wren's friend. We met in university."

The second I hear his voice, football games and afternoons throwing a frisbee around on the lawn of Wren's university fill my head. Someone with Sawyer's physique is with us. No, it is Sawyer. I remember him too.

"Can you tell the court of your relationship to the two parties before you?"

"Yes. Selina or Emily…," he corrects. "Well she was Wren's girlfriend when we were roommates and Seren is her sister that sometimes came to visit."

"How would you describe the two of them?"

Sawyer tells the court of mine and Wren's relationship and then of his and Seren's. He describes one as full of love and adoration while the other is characterized by unrequited emotions and an undercut of tension and jealousy. His stories prove Seren's behavior to be slightly less psychotic but ultimately the same as before she was pregnant.

"So you would agree Mr. Bonavich that Seren Weiss's behavior is ultimately the same now as it was before she was pregnant?"

"Yes."

Sussanah claims that she has no further questions for Sawyer so Seren's lawyer stands to cross examine him. She doesn't get much else from him and ultimately ends up wasting time by asking similar questions to that of the ones Sussanah posed. Eventually the judge asks her to move on.

Next to the stand is Myra Hatton, another friend of mine and Wren's, this one from high school. Seeing her face and hearing her speak helps me to remember her too. I wonder how she's been lately.

Myra introduces herself to the courtroom and claims that she was in our joint friend group throughout high school. She tells stories of Seren's pettiness and each one has a pattern, jealousy. When her lawyer goes to cross-examine her she tries to discredit Myra in every way but all it does is show the jury just how badly Seren's lawyer is grasping at straws.

Susannah's final witness is nurse Carla Hardy. I must have missed her name on the sheet that Sussanah showed me earlier because I don't remember seeing it. She waddles, her stomach having grown rapidly since I last saw her, as she makes her way up to the stand to take her oath of honesty.

"I suggest you tell the truth Mrs. Hardy as jail is not how you want to start motherhood. It's hard to bond with a baby while you're behind bars," Sussanah says with a smile as she approaches.

Carla is pissed but cooperative as Sussanah gets her to confess to meeting Seren in an online chat room for expecting mothers. Carla then goes on to tell a story of being moved by false fantasies that Seren created.

"I was a pregnant, vulnerable woman that was manipulated into withholding essential medicine from my patient and treating her like a second class citizen. Seren Weiss filled my head with stories of how evil her sister was, stories that I now know are not true. I can not take back my actions but I hope that Emily and the court can forgive me."

I roll my eyes as tears fall from her eyes. Someone hands her a tissue. She blows her nose and Sussanah waits until the garbage is discarded before continuing.

"You say that you witholded essential pills from your patient, pills that you reported having given to Miss Weiss. What did these pills do?"

"They are supposed to help with recovery."

"Since she didn't receive this medication could that be the reason why her legs did not work upon waking up? Could it be why she was wheelchair bound until she re-learned how to walk and why she couldn't speak well after her surgeries?"

"Yes," she admits. "This is likely the case for her slow recovery. But I swear I wouldn't have done it if it weren't for Seren. I told her that I hadn't ever had many friends and she used that against me. She made me believe all of these things and told me that I would be doing her a favor, please you have to believe me."

The judge bangs her gavel to bring the attention to her and orders one of the officers in the room to detain Carla for being an accessory to a crime. The woman begins to cry for real this time and part of me does feel a little bad. Sussanah on the other hand smiles victoriously as she's taken away.

"The prosecution rests."

When we come back from a lunch break Seren's lawyer calls her up as the first witness. She takes the stand and is sworn in. Her lawyer tries to make people feel bad for her by painting her as an unlucky outcast her whole life. When it's time for Sussanah to cross examine her she becomes even more emotional and acts as if she is being attacked.

"I have one final question, Miss Weiss. Why is it that you told Rebirth that Wren is dangerous?"

Seren cowers and wipes away phony tears. "I did it as a precaution, just in case, so that she would stay away if she ever remembered. I was just a new mother desperate for the baby's father to be in her life. I didn't want anything to jeopardize that."

"There are no further questions for the defendant, your honor."

Seren is escorted off of the stand by her lawyer, then their second witness is called, a doctor who specializes in childbirth and women's studies. The doctor explains how you can go through a temporary psychotic break after giving birth because of the imbalance of hormones.

"But Seren has yet to give birth. Is it possible for this psychosis to appear during pregnancy?" Her lawyer asks.

"Sort of."

"Could you elaborate please doctor?"

"Well, I am currently conducting a study to see how much male DNA affects a female during reproduction. So far we have found that a male can in fact influence a woman's genes."

"Enough to create a psychotic break?"

"It's unlikely-"

"But it's possible?" Seren's lawyer asks after cutting the doctor off.

"I suppose so but my team has to do more research into it before releasing any official findings."

"But once again it could be possible, yes or no?"

The doctor sighs. Even she is fed up with the bullshit. "It could be a possibility, yes."

"Thank you, that is all."

I bite my tongue but all I want to do is scream about how this is the dumbest argument I have ever heard. I hope that Wren's parents are not here to listen to this crap.

Sussanah stands to take her turn, smoothing out her skirt as she crosses to the doctor. I have complete faith that she will knock this theory off its ass.

"Good afternoon doctor. How are you today?"

She cleans her glasses with her shirt as she answers, "To tell you the truth I have been better."

"I am sorry to hear that but I'll tell you what I'll make it quick because I just have three short questions for you." She folds her fingers together in front of her. "How many times have you seen or heard about a woman murdering and committing identity theft because of her pregnancy?"

"None."

"And in your opinion how likely is it that the baby's father was the one to have caused psychosis from the defendant?"

"Highly unlikely."

"Good and my final question, do you believe that these crimes were even committed in a fit of psychosis?"

"In my professional opinion no, I do not believe so."

"There are no further questions, your honor."

The jury is quick to deliberate, taking under a half an hour to make a unanimous decision. The courtroom congregates back together and everyone rises as the judge approaches the bench. He then announces for us to sit and someone from the jury to come forward. A woman in the front row rises once more and announces the verdict. Guilty.

All in the room celebrate except for Seren and her lawyer. When the gavel comes down everyone settles and the judge dismisses court for the day. It will resume on Monday which is when Seren will be sentenced. Wren's parents invite me to dinner to celebrate but I politely decline and excuse myself for the night.

On the way back to my hotel room a newsstand catches my eye. The daily paper's main headline is a blown-up picture of me after surgery a few days ago with the details of my case underneath. I don't know how these pictures of me got out or who leaked the story but I grab every last copy and dispose of them before hibernating away in my room.

I order room service for dinner and read every article about myself over and over again on my phone. By the time my food comes I am too nauseous to eat.

I feel like a ghost possessing somebody else's body. How is all of this happening to me? It can't be, that's the answer. It's happening to somebody else that right now I think is me. This is not my life, or at least it wasn't supposed to be.

Chapter Thirty-One
Saturday, April 8th

Something falls off of the bedside table. I wouldn't care except for the fact that whatever it is is loud and ruining my sleep, which took a long time to come to me. I feel for the object, flopping my arm around to do so. My fingers brush the floor a few times but I have to inch my body closer to the edge to fully come in contact with it. My phone is the culprit.

I open my eyes and let them adjust as I hold it to my face. Gradually a caller ID comes into focus, it's a number that I don't recognize. I sit up and attempt to pull myself together long enough to answer.

"Hello?" I mutter groggily into the phone.

On the other side of the device is a woman's voice. My brain isn't computing the words she's saying as I begin to fall back asleep against the headboard of the bed.

"Selina dear, are you there?"

"Selina?" It takes me a minute to remember that that's me, I am Selina. I was Selina.

"I'm so sorry Emily oh my word, I didn't mean to call you that. It just slipped my mind." It's Wren's mom.

"It's alright Jia, no need to apologize, I understand. What was it that you were saying?" I lean over to switch the lamp on in an attempt to stay awake.

"I was just asking if you would like us to pick you up

on our way to the airport for our flight to Alnerwick.”

I had completely forgotten about the funeral. I bite my lip as I go through in my head how to break the news. “I’m sorry Jia but I can’t afford to go.”

“What are you talking about? We already bought your ticket. You just need to pack a bag and meet us outside of your hotel in five,” she persuades.

“You paid for my ticket?”

“Of course, we weren’t going to allow you to pay for your own dear, I thought that that was apparent.”

“Oh.” I stare at the clock on the wall, watching the smaller hand tick a few minutes past twelve, marking the start of a new day.

“We’ll be there to pick you up shortly if that is okay with you. Where are you staying?”

I give Jia the address of my current location and thank her many times before ending the call. Then I look around at what little belongings I have with me and practically fall out of bed in a rush to gather up the clothes haphazardly laid around. I try to stuff them in with some sort of order and just barely zip up the chaos of mess before I run to the bathroom to splash water on my face and brush my teeth. I spit in the sink then put the toothbrush back between my teeth while I slip on the coat hanging against the outside of the bathroom door. Once it’s on I wipe leftover spit from my chin and rush to the elevator. Hopefully, there’ll be time to try to change in the airport before boarding but for now my pajamas will have to suffice.

I run down the hall while trying to keep the straps of my duffel up on my shoulder. Luckily people are not quite back from the bars yet so the elevator arrives quickly. Upon entering I hit the button for the lobby and finally have a minute to take the toothbrush out of my mouth and slip it into the holder I have for it.

When the elevator lets me out I see a car pull up, the windows are shaded but once it comes to a complete stop a woman gets out, Jia. I grab my bag and run towards the car without looking back.

The car ride is short but Amaro has been asleep on his wife's shoulder the entire duration. When we pull up to the front entrance of a small airport she gently shakes him awake and right away he jumps to help the driver get our bags from the trunk.

We head towards the check in area after dropping off the couple's bigger suitcases at the weigh-in station. They tell me afterwards that they are the belongings that Wren came here with. My stomach gets queasy hearing this information.

Once we find the gate, Amaro excuses himself to find the bathroom and Jia invites me to walk around with her. I accept her offer and we head towards a stand selling books, one of the only shops open at this hour. I'm not interested in many of them since they mostly consist of cheesy romances with half-naked men on the cover but I still pick one up and am about to pay when Jia takes it from my hands and places it back on the shelf.

"I have some better reading material that you might like." She says with a small smile as she grabs my hands and lures me back towards our bags.

She takes her time pulling it out but once she does I see that it's a brown leather notebook. I notice in her face that she struggles with giving it away, whatever it is, but eventually, she does hand it over.

"What is this?"

"You mentioned in court that Wren was trying to give you something before he died. I believe that this is what he was referring to." Suddenly the notebook in my hands becomes much heavier, the weight pulling my whole body down, forcing me to sit. "After you two split up he fell into a deep depression and almost flunked out of school so my husband and I forced him to go to therapy, which is when he started journaling. Each entry is addressed to someone but most of them are to you."

I can't peel my eyes away from the journal. The sensation feels similar to watching a horror movie or a car wreck, you want to look away but you can't. These pages are scary and vulnerable and not meant to be read in the middle of an airport nor on a public plane so I slip the book into my already filled bag and thank Jia for her kindness in giving it to me.

"I'll return it as soon as I'm finished."

She shakes her head. "It was always meant for you my dear."

Amaro is once again asleep, this time upright in a chair, and Jia is engaged in a vigorous discussion with some strangers that has been going on for twenty minutes now. I'm not sure what they talk about. Meanwhile my phone is dead and we're to begin boarding at any minute now.

My boredom starts to get the best of me and in result I'm about to pull out Wren's journal when I spot someone staring at me from across the way. I squint my eyes to investigate and find that it's Miles leaning against the wall with a black baseball cap and sweats on, unusual attire for him. Once he notices I've seen him he jerks his head in the direction of the bathrooms and heads that way. I follow after him, weighing his motive for being here and how he got past security without a plane ticket.

I glance behind me to see if either of my fellow travelers have noticed my departure, they have not. When my head whips back around I run into Miles. I step back and take him in. Then before I realize what I'm doing I wind up my arm and slap him across the face. We are both stunned.

"Ow," he comments as he rubs the now tender red spot on his check.

"What the hell happened to you?"

"I quit."

"You what?"

"After the other night I decided to resign. I wanted

to surprise you in the morning but when I showed up to my office they pulled me into an interrogation room and showed me a surveillance video of us behind the bar. I had to admit everything and was only officially released an hour ago."

"What did you tell them? What are they going to do to you?"

"I told them that I initiated everything and they said that they would talk to you and make sure that it was consensual but as long as you're okay with it they won't come after me legally. I was incredibly surprised but I think that they are still trying to make up for their mistake with you and think that this will help." A weight feels as if it has been lifted off of my shoulders. Miles is no longer in harm's way. "Say something. This is good, isn't it?"

"Yes, of course it is."

"Then what's the matter?" I pull the sleeves of my shirt to my fingers and fold my arms against my chest to hide away within myself. "Emily? This is when you're supposed to wrap your arms around me and I'm supposed to kiss you and all of that happily ever after junk." He smiles at me and caresses my cheek. I lean into his touch.

"I do want that, but I remember everything now," I confess. "And in a way I feel as if I can finally mourn my losses properly. But I need time to do that and I need to do it alone."

"Oh." He pulls his hand away from my face. I hate that he feels so far away now. "I understand."

The intercom above crackles to life, announcing the beginning of the boarding process for my flight. A line begins to form at the plane's passenger boarding bridge entrance. Behind Miles' shoulder I see Jia waking her husband and searching around for me.

"I have to go."

"Yes, you do. Have a safe flight, Emily." Miles plasters on a weak smile and gives a polite nod of his head before walking off. He stuffs his hands in his pockets as I watch him go.

We land at 9:30 in the morning according to Amaro's watch but don't deboard the plane until ten. He and I slept the whole way. Jia on the other hand has kept herself busy by reading the entirety of a trashy novel and flipping through magazines.

The car ride to their house is somewhat long and stretches through three neighboring towns before we go through the one that I grew up in. I appreciate the distraction from Miles that Jia provides as she points out each place that I could possibly ever have a memory of. She doesn't know that I remember everything now and I'm not exactly sure when to bring it up but with every mention of an event I recall it in great detail.

As the park comes up in view she begins telling me a story of when Wren once ran a marathon with his high school soccer team and how I was there at the finish line waiting for him with a sign and our school colors painted on my face. She narrates for me how I was wearing a cute yellow sundress and a store bought flower crown of daffodils. I want to correct her and let her know that the flowers were actually daisies that I had braided together myself when I got bored of waiting but I keep my mouth shut and let her have her version of the story.

Their house is at the end of a cul-de-sac and we have to go through two guarded gates to get to our final destination. A dog barks at the couple through the window and Amaro jumps out of the driver's seat with the car still on to greet the animal. Jia takes the keys out of the ignition for him and pulls up the parking brake, rolling her eyes at his carelessness.

"Come on dear, we'll give you a tour before we have to get ready to head off to the funeral home."

I'm carrying my duffle and one of Wren's bags of belongings inside when the dog leaps on me, knocking me to the floor. I can't help but giggle like a child as she takes to licking my face and ears.

"I missed you too Pig."

Part of me is surprised at how naturally the name rolls off my tongue until I remember that she was my dog, well mine and Wren's that is. But my shock is nothing compared to the couple now in front of me. Jia has lost hold of her pocketbook, its contents now spilled across the hardwood floor. Change rolls on the tile and a credit card or two have come loose.

"Y-you remember her?" Amaro asks with a stunned look on his face.

I look up sheepishly, unprepared to explain the phenomenon. "I started to have memories after experiencing a head injury a few weeks back. At first they were fuzzy and vague but since then everything has become a lot clearer. I think that I remember everything from before."

"But how?"

"My theory is that it's partially from the kick in the head I received and also from not taking the proper vitamins before and after my Rebirth surgeries."

Jia slowly crumples to the floor at this news, falling to her knees next to me. She stifles her sobs by burying her face into my shirt and wrapping her arms around me. Amaro follows in suit, looking particularly teary eyed himself. We sit here for a while in the moment as Pig barks trying to get in on our embrace. At some point we open our triangle up to her too.

When we rise from the floor Jia abandons her idea on giving me a tour due to my newfound memory. Instead she tells me to get comfortable in Wren's old room and to use the bathroom attached to it to get ready. She then goes off to touch up the makeup she's been wearing since the early hours of the morning.

I climb the stairs and head into Wren's room with my bags. Walking in floods me with memories of the early days of our romance, particularly the first time I slept over. It was when his parents were out of town and Seren had convinced, or more so pressured him, to throw a party that was supposed to be confined to the basement but had somehow escaped to

upstairs. The cops ended up getting called and Wren's parents
fined for having underage drinkers in the house but not before
we found Seren getting it on with someone in Wren's bed.
That day left our friend group fractured for a good while with
people either outright picking our side or trying to sidestep
the drama in general.

"We have fifteen minutes dear before we have to head
out," Jia reminds me as she passes by. This motivates me to
get my feet moving towards the bathroom.

When I enter the room I grab a washcloth from off of
the towel rack and my face wash from inside of the shower.
My fingers just make contact with the bottle when his scent
hits me like a bag of bricks. The grief knocks me to the
ground, causing me to fall against the wall. I stay here for a
while, staring into his bedroom with all of his belongings in
it as I think of all of the times he might have touched or used
them for the last time without knowing it. It isn't until Jia
calls out to give me a five-minute warning that I stumble back
onto my feet.

I hold onto the sink with one hand for support as I
wash my face and put on some of the spare makeup I keep
in the cabinet behind the mirror. I purposefully avoid the
mascara.

Jia comes to check on my progress once more to find
me crouched on the floor digging through my bag. I confess
my situation to her, that I do not have proper funeral attire,
and in response she helps me up and brings me to her closet.

She pulls down a few different options and lays them
out on a chaise lounge for me to go through. She does the
same with her shoes. Then she goes off to help her husband
with his tie.

"We'll head to the car, meet us there when you're done
dear."

On the way to the funeral home we pass by my old
house. A new family lives there now. They play in the yard as

we go by.

When we pull into the parking lot Jia and Amaro immediately go up to talk to the funeral director. The wake will start shortly. I should be paying attention to the words being exchanged but instead I tune the conversation out and slip away. For some reason I know exactly where he is as if his ghost is holding my hand and guiding me towards him.

It is just me and Wren's lifeless body in the room. The casket is made of dark wood and has his high school jersey number inscribed on the end of it, a tragic reminder of how young he was.

To the right of the casket are photos from throughout his life spanning from childhood to his college graduation. I peel off the corner of one of the ones of us, it comes loose easily. A love letter to me is written on the back. I read it and smile before pushing it back onto the poster board it was taped to.

When I go up to him my legs feel like they're made of paper mache that hasn't quite dried yet. I put my hands on the edge of the casket to keep myself upright and squeeze so hard that my arms begin to shake. I'm not sure if I can look at his face.

I jump as two cold hands are placed on my shoulders. Amaro stands behind me, tears in his eyes, and nods at me in silent camaraderie. We can do this together. Slowly I lift my head, moving my gaze from the carpet to the suit he's wearing. This is as far up as I look though before I become hysterical and fall into Amaro's arms because he is wearing the same clothes that he wore to prom my senior year.

Amaro drags me over to a chair off to the side and pulls me into him as Jia rushes over to dot the tears off of my face with a paper towel. I cry into his chest for the next half hour until the guests start to arrive, which is when I pull myself together well enough to robotically greet old friends of ours and family of his.

I never do look at his face. I'm afraid that if I do I might just climb in with him and let myself be buried too.

Just as the funeral is to start I see a police officer talking to the director in the corner of the greeting room. I move closer, letting my curiosity get the best of me, and begin to eavesdrop. Just as I'm about to though the pair of them start moving towards me. The officer even goes so far as to point in my direction. I freeze, losing my chance to pretend I didn't see them and make a getaway.

"Miss Weiss?" The officer calls out to me as he approaches. "Will you come with me please?"

I turn over my shoulder to see Jia and Amaro prepping each other for their speeches. They asked me if I would say something during the open remarks section of the program but I don't think that they expect me to still go through with it now.

"It will be quick, I promise."

"Okay." I go along with him, heading out into the early afternoon air.

"You might want to take a seat." He gestures to the bench on the front porch of the home. I nod and together we sit. "Miss Weiss, I have some bad news. It's about your sister." He holds space for a response. I don't have the energy to give him one so he goes on, "She passed away this morning."

"Seren's dead?"

"Unfortunately so. Extreme stress caused her to go into early labor and she passed away during the delivery. You're the child's only next of kin."

I try to hold back a chuckle once I realize what this means but I can't help it. A full fit of roaring laughter ensues from me. This is absurd. My sister and my ex/childhood best friend are both dead a week apart from each other and now their child is my responsibility. A child that technically has the same DNA as me. How fucking funny fate is.

The officer looks frightened at my response. "It is recommended that you head back to Croyden as soon as possible."

Chapter Thirty-Two
Saturday, April 8th

After explaining the situation Jia tosses me the keys and assures me that they will find another way home. Amaro then crosses the distance between us and pulls a wallet out of his back pocket. He hands me a couple of hundred dollar bills and folds them within my hands before pulling me into a hug.

"I hope that can cover a last minute flight but give me a call if it doesn't. We'll come visit you and our grandbaby soon."

"Thank you two for all of your help, I'm sorry that I couldn't stay longer."

Jia waves away my apology and says a final goodbye before heading back inside to start. Amaro on the other hand doesn't leave the porch until I successfully drive off and lose the funeral home from sight.

The entire way back to the Rivera's house my body is filled with adrenaline. I am now responsible for a human life. I will have to raise this child and send them to school one day and watch them get married and I will do it because it is Wren's child and I loved him. And despite all odds I still love my sister.

The root of her downfall had to do with the comparisons that other people would force on us. It made her feel in competition with me and she always let it bother her which only ended up eating her alive, making her bitter. It's why she constantly tried to chase my happiness instead of finding her own. She had traits or qualities that I envied too at times but the difference between her and I is that I never let the jealousy consume me or impact my ability to love her.

I pull up to the Rivera's house and practically jump out of the car. Pig tries to greet me at the door as I let myself in. When her first attempt is unsuccessful she follows after me, watching as I repack my bag and include some of Wren's clothes. Once she realizes what's happening she lays at the entrance to the door and whines. It breaks my heart so after I call for a car and change I sit with her to say a teary goodbye.

The ticket counter halts my momentum from running, acting as a roadblock. "I would like to book the next flight to Croyden as soon as possible please." I slur my words together so fast that I'm surprised the attendant manning the counter even understands me. She does though because she tells me to hold on a moment and begins to tap away at her keyboard.

"It looks like our next direct flight to Croyden will be in an hour from now but it will be a little over six hundred dollars after taxes and fees."

My mouth falls open at this price until I remember the money that Amaro lent to me. I dig inside my pocket for the bills and carefully count them out before handing them over. The lady, slightly shocked by the pocket change, gives me any leftover money and prints out the ticket for me.

I head over to my gate and settle in, restless as ever. I need a good distraction and a phone charger. Luckily this airport is much larger than the one we left from early this morning so all I have to do is turn the corner to find a stand selling phone-related gadgets. I show the man my device and he rings me up for the specific charger I need.

I plug it into an outlet and watch the battery ever so slowly start to fill up. Eventually, the device powers back on and all of the missed calls from my lawyer, an unknown number and Miles come flooding in, the sight of which overwhelms me so I abandon the phone idea and leave it to finish charging.

Instead to occupy my time I pull out the leather-bound notebook that I have had stored away in my bag since the early hours of this morning. There's no point in avoiding or procrastinating the task. I have to read. It's the only way to begin healing.

November 11th

I started therapy yesterday. I decided that I needed it after the mistake I made last week. Anyways, my therapist recommended that I get a journal to help document my highs and lows so here I am. I'm not really sure how this works. I guess I just write down my stream of consciousness? Okay, starting now. It's her birthday today, which is both a low and a high. It's the first one in years that I haven't been with her for. She turned 20. Everything reminds me of her. But this is for the best, for now at least, because I want her to take the incredible opportunity that the world has gifted her. A future blockbuster hit, maybe even a red carpet and film festivals. It will be all of her eleven year old dreams come true. I wish that I had been more supportive about it in the moment but I was so blindsided by our plans changing and hurt that there was no discussion with me involved. I failed her. So now I have my dream school, a rare scholarship and an ex-girlfriend who changed her mind. But I can't blame her for doing so. I never should have pushed her to move back home for me. It was selfish and it haunts me that I ever did that to her, that I ever made her feel as if she had to choose between me and her career. I've always known that our hometown was not where she was meant to be nor wanted to go back to but I guess part of me just hoped that she would change her mind because it's where I want to be.

November 14th

Dear Lina,

My therapist has suggested that it might be easier to write these entries if I address them to someone in particular so here I am, writing you a letter that you will never read. I found one of your socks mixed in with mine today. I almost broke down in

the laundry room. You should be getting ready to move soon, to be
closer to the studio. I wonder who you will call now to move the
heavy boxes into the truck for you now that your father is gone
and we are not together. This thought has been plaguing my mind
all week so I have been trying not to think about it. Mission failed.
-Wren

The next handful of entries are addressed to Wren's
roommate, therapist friends or parents, thanking them for their
contribution to helping him get out of his so-called slump.
I skim those pages, the ones that detail his life experiences
at his new school. Sometimes I find my name sporadically
throughout but most of the time I don't.

February 26th
Lina, you came back tonight. I've never been happier.
-Wren

February 27th
Dear Lina,
You seem different but I can't quite place why. Maybe
it's that you're quicker to temper than usual or that you're not
remembering things quite right but you're just... different. I can't
complain about it though because you being here is an early Christmas miracle.
-Wren

February 28th
Dear Seren,
I know that it's you. When I found the test hidden
away in your belongings I thought that I had made sense of it.
I thought that that was the reason why Selina was acting so
strange the past twenty-four hours since coming back into my life,
because she was pregnant. But then I realized that if you really
were Selina you would be much farther along by now. So what did
you do to her and why can't I reach her? When you come back from
the store I will find out and I will put you behind bars for it because guarantee whatever it is is that you did is fucking psychotic.
-Wren

March 15th
Dear Lina,

I found you today. Seren may have altered your appearance and stole your memories but i'm glad that she couldn't do anything to take away your spirit or your low tolerance for alcohol. I love you.

-Wren

March 16th
Dear Lina,

She warned you about me, I know that she did, therefore you can't know who I am yet, not until you trust me more. I saw the fear in your eyes when I told you my name. It broke my heart. It's okay though, I can wait. I have planned to give you some time in this life anyway to see if you fall in love with me again or not. If you don't then I will let you go for good but if you do... well I know I can't give you back what she took but I will do my best to fill in the blanks and confirm what has been fabricated and what has actually occurred, at least once the time is right.

I'm also working on trying to forgive Seren for what she has done, enough to look her in the eyes at least. If it weren't for the baby I would never speak to her again but these are the circumstances that I must accept.

-Wren

March 18th
Dear Lina,

We went on another date today, this time to a gala. Your dress was stunning. I was telling stories to other attendees of the life you lived before as a hint but I don't think that you were listening, I could tell that your mind was faraway. You asked me if I was the Wren from your past, I said no of course, and tech-nically I did not lie as I am not the same person I was when you left, nor am I even the same as when you were taken. Anyway, we kissed again which was nice. If it weren't for the man that has been around you a lot lately I would feel a lot more hopeful about it though. Yesterday he was waiting for you at your door and today he was in your house. I've been trying to not think about it but I can't help it so for my own sanity I'm choosing to believe that he is your Rebirth mentor. I hope i'm right but in case i'm not I hope you know that it is okay if you don't choose to come home with me in the end. I obviously want you to return back to Alnerwick with me and take advantage of this second chance that in a way we have been given but I will understand if this is not what you choose.

-Wren

March 20th
Dear Lina,
     I joined your play today. It's made me immensely proud to watch you persevere through your challenges and find joy in new mediums. I hope that you still write in your spare time though as that has always been your main, true love. I've been sending some update emails to my parents as per their request, they tell me that they are proud of you too.

-Wren

March 25th
Dear Lina,
     I took you to breakfast this morning before our first rehearsal. We made a wager on our next date. Speaking of, I got a temporary job taking care of some barn animals at a nearby farm. I made sure to tell the guy that I haven't finished veterinary school yet and that I've only interned at a family clinic but he seemed desperate for help as his place isn't that close to the rest of town and no one else has been willing to make the trek. I'm forever grateful for him taking a chance on me, especially because there was a pregnant horse that I helped deliver today. I have been present and assisted on multiple animal births but have never done one alone until now. It felt indescribable to be able to do that and have a new life in my hands. But what was even better than that is the voicemail you left me today. You said that you missed me. I don't know if you were intoxicated again and just meant you wanted me out with you at the bar or if you are starting to remember who I really am but I can't ask, not yet, just in case.

-Wren

March 26th
Dear Lina,
     I took you to ride horses today. It was going well until you got hurt. I had to call Miles to come help. Knowing that my intu-

ition was right about his role in your life felt like a breath of fresh air. Although I am starting to wonder how close you two are still since he is risking his job and crossing into unprofessional territory just to be in your show. Has he manipulated you? Taken advantage of you? Maybe that's just what I hope has happened, not that I would ever wish that upon you. It would just be my worst fear if you were actually falling for him. I see the way you two look at each other, it's the same way that you look at me... or looked at me.

-Wren

March 30th

Dear Lina,

  Seren stopped by today. She convinced me to go with her to her doctor's appointment for the baby. Seeing the sonogram made everything so scary and real. She's having a girl though. I've started to think about baby names, which I never thought I would be doing without you. My top choice right now is Elanora, in honor of my late mother. I don't know if Seren has any ideas, I haven't discussed it with her. I'm starting to think that she only sees this child as a bartering chip to use against me instead of as an actual soon to be living person, it's deeply upsetting.

  I only got through the appointment by pretending it was you I was with and after it was done I went straight to the library, hoping to find you there. I took you out for ice cream, hoping the flavors would jog your memory and give you some reminder of those few months we spent trying out every shop in Merdin, a new flavor for each week. Then I took you biking. I think you remembered something and that's why you got distracted while riding, unless that's just some delusion I'm telling myself to feel better, which is much more likely. God, I really hope you weren't thinking about Miles though.

-Wren

March 31st

Dear Lina,

  For our next date I want to take you to a drive-in movie like the ones we used to go to over the summer in high school. I haven't been able to find any in close proximity though so I might see if I can pull something together, a last-minute thing, for you. I'll even get a copy of your favorite movie and it will all be worth it

That's the last entry, there is nothing after it. Those were the last words that he had written down. This is what he was trying to show me that night, his confession.

"Flight 414 with nonstop flight to Croyden, Accrington will begin the boarding process now."

Chapter Thirty-Three
Sunday, April 9th

"Hi, I'm here to see Seren Weiss and her daughter."

For just a second I forget that she's gone and am about to correct myself when an officer interrupts, "Right this way ma'am."

He leads me into an elevator and instead of up we go down to the basement level. I'm about to ask why when the doors open and across from us is a room labeled 'morgue.'

"Unfortunately ma'am I need a family member to make a positive ID and give consent for an autopsy, if that is something that you would like." the man explains. He knocks on the door and a tall, darker woman opens it from the other side. She beckons for me to come in.

The room is a touch above freezing and causes me to pull my sweater tighter to my body. I keep my head lowered, afraid to look around me, and watch the officers' feet to keep in the right direction. She stops in front of a metal gurney so I do the same.

"I'm going to slowly pull the sheet back to her neck and you just nod if it's her, okay?"

"Okay."

I force myself to look as inch by inch the white sheet reveals her. First the top of her head with her raven, black curls we at one point shared then her eyes, nose and lips.

I nod. "It's her."

Then she's gone again, covered back up, and the doctor begins to talk me through what to do with the body from here. She lets me take a seat in her office and hands me a pen but I'm too wrapped up in my head to listen so I end up brainlessly signing when and where she tells me to. I think I consent to an autopsy, I'm not entirely sure.

When I'm done the officer gently guides me back into the elevator and we go back up. My brain is running at warp speed. The elevator is tilting. Why is it tilting?! I try to place my hand on the wall for balance but I miss. I think I'm going to throw up if we keep moving. I lean forward and gag but nothing comes out. When was the last time I ate? Room service two nights ago.

The officer presses a button on the wall panel that emits a god-awful noise but at least the world isn't spinning anymore. He helps me to stand upright and instructs me to take a few deep breaths. I still feel sick but not as nauseous after doing so.

"What you're going to see next is not going to be pretty either, okay? The child is very premature. She's being kept alive only by tubes and wires and the doctors around her." My breathing threatens to become labored again as this knowledge settles with me. Is she going to die too? Is she next? "I have to start the elevator back up again but at least now you know what you're walking into. Ready?"

I nod and he presses the red button once more, causing the elevator to kick back into gear. We rise another floor up and then the doors open. It's quiet when we step out and the officer, whose name I still haven't caught, talks to the staff at the desk. They tell me to leave my bags there before bringing us across the hall to a large room filled with children in clear incubators. Seren's child is near the front of the room wearing the tiniest diaper I have ever seen. I notice our last name on the outside of the box as we approach.

Upon getting closer I see the full extent of what the officer was referring to. There's a tube in her mouth,

obstructing most of her facial features, and pasted patches on
her stomach with more wires leading to the machine beeping
next to her. Her body is so small, no larger than my hand. I
want to reach in, to let her know that someone is here and that
somebody alive loves her, but for now I have to settle with
touching the fiberglass.

A doctor in a baby pink lab coat and scrubs introduces
herself to me. She seems weathered and exhausted. "I'm sorry
about your circumstances Miss Weiss. It is truly unfortunate."

"I appreciate it."

"Your sister's baby is in stable condition for now
but I predict that it will be at least another few weeks in
the NICU since she is a micro preemie." I nod to show my
understanding. "And I know that the circumstances are
strange but have you thought of a name Miss Weiss?"

A name? I think back to what Wren said in his journal.
"Elanora."

"What a beautiful tribute Emily," Jia whispers in
my ear as she hugs me. Amaro sits in a chair off to the side,
cradling Nora to his chest. It's late, the moon just becoming
visible in the sky, and the couple are fresh off of their flight.

Susannah walks into the room, emoting confidence,
with a briefcase in her hand that she places on a tabletop. She
unlatches it and pulls out packets of paper before going on to
explain the status of everything going on.

Prosecution will still be done to anyone who assisted
Seren in her crimes, such as the nurse from the ship, but since
she is dead there is nothing else that can be done in terms of
her. As for Rebirth, they have offered me a sufficient amount
in hush money- enough to cover the expenses of all Nora's
medical bills, purchase the two of us a more suitable living
arrangement and more. Sussanah has warned me that I could
acquire another million if I took them to court but with the
state Nora is in, Jia, Amaro and I agree that it might not
be worth it at this moment. Amaro even double-checks the

contract for me, since he has a background in law, as Jia takes a turn holding Nora.

"Everything the lady said checks out," Amaro announces to the two of us.

Sussanah gives a sarcastic thanks as she grabs the paper back from his hands. She places it on the tabletop and slides it over for me to sign. And with the lift of the pen on my final signature I now officially have wealth far beyond what I could have imagined for myself.

Six Months Later

I sit at the computer that I bought last night, a birthday present to myself. I was going to take Nora's nap time to set it up but this morning Tabitha offered to take her along to do some errands and allow me some alone time. Our number one dinner topic as of late has been my book and how I have been having a hard time coming up with a proper ending. Our second hottest piece of discussion has been the play coming up.

I finally recast the roles this past month and am rushing to put it together before the end of the year. Bee took on Seren's role as well as her own and Ellie and Angie convinced their band member Scott to fill in for Wren. He wasn't too thrilled about it at first but he's got a natural talent for performing and has grown to love the stage, whether he'll admit to it or not. Our only issue is with Miles's role. If we still can't find someone within the next few weeks then I will just have to take on the character myself, though I hope it doesn't come to that.

I open up my writing browser and am about to begin when the doorbell rings. I groan and walk down the hall past the nursery and guest room, which still has Tabitha's unpacked boxes from when she officially moved in a week ago.

"I'm coming!" I call out as I jog down the stairs.

The front door is made partially of frosted glass so I can't make out who is on the other side but I do see the silhouettes of two people around my size. Definitely not Tabitha and my six-month-old child.

I pull the front door open and streamers go off in my face. Ellie and Angie pull them out of their mouths to simultaneously yell, "happy birthday!" They each have a brown paper bag in their hands filled to the brim. On the top I spot balloons and cake candles.

"What is all of that for?"

"Your party," Ellie explains as the two walk past me into the dining room. I shut the door behind them, making sure to leave it unlocked in case Tabitha forgot her key again.

"I thought I told you two that I didn't want a party." I fold my arms across my chest and raise my eyebrows but I can't help the slight smile that turns the corners of my lips up anyway.

They avoid eye contact and begin to set up. "I don't remember that, do you El?"

"No, Angie I don't."

"Okay, fine, but everyone must be gone by eight so I can get Nora to bed on time." They give each other a sly look of triumph and start blowing up the balloons.

I'm about to leave them to return to my writing when Tabitha comes in with Nora on her hip and a bag of groceries in both hands. "Oh good, the girls are already here. Emily, could you take the child?"

Nora begins to bounce against Tabitha's hip excitedly at the sight of me and reaches her tiny arms towards me. I grab her and snuggle her against my chest before fixing her hat. Then I head after Tabitha who makes her way into the kitchen.

"Did you get any writing done?" She asks as she begins to put stuff away.

"No, I just finished setting it up. What is going on here?"

Angie and Ellie enter the kitchen too, surveying the

groceries that were just brought in. "Did you get a cake?" One of them asks.

"I ordered one, it has to be picked up from the bakers in an hour if one of you can run back out around then and grab it."

"I can," the other one volunteers. What an unlikely team the three of them are.

"I really thought that I asked not to make my birthday a big deal guys," I remind the group of them.

"But you're turning twenty-one. That is a big deal Em," Ellie protests as she unloads cheese and crackers from the grocery bag.

"When did you tell everyone else to be over?" Angie asks.

Tabitha checks her watch. "At noon."

"We better get started on the food then."

A half-hour later appetizers are placed on the table as Bee and James show up on my doorstep. Doctor Pierce arrives next, bearing a bottle of scotch with a bow wrapped around the handle and Scott and Evan are the last to show. We wait for them to sit at the table. Jia and Amaro apparently couldn't make it but sent a gift and card in the mail earlier this week with a picture of the two of them visiting family in Aelville so I'm not too troubled by their absence.

"It smells delicious Tabitha," I compliment as I spoon a mouthful of smashed peas into Nora's mouth. I wipe the excess from her chin with a napkin.

"I can't take all of the credit, Ellie helped."

"I prepped part of the desert," she clarifies to the group of us.

"Speaking of dessert, should someone head out to pick up the cake soon?" Angie poses the question as we all begin to dig into our meals of potatoes and steak. I try to take a bite of my own food but put the fork down mid-bite when Nora babbles, my signal to give her more peas.

"I have somebody on that already."

I give Ellie a puzzled look and am about to ask what she means when someone knocks on the door. Everyone's heads turn towards the noise. "Can you continue feeding her? I'll be right back."

I push the small bowl filled with green mush towards Tabitha and step away from the table. Behind me she sings to Nora to distract her from the fact that I have left her eyesight.

The frosted glass on the door once again does not help to reveal my mystery guest but I'm assuming that it's just a delivery boy as I can see the large cake box in their hands. I turn the handle and swing the door open, becoming frozen at the sight in front of me. I don't blink or move a muscle in case what I see fades away like a mystical illusion or a trick of the light. Miles does the same, frozen in time except for his eyes which can't seem to settle on any part of me. He looks the same as the last time I saw him except with some stubble on his cheeks and chin that make up a beard. I'm only used to his clean-shaven look but both suit him well.

"What are you doing here?"

"I promised that I would be with you on your birthday, remember? No matter where I would end up I said that I would come back to see you."

"Right," I breathe out in disbelief. "And where did you end up? I mean, where have you been?" He holds the cake box out to me. I take it from him.

"I have an apartment in Croyden and work for my parents now at the restaurant."

"Wow! And how are you liking it?"

"It's a dream really, I didn't know what I was missing."

"That's great, I'm really happy for you."

"Thanks."

"Would you like to come in? We could fix you a plate."

"Sure, I would love to."

The meal is joyous and filled with love. Evan and Scott

tell everyone about the upcoming album they're planning
on making with the band and Ellie and Angie talk about
when they're planning on moving into their own apartment,
just the two of them. Doctor Pierce even contributes to the
conversation by talking about how work is going for him. At
some point, the status of my book comes up and I become as
vague as possible, detering the conversation faster than Nora
can throw things off of her high chair.

Once everyone finishes their plates Tabitha collects
them all as Angie and Ellie set up the cake in the kitchen.
People take the quick transitional period to go to the bathroom
or take a smoke break and soon it is just me, Miles, and a
sleeping Nora at the table.

"I'm really glad you're here." I reach under the table to
find his hand. I squeeze, wanting our skin to be as close as it
can be for as long as possible. He squeezes too.

"I was wondering if we could talk later."

"Of course."

My throat gets dry and my stomach becomes flustered
with anticipatory anxiety. After a six month absence the
butterflies feel so foreign now.

Once everyone comes back together they all sing,
quietly so as to not disturb the sleeping girl to my left, and I
blow out the candles with the numbers two and one displayed
on top. A kitchen knife then distributes out slices to everyone
and we all shuffle into the sitting room to eat there.

Conversation slowly picks back up once we're all done
eating. Someone suggests doing presents now so I make sure
to put Nora in her crib before we start, that way my guests
don't feel any more pressure to keep quiet.

When I return I settle on the couch and Bear crawls
into my lap. Dr. Pierce starts off by uncorking the bottle he
got for me and filling a glass that gets placed beside my chair.
I wrap the ribbon that came with it in my hair and promise
Angie to do a round of shots later, but only if Nora doesn't
wake up by then. She celebrates excitedly before wrapping an
arm back around Ellie's shoulder.

Scott, Evan, Angie, and Ellie announce their joint gift next, two roundtrip tickets for Nora and I to visit Jia and Amaro for Christmas. I make sure to thank each of them individually with sincere gratitude before pulling Tabitha's present into my lap.

I open the small cardboard box and pull aside the tissue paper to see that underneath is an exact replica of her red scarf. I run my hand along the stitching and wrap it around my neck before getting up. I make my way across the carpet to the recliner in the corner and bend down to meet her level, wrapping her up in a hug.

"I must tell you something later," she whispers into my ear. I nod so she knows I have heard her and go back to sit in my spot.

Miles is the last to produce a gift, which he has to run to his car to grab. Upon coming back inside he hands me a bouquet of thriving flowers of all colors.

"They're from the garden that we planted together," he explains. "I know it's not much but I thought that you would want to see what the flowers grew to look like before it got too cold outside."

"The gift is perfect Miles," I reassure him as I admire the beauty in his hands.

Shortly after presents everyone starts to head out and Miles offers to help in the kitchen with the dishes. I'm glad that he's not leaving just yet. I thank him for the offer and let him know that I will come help in a minute. There's someone that I need to talk to first.

I sit on the ottoman across from her and look at Tabitha expectantly. "First I want to say that I am proud of you," she starts off with right away. "For putting together the play, your perseverance, the community you have surrounded yourself with, your heart and the mother you have become to Nora."

"Thank you, that-."

"But," she holds a hand up to insinuate that she is

not done and cuts me off. "I also have something to confess to you." My eyebrows furrow as I search her face for clues. She inhales deeply. "I wrote the script that I gave to you all of those months ago and everything that I wrote is true." My mouth goes slack and my eyes bulge. I can't believe what I'm hearing. "Raelyn's character is based off of me and my best friend is, or was, based on Elena."

"What happened to her after she took the fall for you? Did she ever contact you after getting out of prison?"

Tabitha's face stretches from serious to somber. "No, she went crazy due to the trauma of it all so her family ended up volunteering her for the first round of Rebirth testing. She died a few years after but I refuse to know why. She's the one that made me this scarf. I always wear it to hide reminders of that night."

She moves the material back to reveal a long ago healed scar that runs from behind her ear to the center of her neck. I come closer to inspect it before she covers it back up.

"Perfect casting with Angelina and Ellie by the way, they very much remind me of me and my friend."

"What do you mean?"

She's about to reply but shuts her mouth when Miles walks into the room with a crying Nora in his hands. He looks panicked and unprepared. It's cute. I get up to grab her but Tabitha beats me to it, intercepting me and walking off with her before I can get to them.

"Now it's your turn to talk Mr," she says over her shoulder to Miles.

"Would you like to go on a walk?" He suggests.

The October air is chilly but Tabitha's scarf wrapped around my neck helps. The technicolor leaves fall, blowing around us more rapidly the farther away from town we get. Neither of us knows where we're going nor have we said a word. At one point as we walk past the bakery, where the smell of fresh bread fills the air, our hands brush against each other. I go to pull away and apologize but instead Miles reaches back out for me, making the conscious decision to entwine our fingers together.

"I miss you."

There's a heavy vulnerability in his words that pulls me to stop, to breathe. "I miss you too," I admit. He blushes as the confession.

"I heard what you did for the town by the way, donating some of the money you won in your settlement for new handicap ramps. That was very kind of you."

"It was needed," I explain, shrugging off the compliment.

Then we walk along in silent solidarity once more.

Later that night Miles lies in my bed, half naked and covered in a blanket. The moon shines through my window, illuminating the floorboards in the room. The only other light comes from my computer. I type vigorously, rejuvenated with inspiration, while still trying to not wake Miles with the clicking sounds of the keyboard.

This time apart has brought me the realization that I do not need him, I never did, even if it was his job to be there for me. He is a luxury, not a necessity. And he has allowed me to grieve the lives I have lost while discovering who I can be on my own. I have lived twice, I have loved twice and I have discovered myself twice. I can do life without him but that doesn't seem as fun as doing it with him.

I started my story, this story, when I was a shell of a person, barely able to walk and confused. My sister had stolen from me my identity, my life and my memories which I have since taken back.

In a way I have truly been reborn.

-The End.

Acknowledgments

My first thank you goes to anyone who has taken a chance on this book. Thank you for lending me your time and reading the thoughts that I have created. Thank you for living in this world with me for a moment and for bringing the book to life in your own imagination.

Next, I would like to thank those who helped during the production design process of the book. Thank you to Sydney for the beautiful hand-painted cover art, I will always be amazed at your talent. Thank you to my partner Nate for the incredible cover, spine, and interior formatting. And to my Mom and Dad thank you for being some of my beta readers, believing in me, pushing me to publish this, and always nurturing my love for literature.

Finally, this may seem silly but, thank you to Taylor Swift. Not that you'll ever see this but your music is the bulk of my playlists and your lyricism truly gives me endless creativity and inspiration.

About the Author

Julia is an undergraduate student at Salve Regina University studying creative writing, publishing, and theater. Besides writing she enjoys performing, reading, and spending time with family on the beach. Her biggest writing inspirations are Taylor Swift and Suzanne Collins. When not in school or writing Julia works as a barista in Newport, Rhode Island where she has been residing for the past few years with her partner Nate.